HIGH BODY COUNT

A NULL
&
BOYD NOIR

GARY S. KADET

For all those who lived and chose not to talk about it—and especially for those who did.

"There is a place on earth that is a vast desolate wilderness, a place populated by shadows of the dead in their multitudes, a place where the living are dead, where only death, hate and pain exist."

— GIULIANA TEDESCHI

PRELUDE

"How's the food?"

"Not so great here at Lemuel Shattuck. It would be better if I was at some ritzy place like McClean's, but my health plan only covers this place."

"But it's not too bad."

"Edible. It's not like I'm looking forward to eating."

"What are you looking forward to?"

"Nothing. I have nothing to look forward to."

"They tell you that's not true?"

"Yeah."

"They would."

A shadow passed repeatedly over the big picture window of the solarium at the Lemuel Shattuck Hospital visiting area. The middle-aged woman was dressed in pajamas and a robe, her face bedraggled and puffy, pretty despite no make-up. The man sitting across from her was a horror of scars on his wreck of a face, shaded drastically in a porkpie hat, his scrawny body engulfed in an overcoat.

He lit a cigarette, and she accepted it gratefully.

"How's the detox?"

"I'm out of it."

"Still need a drink, though."

"Like God needs worshippers."

The shadow swung past like a pendulum.

"You know it will kill you."

"I'd like to die, so fine."

"That's why you're here."

"It's what I get for being honest in therapy."

"This time you know it's not your fault."

"I don't know anything."

"You know who I am?"

"A criminal. A monster. And I made you."

"You did. But this time you didn't make what happened."

"Sure I did. I went after them."

"You made kiddie porn an OC deal."

"They needed to be gotten."

"And did you get them?"

"I got some. It wasn't enough."

"There's a lot of them."

"There are."

"And they got to you."

"They did."

"They got to Rudy."

"I don't need to tell you."

"You don't. It was by the numbers: They did some opposition research, found out all about you."

The cigarette went flying, making sparks on the floor. Her hands were trembling, eyes glazed, darting.

"Rudy's daycare!" she cried and restrained herself. No one came in response. She was nervously looking for possibly a milieu therapist or a nurse.

"That's right. Rudy's daycare. Edward Brooke Child Services. They snatched him. Paid the staff not to know anything, scared them out of their wits with one or two big guns, whisked him away."

"Don't say it. Just don't."

"But it needs to be said, don't you think?"

"You can't hurt me."

"I'm not trying to hurt you."

"That's all you do: pain and death."

"That's right. All I do. Sometimes life even makes me do other things, though. This is part of that. It needs to be said; either you do it or I will."

"No." Tears now, her frame crumbling into itself, slumped in the robe in her seat, shaking.

"I gave him to you to love. And did you?"

"You know I did." Trembling. Loud: "I did!"

"Then he had at least some love in his life. More than some ever get."

"It wasn't enough."

"It's never enough. Just say it."

"Go fuck yourself."

"Fine. I will then. It was time to make you stop. So, they took him. They made movies with him. Even left you a thumb drive full of them. They played him out fast. Then they served him up to a special man. If you want to call what he is a man."

"Shut the fuck up!"

"Right. He anally raped Rudy's seventy-five-pound little body until the kid went limp. Then, when there was nothing left in him anymore, and he was done, he broke his neck. Must have been like breaking the neck of a chicken. Easy. Clean as you please. No real resistance."

"They laughed," she sobbed.

"No. Nobody laughed. It was a job. A somber job. The special man might have smiled, though. Special."

"It was revenge. I was stupid."

"No. You were playing by some rules. They play by no rules at all. Big advantage."

"It's my fault."

"No. It's their fault."

"And what happens next?"

"Criminal investigation, right? Boston's best bringing them down—it's personal now, being one of their own. They'll take care of it, right?"

"You don't believe that."

"Cigarette?"

"No, they disgust me. I disgust me. Why are you here?"

3

"You know why."

"Nobody gets your agenda, Null. Nobody. Not even me."

"Who am I?"

"Joseph Xavier Null. You're a criminal, a murderer—and I guess now the crystal meth king of Boston."

"All true, especially the latter. So, who better than me to put the squeeze on KP to find who murdered Rudy?"

"For what? To kill him for me?"

"No. I was hoping you'd do that after I gave him to you."

"I'm not a murderer, Null."

"Tell that to Dr. Benway."

"You know he had to die."

"I know it. Just as you know the human filth that fucked a child to death for fun has got to die. Only he has to die in pain— a long stretch of agony. Nothing else will do."

"As if that would solve it."

"It wouldn't."

"And it wouldn't bring Rudy back."

"No." Null gave Boyd his deep, empty look, smacked his lips. "But it might bring *you* back."

"So, fine—do it. Go ahead. I don't care. I can't stop you. Just leave me alone."

Null shook his head. "No. I have plans for you."

"You're going to try and make me a murderer. No thanks."

"You're already that. But you're going to help me."

"Help you what? Find the guy?"

"No. I'll find him. But what I have to do is a bigger job, harder."

"You're insane."

"That was my last clinical diagnosis."

"I can't stand this anymore!" She stood wildly, lurching to leave.

Null's quiet, cheerless voice stopped her: "It's bigger than one guy. A lot bigger."

"There's nothing bigger than that to me."

"Maybe there is."

Null looked up at her with a wounded, steely expression on

his scarred face, spoke just above a whisper. "I'm coming after them all, you know. All of them. All."

"All of whom? What are you talking about?"

"The KP operators of Boston—maybe all of New England. Every single one."

"And do what? Kill them all?"

It was as if he were describing the weather outside: a sun-dappled, gray streaked Boston day. "That's right. I'm going to kill every single last one of them."

"You actually think you can do that? You think that'll work? You're snorting your own fucking product is what's happening."

He nodded. "Every now and then, yes. Doesn't change the fact."

"And mass murder will be your justice? Drop the meth!"

"Exactly. And I will make them die in pain, for the sake of an ethical kind of justice."

"Since when can torture and mass murder be made an ethical justice?"

"What I've read in Ludwig Wittgenstein's *Blue and Brown Books* asserts that possibility. I'll test it out. I don't mind a few—casualties. Similar reasoning worked for George W. Bush."

"You're sick! You should be in here, not me!"

"It's a fair point. But it's the pre-determined course of my drive to continue living. I will, as you say, torture and murder every single person involved in the kiddie porn business in Boston, no matter who they are, where they are, what they are, even if they just invested in it or acted as a key grip on a movie set. Every single one of them involved will die, screaming in agony, if I'm lucky."

"It can't be done. They'll kill you."

"If so, then that will solve my end of the problem. But I've been very lucky insofar as staying alive. I should have been killed a while back. Chalk it up to God, if you want.

"We both know there is no God."

"And I'm even luckier with killing."

"Your luck will run out."

"Maybe. But fortune favors the favored, now doesn't it?"

Her eyes narrowed and her posture straightened. The rage was present. She threw up her hands. "What do you want me to do, you sick fuck – give you my goddamn blessing? Well forget it!"

"No. I just wanted you to know what was going to happen. Maybe it'll help you get out of here. Maybe you'll want to join in."

"Why would I?"

"You said revenge is not enough?"

"There is no enough anymore."

"Bringing you back was a thought."

"I don't know. I can't think. I can never come back."

"But you will—and none of them will. They're guilty. They *all* killed Rudy. And at the very least, I will be avenged."

"You? What does this have to do with you?"

"You forget. I rescued him from the pedophile gangsters, made them pay. Gave him to you. And now they've taken him back and murdered him. Should I let that go?"

"So, you'll make them pay again?"

"Yes, and this time I'll take everything from them. I will leave them nothing—nothing for anyone to inherit. Nothing to mourn. Scorched earth."

"You've lost it, Null. You have no idea what you're going to do, do you? Of course you don't. You need to check yourself in here. You're fucked!"

"Oh, I'm beyond the planning stages at this point. I'm good to go."

"Really? And just how is that going to work?"

"Simple."

She glared at him with glassy eyes reddening in a spreading vascular pattern, her face flushed, nostrils flaring. "Nothing with you is ever simple. One of the many reasons you suck."

"Make me a list while you're in here. Give you something to do."

"Just don't do anything, Null. Leave it alone, for Christ's sake. You'll only make everything worse."

"I don't deny that. Worse for whom, though, would be the issue."

"You can't possibly believe you're going to do this and have it work."

"I believe in nothing, but I know it will work. Just as I know when it comes time, you'll help me."

Her voice shifted to a tone of ironic hope: "You have a place to start, then?"

"Yes, I do."

"So, what is it?"

"I'm going to start at the top and kill my way down."

ONE

"What made you come directly to me, Mr. Null?"

"I wanted to start at the top."

"You've managed that. I'm afraid I'm not entirely comfortable with the fact."

"Comfortable enough to take my deposit?"

"Of course."

"Why uncomfortable?"

"Your reputation precedes you."

"You mean that I'm supposed to be dead?"

"No. I don't think anyone in Boston is fooled by that tale anymore."

"BPD thinks it's pretty credible."

"Yes, but really, who are they?"

"Exactly, Mr. Finnerty. You know, I was hoping we'd do this in your office at city hall. You are the head of code enforcement, after all."

"There are some things I don't care to do while on the people's dime."

"This One Boston Place office is pretty swanky, though. Nice view."

"May I review the deposit?"

Null produced an attaché case resting by his chair near his feet and placed it gingerly down on the conference table. "By all means. All in cash, as requested. You can count it if you want. I'm patient."

"That's another reason why I agreed to meet this way—

a purely cash transaction. Kind of a rarity these days." He snapped the case open, revealing neat little bundles of paper money. Appreciated the feel of it.

"Nothing funny about what's in the case."

"Apparently, your being Boston's meth king makes you pretty free with the cheddar."

"I have more than I know what to do with."

"Only people lacking imagination have that problem."

"I admit it: I lack imagination."

"Not good for a king to lack imagination."

"I never wanted to be king. Is the deposit enough?"

"It's actually a little much, but I'll make sure it'll be fairly applied to your account."

"And you're saying I get a two-to-one return on my investment, after I finish the first payment?"

"Exactly—with a very short turnaround."

"You seem nervous, Finnerty."

"I am. All of Boston knows what you've done. I hear things"

"Gossip always exaggerates."

"Maybe so, but there isn't anyone doing business in town who isn't a little afraid of you."

"Do I inspire fear?"

"In all honesty, yes. And we'll have to hurry this meeting along, regardless. I have city business going too, you know."

"I need a few verifications from you before I leave."

"Go ahead and ask."

"The money is going directly into the KP end of the business."

"Yes, that's why it's a high investment, high-yield, short turn-around proposition."

"Are you involved in that?"

"No. I have nothing to do with the nuts and bolts day to day."

"No contact with the, um, subjects?"

"Never. I never touch them."

"So, you're removed from the whole thing?"

"I can't say that. I actually run it. This is how I can ensure your investment dividends. I manage the ebb and flow of product and profit."

"You're the boss—covering all of New England, correct?"

"All of it that counts; there may be a couple of gypsy outfits out in Rhode Island and Connecticut, but they can't last. New Hampshire's a joke. We eventually absorb them."

"No need to be nervous, Finnerty."

"Why are you here? You could have had the cash delivered. Wire transfer would have been just fine."

"I'm not the most trusting person. I like to know who I'm doing business with. And I prefer doing business with the boss. Take it easy, Finnerty. You're sweating."

"This doesn't feel right, Null. *You* don't feel right."

"If you're that uptight, why not call security?"

"You're going to let me?"

"Probably not."

"There's not much you can do here. Just go. I don't want your money."

"Too late for that, Finnerty. You've earned it."

"What do you want?"

"Nothing. Literally. What I think should be done, though, is another issue."

"I don't understand."

"Why so worried? I'm not carrying any weapons. Your boys outside in the hall and down in the lobby made sure of that. You have four inches and maybe sixty pounds on me. You should be pretty confident you could take me. If you had to, I mean."

"Listen, I've heard stories—"

"I'm not here to tell you any stories. But you can tell me a story. The children. Just what are they to you?"

"What are they to anyone? Nothing. I don't know them. They're a commodity, to just about anyone. Not even human, if you really think about it."

"Not human?"

"They're like animals. Desperate, scrounging, no families, no one involved with them. What kind of life and future do they face? They'd starve to death or freeze. Wind up abused, molested and killed. At best, a drain on society. At least with us, they have a purpose and are well-treated. Rewarded even."

"To be abused, molested and killed? That's well-treated?"

"Not at all. My operations are clean. They're fed, clothed, sheltered. We use them up until there's nothing to get out of them anymore, that's all. They age out just as they would in any foster program."

"Then what?"

"We do the only logical thing: we sell them outright to make room for the next batch."

"Batch?"

"One of the great things about this business: We never seem to run out of product."

"Who do you sell them to?"

"Solid, substantial people. Qualified buyers. The crème de la crème in most cases."

"Sounds like an excellent starting position."

"I don't know what you mean."

"Your office here—sound-proofed, am I right?"

"You are."

"I think now might be a good time for you to go and call security."

Nervous, tightening: "You're going to do something?"

"Let me ask you something—"

Finnerty's face went gray, his lips dragged down into a frown; beads of sweat dappled his forehead as he looked back toward his big, impressive cherrywood desk. He seemed poised. Ready to jerk from the table and get up fast, making whatever move he could. "What?" he asked by reflex just before.

Null's eyes narrowed. "Got a pencil?"

———

Finnerty lay on the floor flopping on his back, his corduroy jacket strewn on the rug, his paisley tie loosened, panting like a freshly caught fish. His blue Brooks Brothers shirt was spotted with deep spreading vermillion patches of blood. Null was on him, stabbing him strategically, methodically and with odd calm, with a pencil.

"Too bad you missed that call for security."

The pencil, with its now broken tip, nevertheless went right through Finnerty's left arm and he let out a guttural scream.

"Sound proofed. Don't you remember? Clever."

Null stabbed him in the abdomen.

"Messy work."

Finnerty rumbled up from his throat with a difficult whine: "Please stop! I'll give you anything you want!"

"Yes, I believe you." Null stabbed the right arm as Finnerty struggled pointlessly. "Trouble is, I don't want anything."

"You're killing me!"

"Yes. That's the plan."

He bucked up hard, trying to dislodge Null from his position on top of him. It was a no go. Null punched him hard in the jaw to quiet him down.

"You have two options here: One is to die slowly in agony; two is to die in agony faster. That's it. You're not surviving this meeting. I guarantee it."

"Fuckstick! My men'll kill you on the way out!" He spat flecks of blood.

Null shrugged. "Could happen. But I found your gun. I knew you'd be keeping one around just in case. No flies on you, Finnerty." Null produced a Heckler & Koch P7 from his over-coat. "I like the suppressor."

"You're dead, Null!" Finnerty screamed.

"I hear that a lot. I think it's at least half-true. But you will be fully dead and there's no way around that." He sank the pencil into his abdomen and Finnerty squealed. Blood congealed in muck about the stomach. Null took his hands off the pencil for a moment and let it waver there with Finnerty's breathing.

Null fumbled his smart phone out from his coat pocket and snapped a picture of Finnerty's face, who winced with the flash.

Null muttered, "Premature, I think," and pocketed back the phone.

"Please—!"

"Make up your mind about how you want to die."

"Anything you want!"

"Great. Dying in faster agony for you then."

Finnerty began to cry, sobbing wounded and vulnerable, just like—

"Crying like a child? Maybe you want sympathy, mercy, humanity?"

"Please!"

"I can't. You sold it all to rich perverts after it aged out. It's all used up and dead, Finnerty. Just like you."

Null stabbed him with the pencil deep into his shoulder, which produced a gasp of air from Finnerty that sounded like a sigh, combined with a whimpering.

"You're like a child on the chopping block, ain't you, Finnerty?"

Finnerty tried again wildly. "Anything!"

"The list of clients you sell the aged-out children to, please. Also, it would be nice to have a breakdown of the entire operation. Flow charts, hierarchies, payout information. That would be handy and helpful."

Finnerty coughed, drooling. "The laptop on the desk. Has everything. Just take it and screw!"

"I don't need anything else?" Null punched him dead in the face as he tried to rise, then stabbed him again with great force carefully in the thigh. "Nothing else?"

Finnerty screamed, high pitched this time, frail sounding. Null gave him just enough time to recover himself. "No," he managed to rasp. "All there." Wheezing.

"That's all I need then," said Null, stretching his arms.

Finnerty stifled a cough, heaved breathing, struggled to speak: "You— You'll be dead before you get to use it!"

Null sank the blood-debauched pencil firmly into the center of Finnerty's chest.

"That'll make two of us then."

———

"Kill him!" hollered the first one running down the hall, firing a powerful automatic. Null dropped to the floor, twisted out of the spray. "Kill the bastard!"

With soft, suppressed bursts, Null took out the young man's throat, and he promptly dropped like forgotten baggage. Null stood, spotted with gore on his overcoat and porkpie hat, his arm extended with the Heckler & Koch P7, carrying the attaché case with the laptop in it, walking toward the elevator bank.

Null shouted clearly, "It's inevitable that you're going to die, probable that I'm going to kill you, but you don't have to die today! I need some time to look at Finnerty's laptop! So, if you were to run, I'd have much better things to do than catch you!"

Nothing. The quiet, somber buzzing of fluorescent lights and security cameras. The bell of the elevator.

"Could it be you going down? Let's hope."

Instead, a man rounded the corner from the elevator bank, started to raise his arm.

Null blew his face away with half a clip of the Heckler & Koch P7 before he could clearly see it.

"This is a good gun."

He stepped over the corpse on the floor.

"Not your lucky day. I'm not sure you're the right one, but every endeavor affords a margin of error."

Null noticed a shadow behind him, fired into it without looking away from the corpse.

A blonde-haired boy, Null guessed at around 18-years old, fell to his knees and coughed blood, fired single rounds into the walls going down. Null had managed to hit him in the chest, the belly and the groin without looking. He stepped over to what was left of his assailant.

"Just a kid. Another KP casualty—backwards."

He snapped pictures with his cell phone.

He went back to the corpse at the corner of the elevator bank and fired two rounds directly into the head, shrugged, and took the next elevator down, his gun drawn in the event he had a meeting in the lobby.

"This suppressor is impressive," he said to absolutely no one.

He exchanged the clip in the gun for a full one going down.

The elevator doors parted for the final time and a middle-aged, dark-haired man with a pock-marked face sized him up, turned toward him.

Null shot his lights out before he could make any clear determination about the man.

"The margin for error here appears to be higher than expected."

People in the lobby scattered off to the sides, cutting Null a wide berth as he left, walking at a moderate pace, the Heckler poised and ready. When he hit State Street, he pocketed the gun in his overcoat and sauntered past a couple of cops who elbowed their way past him, shouting for him to move.

"All in a hurry, but with no real place to go. No, not this time."

Null strolled toward the Orange Line near Faneuil Hall, whistling the blues tune through his teeth, "I Asked for Water, but She Gave Me Gasoline."

TWO

It was a squat split-level house on Dedham Street in Newton that was impressive fifty years ago but had since developed a shabby gray layer in the passing years and a passive sort of sag to its stature. Danish modern, now dilapidated passé, and yet an exorbitant dwelling on a pricey street that priced out all the actual middle class for whom it was originally built. It was a little after one in the morning and some lights in the house were still on. Bernie Franking, late forties, slump-postured, pot-bellied, bespectacled wandered into the den of the house from the bedroom at the end of the hall where he had been napping. His computer was running, and the television was still on at a low volume crooning continuous cable news.

A man draped in a dark overcoat wearing a porkpie hat rumpled up and looking himself to be a kind of shadow was slumped in a leather recliner. Bernie stopped cold and shuddered for a moment. He cleared his throat. He knew what this was.

"Street," he grumbled. "I'm not *street*. You've got the wrong guy. If you have a problem with the company, I can give you a name and a number."

"Exactly what I came here for," said Null softly. "I'll want that name and number."

"I'll get it for you," Bernie said.

"Not yet," Null replied and pulled the Heckler & Koch P7. Aimed it straight, relaxed in his lap.

Bernie was cool, stayed still.

"What do you want?"

"Everything," said Null, unblinking, almost in a whisper. "I want it all."

"There's no cash on hand. Nothing of value here. My wife and kids are asleep down the hall."

"I'll try not to wake them."

"I see." He rubbed his chin, slumping a bit as he stood. "If you let me, I'll get you what you want."

"Do you even know what I want?"

"Manny Legere's number. He's the guy to talk to."

"You mean he's the guy who'll whack me out?"

Bernie smiled and shook his head, stroking back his receding hairline. "If that's what it takes, sure. He's street. He deals with bums like you. He has people to take care of problems like you."

"Good to know. So, how smart is it really, do you think, to call a guy with a high-powered semi-automatic pistol and suppressor aimed at your face a bum?"

"Makes no difference. If you were going to kill me, you'd have done it already. But your little plan won't work—they won't be giving you any money for my safe return. They'd see me die before they gave you a nickel."

"I believe that's true, Bernie. I'm not here for that."

"So, what are you here for, then? Get to the point. I'm tired and it's late."

"You have balls, Bernie, I'll give you that."

"It's easy to have balls compared to a sack-less low life like you. Do what you came to do and screw, already."

"You're next. You're number two."

"What the fuck are you talking about?

"Finnerty."

Bernie scrunched up his face, adjusted his rimless glasses. "Jesus. You're the whack job that offed Finnerty?"

"With a pencil."

"A number two pencil?"

"*You're* number two. Which means you're next."

"You're talking about Hebe Group."

"If that's what you call it."

"That's the name of the financial entity whose money I move to and fro."

"You're the accountant."

"No, we have several of those. You could say I'm the comptroller."

"But you know about the street."

"I know enough to know I have nothing to do with it. And to send schmucks like you packing."

"You're clean. No contact with the filthy little kiddies?"

"None. I do the money, oversee the legal end, manage financial compliances, investments, employee benefits."

"Benefits?"

"Second and third-tier employees get a modest benefits package, ala carte health, 401k, dental."

"You're very forthcoming, Bernie."

"I just want you to go, so I'll tell you whatever you need to know."

"You have the wrong idea about this meeting, Bernie."

"Why do you say that?"

"Because it's highly unlikely you're going to survive it."

"The sound of shots will wake the wife and kids. You intend to kill them too?"

"No, not if I can help it. The suppressor attached to the barrel here does a pretty good job with the noise. Hardly makes any."

"What do I have to say to make you leave and not kill me?"

"Answers, Bernie. I want answers."

"Just ask."

"You think it's alright, what you do, making porn with children, forcing them to have sex with men—"

"Women too."

Null nodded. "Okay. Women too. Log-boys, "young friends" they call them on the dark web: little children fucked constantly for content, live streaming playhouses, special DVDs, one-on-one camera sessions for the goofs, then sold off as slaves when they hit puberty. Or just outright killed when it suits your purposes—when the product is too damaged to sell. You have someone break their necks."

"You make it sound ugly, inhuman."

"You mean it isn't?"

"It's like dealing with loaves of bread, really. We think of it that way. They're just a commodity—we invest in the product, perfect it, package it, leverage it then sell it. It's a straight up business—nothing more."

"What do you think of these little, innocent children you whore out and murder?"

Bernie chuckled. "Innocent? Really. You're not that naïve. Most of the kids we get have been whored out and raped long before we came into the picture. They come from nothing, from abuse and horror, headed for nothing. We rescued them, gave them medical attention, fed them well, even gave them a little tutoring—"

"How many of them are there?" Calm, almost unctuous.

"Recent count?"

"That will do."

"Two twenty, including the ones being readied for sale."

"You're like me. You feel nothing."

"What's to feel? They're barely even human. Little beasts, crying monsters of savage disgust. Hebe Group is their salvation. We make their terrible lives livable; give them a chance."

"I don't think you're lying."

"I'm not."

"There's something in that. I believe you believe what you're saying."

"As far as I know, it's true. You've got what you need?"

"No, I need total Hebe Group employee information—everything. Home addresses, hours they work, physical location of where they work. Birthdays, salaries, the works."

"I have all that, but it might not prove to be, umm, totally accurate. And we have some 1099 contractors who might, uh—"

"Might not actually *be* on a 1099."

"Exactly."

"How do you plan to give it to me?"

"I can send it to you in a zip or rar file."

"No, I have to leave here with it in my pocket." He leaned toward Bernie, expressionless. "Give me the remote address of your VPN, the IP address and all the passwords and we'll be done."

"Sure. Easy-peasy. How do you know I won't change them before you gain access?"

"Let me worry about that."

Bernie breathed a sigh of relief. He was getting off easy. Maybe he'd give him a day, just to be certain, then make the necessary changes. He'd have to meet with Legere about security. Now that he was de facto the one in charge, these kinds of incursions had to be prevented. Legere would track this thug down and murder him neatly and quietly in some occult venue, same as always. Still, this was a curious mess that had to be accounted for and prevented in the future. No telling who else knew about the group and how much information this joker had gotten from Finnerty.

Oh, well, soon it would be a moot point.

Bernie was given leave by Null to sit down and write out the information. He handed it to Null, who had by then put away the Heckler & Koch P7. He pocketed the paper, turned his back on Bernie, who for a moment actually thought of doing something, maybe battering him on the head with one of the pots in the foyer, but thought better of it and decided just to let him go.

Getting rid of him was the key point, and that was happening.

Null left the house, quiet as a whisper.

By the time six in the morning had rolled around, Bernie had barely slept. He was anxious to get back to the office on Beacon Street and meet with Legere and some of management to attack this security breach and the potential problems it might cause, even after Legere disposed of the criminal, and he was obviously a criminal, not a person of substance like them. This could turn into something serious, jeopardizing the bottom line. Rules had to be tightened. He was getting used to being in charge. So far, he liked the fit.

It was a gray New England morning—misty—just past dawn. He was leaving early today. Bernie opened the driver's side door of his Audi, humming "What a Fool Believes," as Null came up silently behind him with the Heckler & Koch P7, suppressor pointed squarely at the back of his head and blew his brains out with a single round.

Then he flipped the body over and snapped a picture of what was left of Bernie's face with his phone.

THREE

Null drove a flat black painted Ford Escort from back in the 90s to University Place off Beacon, to the retrofitted help center — multi-service center it would have been called decades ago, with new MSWs and humanities graduates dealing with social awareness of issues of alternative sexuality, STDs, runaways, drugs, all for a pittance or a stipend long ago when youth was far more epidemic. Now, the parcel of prime rental real estate was occupied by the Dapper O'Neil Shelter and Service Group, a final stopgap before the street for dispossessed gay men. But he wasn't even sure it did that anymore. Ever since the death of Kenny Embers, he no longer knew exactly what social service Dapper O'Neil provided but he knew one thing:

Ruth Coelacanth was still there.

The replacement institutional door was mismatched with the concrete façade of the building with a window cross-hatched by chicken wire. He had to be buzzed in by some weedy looking graduate student with stringy hair, a slouching gait and hollow eyes. Null elbowed past him and some older looking volunteers to where he remembered Ruth Coelacanth's office should be.

The door was open.

The hour was late, especially for a halfway house, social services stopover for the doomed, but there she was, hunched over at her desk typing on a generations-too-old laptop. He watched her for a moment, silent and still, and he remained invisible to her. He broke the silence in a small voice.

"Mrs. Coelacanth."

She started in her seat, then rose up abruptly from the desk.

"You!" she scolded, approaching him warily.

"You remember me?"

"Yes, Mr. Null. I remember you."

"It's been awhile."

"Not nearly long enough."

"It seems a lot of people feel that way about it."

"Your protégé left us long ago. I can't tell you anything about him."

"I know what happened. He's dead."

"I can't say that's unexpected from what I see here every day."

"No, it wasn't unexpected."

"May I ask?"

"I ripped a knife out of his chest and he bled to death."

Silence and obvious disquiet affected Ruth Coelacanth as she shifted her weight from one foot to the other. She took a hard breath.

"You didn't kill him?"

"I made it happen, but there was no way it wasn't going to happen. And the ones that took him out don't walk the earth anymore."

"What in God's name do you want from me, Mr. Null?"

"I need to know what to do with some children."

Her face was deeply perplexed, as if she were waking from an absurd dream.

"I don't understand."

Null seemed patient, relaxed. "It's simple: I am going to have a bunch of children and I need to find a place to put them."

"What kind of children?"

"All kinds."

"Are you taunting me, Mr. Null?"

"No, honestly, I'm not."

"Where are the children and where are they coming from?"

"I don't know exactly where they are, and they're from a kiddie porn business that very soon is going to go belly up."

"I don't believe it."

"It's a fact."

"Mr. Null, do you know what you're talking about? Do you know what you're actually *saying?*"

"I'm not sure I do, when you think about it."

"You mean when *you* think about it—I'm not about to!"

"No need to get excited."

"Well, it's monstrous." Beads of sweat had collected across her furrowed brow just below the hairline where the hair was a grim, grayish white. Her rimless glasses hung heavy on her face. She looked frumpy and tired, but her eyes burned.

"From where are you getting these children? This really isn't a set up for children, you know. They can't stay here."

"You're the only person I know who might be able to help me. I travel in a much different circle than you do."

"I don't want to know about that."

"You don't."

"How many children are we talking about, and knowing the age range would be helpful?"

"All ages, but none in their late teens, I think."

"You think. Finding an available bed these days just for one child even for one night is an exhausting problem." She let the silence mount as Null considered what she was saying. "It's all about beds," she said wearily, shuffling over to her desk and sitting back down at it. "A bed means a place to stay, period, not just a place to sleep, although sometimes it can mean just that."

"Then you'll be needing some beds."

"And how many beds would that be, Mr. Null?"

"Approximately two-hundred-twenty-five of them, give or take."

Silence again glissading over palpable shock. Mrs. Coelacanth blinked once, swallowed something back and sputtered, "That can't be real. Give or take."

"Granted. It's an approximation. There very well may be some attrition involved. I don't know how many of them have died since the last headcount was done. The comptroller wasn't able to get very specific when I—"

"I don't really need to know that, do I, Mr. Null?"

"No, I suppose you don't."

"What happened to so many children? Have you seen them, evaluated them, even spoken with them?"

"No, I only saw them accounted for in a spreadsheet. I'll have to take inventory myself when I find them. I don't know where they are. I only have the corporate books."

"Corporate books? What kind of corporation does such things?"

"A profitable one."

"Well, if you know the company name, and the particulars, why not let the police handle it?"

"Because they'll be too fair to those involved. Give them a shot at justice, plea deals, or maybe just blow the whole thing on clumsy forensics, bad evidence chain of custody and legal technicalities. I can't allow that."

"It's how justice works, Mr. Null."

"Not this time."

"And why is that?"

"This is not about judgment. This is only about execution. Guilt is presumed."

"What are you talking about?"

"I am going to kill them all. Every single last one of them. Down to the zero."

She raised her hands to her ears reflexively but did not cover them. "Don't tell me that, please. I can't hear that. Don't tell me that. I don't want to know anything at all about *that*."

"Okay, Mrs. Coelacanth. That's my business. Finding beds is yours."

"I have no idea how I'm going to do it."

"But are you going to do it?"

She sat back and sighed, removed her glasses and wiped the lenses thoughtfully with her sweater. "Yes, I'm going to do it. If what you're saying is true, someone will have to do it."

"And it might as well be you?"

"Who else have we got?"

"That is exactly my point, Mrs. Coelacanth."

"Do you know anything about kiddie porn, Mr. Null?"

"No, I don't think I do beyond the basic idea."

"Well, for the children, it's the deepest kind of hell. They come from abuse, torment and rape, from terrible parents who should be criminally prosecuted. Some of them are kidnapped, lured in by the Internet by some kind of catfishing game. Some younger ones are kidnapped right out of their bedrooms at night and never heard from again. The rest tend to be fall-offs and runaways from the overtaxed foster care system, which is likely where you're proposing we put these children if and when we get them."

"I know all that I think," Null said flatly.

"Do you, Mr. Null? Because these are not going to be easy, happy children grateful for your rescue—they'll fight you tooth and nail."

"But why?"

"You'll be taking away from them the only stability they've ever known. It's all they trust as much as they trust anything at all."

The shadows gathered from the darkening windows as the late spring sun was setting at last throughout the spacious, dusty office with books and papers and archival boxes scattered hither and thither. "They certainly won't trust me," replied Null coldly.

"Why would they? You're a murderous intruder taking away the only protection they have."

"The protection of their abusers, their rapists, their—"

"Family, Mr. Null. We're talking about their family."

"How can they be that?"

"Because the monsters bond with them, imitate kindness and affection. The little ones give in, and the big ones too. The monsters then claim the child wants sex with them, is happy about it, more than complicit, insisting they were asking for it. It's a twisted thing where even the once innocent child doesn't understand the difference between good and evil anymore."

"I'm not sure I do," said Null, pondering what she had said.

"Well, I'm sure you do."

"You're saying this is a lost cause, Mrs. Coelacanth."

"That's what I'm saying."

"The system can't absorb them."

"There is no system anymore, Mr. Null. The Republicans cut it all away. It's been going on for the past thirty years since Reagan chucked all the Federally funded mental patients out onto the street and singlehandedly created the homeless population. There's only scattershot remains where we can try and put them, maybe even some places out of state."

"Maybe you could do that then, Mrs. Coelacanth. Maybe you're just the person to handle it. I don't think I could. My interpersonal skills are a bit—*lacking*."

"I can see that."

"Just get the beds. I'll do the rest. Can I bring them here?"

"I don't know. They have to go someplace, although I have no beds here at the moment."

"Some other place?"

"There is no other pace. Frustrating man. Yes, bring them here."

"At all hours?"

"The last set of volunteers leave at 10:00 p.m.. After that, call my cell. You still have the number?"

"I do."

"Try not to call."

"I won't."

"There's something else you need to think about before you go."

"What is that?"

"They're all drug addicts."

"They drug the kids?"

"They say they don't, that the little ones tire out easily and become complicit, but the truth is they keep them all drugged as much as possible. Heroin and fentanyl are a cheap deal on the street, a quick score, makes it easy to give in, and I'm sure you know all about the meth that keeps them lively. This city has a meth problem as you know."

Null registered a look of surprise at her statement. "You're saying I contribute to this?"

"What do *you* think, Mr. Null?"

"I can't control that."

"Exactly, Mr. Null—*no* one can control it. It touches everyone in the same way or other. You can't stop it, you're not going to be the one who ends it. No doubt it will end you."

"You could be right. But I have a lot of luck with things like this."

"You're going to need it."

"Nevertheless, it's got to be done."

"You'll never be able to do it. And it's bigger than just Boston."

"I know, but I can at least make a dent. What have I got to lose?"

"Your life, for one," Mrs. Coelacanth sighed, shaking her head.

"It's not much of a life and it won't be much of a loss."

"I wish you luck all the same, Mr. Null."

"Thank you. I'll be in touch." Null began to blend in with the shadows as he turned and walked to the door. Before he shut it when he was out of the room, he heard her voice behind him yet again.

"Mr. Null, wait."

He turned to her. "What?"

"When you do what I know you're going to do, will you do something for me as well?"

"Sure. What is it?"

Her voice was cheery and she blinked once.

"Kill every single one of those goddamn bastards you find for me too!"

FOUR

It was another gray, misty Boston morning when Null got off the Red Line at Broadway Station in South Boston. He stood at the top of the escalator for a moment, adjusting himself and his somewhat weighted down overcoat. He walked determinedly with his usual limp all the way down to East Eighth Street to an old warehouse recently retrofitted into commercial rental spaces. There was no security by the elevator banks in the clean, sparse, lobby trimmed attractively in bright green acrylic. He rode up to the third floor.

The elevator opened to an even more sparse lobby with a reception desk, but no receptionist. A homemade, makeshift magic marker confected banner was tacked to the wall reading: "Hebe Analytica." Null left reception and began walking about cubicle-defined corridors of arid dust. It was an unpleasantly fluorescent- lit, nondescript office space with greenish rugs and wallpaper that looked slightly radioactive.

A dowdy, bespectacled young woman stood in his path and said, polite, albeit shaken, "Sir?" she asked tentatively. "Sir, you really can't be in here. This office isn't open to the public. You can't even make an appointment. All we are here is a backbone array of servers and technicians."

Null had obliged her by stopping, cocked his head a little bit to listen to her. He rotated his shoulders, noticing he was a bit stiff. "This is where the chat rooms are served."

"That's old tech. We don't do it like that anymore—"

"And the live feeds. They originate here?"

"No, there's nothing like that here. This is big data—a series of cloud hosts. We just keep things running, hosted, like a relay station."

"A pretty big relay station, I'd say." Null squinted and looked around.

"Big enough, but you have to go."

"I see." Null cocked his head again. "Who do I see if I need to make an appointment?"

"If you really need to see someone, let me get you a card. Just stay right there."

"Sure. I'll wait."

She left hurriedly and emerged from a row of cubicles with a business card for an entirely different business whose names and numbers had been crossed out in pen and others hastily put in. "This is who you need to call. He deals with all outside business. We only deal directly with vendors now and then, and only when we have to."

There were conversations and telephone calls occurring in the background. Nothing out of the ordinary for an average mid-sized office. Some laughter; a raised voice or two.

"So, I should call this guy. Written in on the card."

"Yes. He'll take care of you."

"Who told you to do this? Finnerty? Franking?"

She was getting a bit nervous, he could see No doubt thinking such thoughts as, *"Why wouldn't this jerk just leave already? What was his problem? Didn't he get the point?"* It didn't matter what she thought. "I don't know them, sir. My boss told me—told all of us—that if anyone came here making any inquiries that we should give them that name and number. Even the police."

"And have the police ever come?"

"Why would they?"

"No, I guess they wouldn't. So, do you know who this is? Have you ever met him?"

"Who?"

"The man on the card."

"Emmanuel Legere? Never saw or spoke to him, ever. I never had any reason to speak with him."

"It's too bad that you can't get a hold of him now. It would have proven to be very helpful."

"Why?"

Null reached into his coat pocket and produced the Heckler & Koch P7 with suppressor and put two quick rounds in the young woman's belly. She made a sound that was a combination between a cough and a belch then sank to her knees on the rug.

Groaning, she flopped over to one side.

"That's why," said Null.

"What are you doing?!" she cried, coughing in shock. "Why are you doing this? I don't know you! Stop! Call me an ambulance!"

Other workers abruptly assembled in the corridor, staring in wonder as Null knelt down beside the young woman. They were a rag-tag group of cheaply dressed clerical types, milling about wide-eyed in astonishment. They were expecting perhaps another office surprise party, an impromptu celebration, but certainly not one of their colleagues writhing in agony on the carpet bleeding to death.

They did not expect to be looking down the long barrel of a Heckler & Koch P7 with suppressor either.

"You'll want to stay right there, all of you, and be quiet while I talk to this woman. The first one of you to step forward gets one right to the head." He paused, then added blankly, "I don't think any of you will be calling the police. But go ahead if you want. I'm betting none of you will, maybe because you fear Legere as much as I'm supposed to. For all I know, you may have a point."

A short, squat data wonk type in a Hawaiian shirt stood up and shouted, "Somebody call Legere!" He made for a cubicle which presumably had a phone.

Null dropped him with a short burst of rounds to the thorax from the Heckler.

There was silence after that, but for shallow breathing.

Null broke it, loudly.

"Be sure that I know what I'm doing here, just as sure as you are that you don't have any idea what you're doing at all."

"Okay," volunteered a balding, reedy, obvious middle manager in a tan crew neck sweater in the center of the pile. His followers were murmuring nervously.

"What's your name?" Null demanded of the girl he shot curled up on the floor.

"Please," she whined, gurgling a little. "It hurts so bad. I need help!"

Null studied her.

"Help!" she cried. "Hospital! Hospital!"

Null sounded stern. "Focus, please. Now tell me, what's your name?"

"D-Delores! Please, help me!"

"You know why I'm here, don't you?"

"No, I really don't. Here. Take my ph-phone. Call me an ambulance!"

Null knocked the phone away from her, so it rebounded against the wall and broke open.

Blood, deep, rich and red, was coming down in gouts from her stomach to the rug.

"Too late for that, Delores. You know why I'm here."

"No," she sobbed. "I don't! I don't!"

"Tell me about the children."

"Ambulance!" she screamed. *"Ambulance!*

Null nonchalantly fired another round into Delores's right thigh, and she screamed hysterically. The middle manager, who had been watching in horror, paralyzed at first by fear and confusion, stood up and lunged toward him. Null quickly put three rounds into his midsection, which dropped him down hard to the rug. "Move again, you're next for death."

"Don't let me die!" cried Delores. "Please!"

"But you have to die, and you know why, don't you?"

"Call Legere! Manny! He'll take care of you, you goddamn fucking son of a bitch!"

"Manny," Null repeated softly, knowingly. Then he shouted, "The children. Where are they? Tell me where all the streaming playrooms are at and I promise I'll ease the pain."

"I can't. I don't know. I never wanted to know!"

"She's telling the truth!" the middle manager gulped. "Just stop! Stop this now!"

Null stepped over, shot him point blank in the chest, which quieted him. Then he hovered back over to Delores.

"You know what they're doing."

"I'm in graduate school! That's all I really know! The kids are just the talent!" She was hyperventilating, paused for one deep breath and screamed, "I don't have anything to do with *the fucking talent!* I can't help you!"

"But you know what happens to them, don't you?"

"They live good lives! Don't you see we're helping them to get a better life?" She moaned deep and hard. "It hurts so bad, please! I'm dying." She made a sound that defied category.

"You say they live good lives, tricked out like little whores, fucked online and offline for private clients until they either die or age out and get sold to the highest bidder, in their teens!" He was loud, emphatic, yet listless at the same time.

"They're garbage!" Delores screamed. "Human *garbage!* Just fodder! This is so much better than what they'd get otherwise. Believe me, it's my field of study. Be realistic. We take *care* of them! We're the good guys! Please don't let me die! So much pain." Grunting mixed with spittle to create a fountain of noise.

"It's good to know you feel that way, Delores. You actually feel things. I, unfortunately, do not. But I think I understand you."

"No, you don't! How could you possibly? I'm in graduate school, paying off college loans, busting my ass! I could be of value to the world—*don't throw me away!*"

"Like garbage?"

"No, I have something to offer!"

"What are you going to graduate school for, Delores? What do you have to offer?"

"M-S-W!" she spoke in coughing bursts. "Social—

worker! Please, you're making a mistake. Help me!" She was grunting in agony.

"I'll help you, Delores."

Null stuck the suppressor in Delores's mouth halfway down her throat so that she gagged loudly and bucked up against it. Pushing her back down, he pumped several shots down her windpipe and that was that. Shuffling through his coat pockets, he took out the smart phone, snapped a picture of her face, then pocketed it again and stood up wearily. The middle manager, still alive, squirmed stupidly near Null's feet. He kicked him hard until he lay still.

"Now," announced Null in a clear, loud voice to the huddle of now terrified office workers, waving the Heckler & Koch P7 with suppressor at them. "I think I should have a little conversation with you all about child abuse."

———

Null had some trouble moving quickly enough when they rushed him. He barely had time to produce the new Bushmaster 90291 semi-automatic rifle with 30-round banana clip. He sprayed the rounds into the group just before they cleared the distance to mob him.

They fell, wounded or not.

He gingerly picked up the Heckler from its place on the rug where he had dropped it cavalierly to squeeze off enough shots with the Bushmaster to drop the mob.

Surveying the scene, Null was sure he had killed at least three of the dowdy, nondescript office workers.

"That's unfortunate," he murmured, lost in thought.

Amid the cries for help and moaning of his victims, Null approached and stood over each one, asking questions, getting hysterical responses and cries for pity, mercy and help which an average human being faced with such carnage might be apt to give.

Null instead surveyed the scene gravely.

"Anyone among you able to get up and stand?"

A young woman, much younger than Delores, stood up, raising her hand tentatively.

"Good. What's your name?"

"Michele," she said, just above a whisper.

"Okay Michele. I need you to take some security steps for me. Make sure your floor at the elevator bank is keyed off, make sure there's an outgoing message on the trunk line for the phones, turn off inside access to all the lines."

"I don't have the codes or the key to do that. The office manager does."

"Where is she then?"

Shaking, barely able to maintain an aspect of calm, Michele answered. "She's on the rug behind you. You killed her."

"Inconvenient. Better work out something with your friends on the floor."

"The supervisor might have the elevator key. He has the codes on his computer."

"Well, let's talk to him then."

"C-can't. He's dead over by your feet."

"You're making things complicated."

"No, I can do it."

"Don't try and leave, please. I don't want to have to track you down. And I will, that is if I miss you. You should know I seldom miss."

Michele said nothing but quickly ran to another office off the corridor, then came back holding a key ring. "Mr.—um whoever you are—"

"Null. I am Null."

"Mr. Null. I have to go out to the lobby to lock the elevator."

"Do it. And if you don't come back in a few minutes, everyone else will die. Make it fast."

Michele obliged, realizing as she went that she too had been hit by one of the semi-automatic rifle's rounds. It made her walk funny. Null took notice of the spreading red stain on her sweater as she went.

When she came back holding the keys up so he could see them, Null thanked her, then blew a hole in her abdomen.

He reached under his coat and manipulated something under it, extracting a somewhat short machete.

Machete in one hand, Bushmaster 90291 in the other.

The wounded crowd on the floor made an array of protests and noises: pleas, threats, logical arguments. Null didn't interrupt; he simply waited them out. When a gap of barely murmured silence emerged, Null didn't hesitate to fill it.

"Is there anyone here who doesn't know that nature of the business you're in?"

A weedy young man whose legs had been shot out from under him dragged himself toward Null like an arm-baby. His glasses were half off his face, his breathing shallow and desperate, his complexion was scarlet. He forced the words out of himself.

"We're in data management, asshole. That's all. We don't do anything wrong. You're murdering people for nothing. You're both stupid and crazy!"

"You obviously think I'll murder you for nothing too, while I'm at it."

He coughed out the words. "Take your best shot, motherfucker!"

Null obliged him and pulped his chest with half a clip.

Humming the blues tune, "Who's Been Talkin'?" Null set the machete down and snapped pictures of the dead while the remaining workers cowered in a heap on the floor. He turned to them, holding up machete and Bushmaster 90291 both.

"Now, you're all going to miss meetings and appointments without excuses. You won't be home for dinner. So, obviously we don't have a lot of time, and in that time, we're all going to have a little chat."

"What the fuck do you want?" screamed a male voice from the heap of bodies Null couldn't identify.

"Kiddie Porn. You will tell me where the talent is. When I

leave here, I will know whatever I need to know to find them, even if you don't know that yourselves."

A voice pleaded, "We don't know, they don't tell us. We just have IP addresses."

Null spoke quietly. "When I leave here, I will know where each and every child is. And I will know everything I need to know to find the rest of you—whoever is making this business work."

Another voice from within the pile spoke. "It's not us! Please! Find Legere! I have his number. He can help you."

"Not if I help him first," Null replied and fired a burst of rounds directly into the center of the pile. They quieted after that.

An attractive blonde woman doubled over on the floor nearest Null, who looked dressed as if she were in outside sales, caught his eye. He dragged her closer, knelt down as if to speak to her, but she spoke abruptly first. "Please, God, no. I don't know anything! I really don't! I don't!"

"Of course not," Null replied.

"Thank you," she heaved.

In a cool gesture, he raised up the machete and in a single, neat downward stroke, lopped off her right hand.

"Now," he hissed. "Tell me."

The afternoon had become even grayer than the morning. There were no sirens, but those in the distance—maybe an ambulance or two. They didn't sound as if they were coming closer. Weighed down by the Heckler, the Bushmaster, the Glock and machete under his coat, which added a swinging imbalance to his gait, Null took the long walk back to the Broadway T station.

After fifteen or so interviews conducted with aid of the machete, he was ready to visit his first playhouse.

FIVE

It was a nice yellow and white trim two-family clapboard house just outside of Brookline Village—one of the old owner occupancies from the age of gentrification. With two large Romanesque pillars supporting a porch roof, it was built in the old Georgian style. Quietly prim with well-maintained lawn and shrubbery on a quietly prim street.

On the second floor, Clark Christian, a portly, balding man with a slumped posture wearing a blue terry bathrobe, was getting his little girl ready for bed, standing in the recently rehabbed kitchen with gleaming new fixtures. The little girl, who had to be at least six, maybe just a little older and wearing freshly washed sweetheart pajamas, was named Jenna. She looked very sleepy.

"Daddy, can I have more milkies?"

"No, honey bunny. No more milkies for you. Too much of a good thing."

"Is it loving-time, Daddy, before I go sleepies?"

"Yes, angel. Did you brush your teeth?"

"I did, Daddy, like a really good girl. You like me when I'm a really good girl."

"You're always a really good girl, sweetheart."

She puffed out her little chest at this and smiled. "I know I am! You tell me all the time."

"Now you get into bed and very soon we shall have some lovin'- time."

She squealed a tired, happy squeal and skipped off to the bedroom adjoining the kitchen. "Okay, daddies!"

There was banging coming from downstairs. Christian didn't look out the window. He didn't have to. From the mini-drawer next to the classic premium giveaway gas stove, he withdrew a 38 Smith & Wesson revolver, opened it, gave the carousel a spin then snapped it closed. He put it in the pocket of his bathrobe, which made it hang funny.

He paused for a long time in between breaths, but there was nothing but silence—not even the bedtime murmurings of a small child.

Christian started breathing again, chuckling to himself and shaking his head.

Christian rinsed out the pot, and the unicorn decorated glass from the warm milk he had given Jenna, wiped the stovetop shaking his head at his own foolishness.

He jumped back hard and threw the glass to the side when Null kicked in the door, his shoulders rounded from the weight of his coat, face darkened in shadow from the porkpie hat, wheezing just slightly.

"Shit!" barked Christian.

"Where's the kid?" Null asked, as if he were seeking the time of day.

"Get out before I call the police." Christian grabbed hold tightly of the Smith & Wesson in the pocket of his robe but kept it there.

"There's no chance of you calling the police. But go ahead. It should be interesting if you do."

Christian breathed a sigh of relief, chuckled a bit and looked up at Null with twinkling eyes. "Mister, I don't know what you think you're doing here, but you've got the wrong house. All I am is a retired single dad, living with his little girl. That's all."

"You didn't say she was your daughter."

"I didn't have to. Obviously, she is."

"Let's find out from her."

40

"It's her bedtime. I don't want to disturb her."

"Just you and her. No one else here at all?"

"The downstairs tenants. Why don't you go ask them and leave us alone here?"

Null looked about, wandered off into the dark hall then wandered back.

"Pretty nice set-up here."

"It should be. My life's work."

Null picked up a small bottle from the counter beside the stove. Examined it. "Liquid Thiopental. Must be hard to get." He put it down.

"It's prescribed. Any good pharmacist can prepare it that way."

"Expensive."

"I have health insurance off the ObamaCare."

"You dose her pretty heavy with it?"

"You need to leave."

"I do, but not yet."

"I can make you leave."

"Can you, Clark?"

"So, you know my name. Big deal. Who cares what you know?"

"You'll care. And soon."

"Listen, fuckstick. My daughter is asleep in the next room—"

"No, I'm not Daddy! I-I-I'm still away-ake!" It was Jenna, popping her little head abruptly out the half-opened door to her bedroom. She opened it all the way and shuffled into the kitchen. *"Whosis?"* she asked.

Christian grabbed the Smith & Wesson ever tighter in an already white-knuckled grip in his pocket. He blanked knowing how to play it—and he had been playing it for years. Despite this, he froze.

"This is, um, Mr...."

"Hello, Jenna. I'm Mr. Null."

"Hi, Mister Null. Can you please go 'cause Daddy and I are gonna have some lovin' time soon an' it's *private.*"

Null knelt down to Jenna and looked her dead in the eye. "Daddy and I have to talk about some grown up stuff, so you should get back into bed and I'll come and tuck you in in a little bit."

"What about my daddy?"

"He's going to be very busy."

"He's going to boot your ass out of here!"

"Do you really want to do this with me in front of the child?"

Jenna waddled over to Christian sleepily and tugged on his robe. "Is it lovin' time yet, Daddy?"

"Yes, *daddy*," echoed Null. "Is it time?"

"Milkies, Daddy?"

"Yes, baby." Null watched as Christian heated some milk and dosed it with Thiopental. It warmed quickly and he gave it to her in the unicorn glass. She drank it quickly, then handed the glass back to Christian.

"Now hop on back into bed and I'll come in and tuck you in very soon."

"But Mr. Null said *he'd* tuck me in."

"Mr. Null is mistaken, dear heart."

"Are we still gonna have lovin' time still?"

"Yes, baby, we sure will."

He bent down to kiss her on the head and she scampered back to her bedroom and closed the door.

The two stood there, looking at each other for a moment. Quiet but for the buzzing of the overhead light and uneven breathing.

"You're one guy, Null. Not a very big guy at that. You break in here, and think you can screw with me and disturb my girl? I'll kick your fucking ass, shit-for-brains."

"Make your move, Christian."

He pulled the Smith & Wesson, held it up somewhat shakily. "I don't have to kick your ass. I could just put one in you, maybe two, for good measure."

"You sure you want to wake Jenna with that?"

"She's doped up enough so it won't matter."

"You put that drug in her every night?"

"Yeah—it makes things go dreamy smooth. Now, get the fuck out of here before I kill your ass."

"I'm not ready yet."

"Yeah, motherfucker? Well, get ready."

"Okay," said Null, and in the quick blur of a moment just as Christian blinked his eyes, he had the machete out, raised up and slashing down, taking the hand that held the Smith & Wesson cleanly off at the wrist and sending both to the floor. Christian stood there trembling and wordless, the stump of his wrist dribbling down blood.

"Now I'm ready," Null added, and then put two nine-millimeter rounds directly into Christian's gut before he had the chance to let out an inarticulate cough of shock and surprise and sink down to the linoleum.

"Wh-what do you want?" sobbed Christian.

"I'll take the little girl, for starters."

"No—she's all I have!"

"It doesn't matter anymore, Christian. All you have is gone now anyway."

In response, Christian made for the severed hand and the gun by the stove. Null kicked him in the head to stop him, propped him up against the front of the stove, then broke his nose with a direct hammer blow to the face.

He sobbed gushily, "Call 911! Get me to a hospital—I'll tell you everything you want to know!"

"You'll tell me anyway. And I won't be calling 911 until after you're dead, which won't be as soon as you would like."

"No, I wanna live!"

Null sighed. "I'm going to change that."

"I'll tell you anything, flip on anybody. Just help me."

"I'll be helping you, that's for sure."

Blood drooled out of Christian's mouth. "Please," he managed.

Null abruptly spread his arms and spun about slowly, addressing all corners of the room. He spoke loudly. "This is going to be a different show that what you're used to. There will be no lovin' time tonight. Think of this as a cautionary tale—

what will happen to you when I find you. And I am very good at finding people who don't want to be found. But don't log off. It's too late. Just try to profit from what I'm about to show you."

"You—knew—about the cameras?"

"I did. I knew about the cameras everywhere sent to all you pedophiles by Hebe Group. You're independent contractor entertainers, each with your own wired up, camera-ready Internet playhouses. A franchise of disgust, horror and torment."

"It's-not-that-bad," Christian spat out, heaving. Then he screamed so that Null thought even Jenna could hear it. "We LOVE—our—little girls!" He began to spasm and Null got down on the bloody linoleum next to him. With an air of weary calm, he hacked off Christian's left foot.

"Where did you steal her from?"

"I was saving her—" he coughed bloodily—"*from a bad home*! I was helping her!" His breathing became sharp and shallow and his tongue hung outside of his mouth as Null hacked off the other foot in a hard, single downward stroke with such force and speed there was barely any blood.

Christian wailed.

Null took out his phone and snapped a picture of the craggy, agonized face. "For the files," he said, then asked again: "Where did you take her from?"

Christian spilled it and concurrently peed a great volume on the linoleum so that Null had to jump up and back to avoid getting wet. Christian repeated it to make sure Null could understand him.

"Thank you," Null said in a quiet voice, mopping up the area around Christian with the sponge mop that had been leaning up against the refrigerator, then got back down on the floor, and sat cross-legged.

"We've got a few more pieces to go before I call 911," he said reasonably.

Christian whimpered softly, "Please."

"You need pity," Null observed. "Compassion. Sensitivity —*empathy*. Right?"

He whimpered again in answer.

"Human kindness, right?"

"Yes!" Christian groaned.

Null said it firmly, coolly. "These are the things you happily destroy when you rape and sodomize a child. The absence of these things is what you invite when you do it." Null raised the machete.

Christian answered back stertorously, weeping: *"Nooooo!"*

"I am the absence of these things."

Then Null went quietly and diligently about the serious task of hacking Christian to little pieces.

SIX

"Why'd you make me wear a pillowcase over my head, Mr. Null?" asked Jenna.

"Some things a child should never see," said Null, turning the flat black Ford escort onto the Mass Turnpike.

"I'm *not* a child," Jenna said, pouting. "I am a grown lady already."

"No, Jenna, you're a child. A very nice little girl child. You should try and hold onto that."

"Daddy says I'm grown up enough for lovin' time. I love my daddy." She hugged herself as if for reassurance over the slightly loose seatbelt—being that she was too small to fasten it tightly around—sitting next to Null as he drove.

"We're not going to talk about lovin' time anymore for today, okay?"

"'Kay," she sighed. "Why couldn't my daddy come?"

"Daddy's asleep, Jenna. He's going to be asleep for a very long time."

"Where we goin'?"

"I'm taking you home, Jenna, to your parent's house."

"Aren't daddies parents?"

"They are."

"Then take me back to my daddy, please."

"I'm taking you back to your real parents, Jenna."

Jenna was upset; suddenly red-faced. "Please, oh please stop the car, Mr. Null!"

"No, Jenna, I can't. We're on the highway and there's no place to put you."

"I can walk!"

"No, you can't. You're a very drugged little girl. I don't know how you can be awake. Or maybe I do."

Jenna screamed, red faced and teary eyed. "Let me out!"

"I will when we get there. I promise."

"Don't take me back to the bad people!"

"Why are they bad, Jenna?"

"My daddy says they're bad, and he knows everything."

"Did they hurt you?"

"I got spankings! Daddy never spanked me!"

"Anything else?"

"They yelled a lot—all the time. Yelling, yelling. They made the house shake."

"And that's all?"

"I didn't get no lovin' time."

"None?"

"Maybe a li'l' kiss sometimes, but that's all."

"That's it?"

"Daddy says a grown-up lady like me can't live without her lovin' time."

Null turned the car onto Spiers Road off Dedham Street in Newton after having barreled down the VFW Parkway from West Roxbury. He pulled into the empty driveway at number forty.

"We're here, Jenna."

"But I don't wanna *be* here!"

"Sometimes grown-up ladies have to do things they don't want to. So, you be a good little grown-up lady and come with me."

Jenna pouted, her head down. "I'm sleepies."

"I'll bet you are."

Eyes and head up, she questioned, "Carry me?"

Null, distant, cool and patient. "Of course. That'll be fine."

47

A dark-haired, frowzy woman with sad, bedraggled features opened the door and seemed to sag right before them. Null held Jenna in one arm and she nestled her head into his shoulder.

"What do you want?" she asked, near slurring. Then suddenly her face came alive before Null could explain. She became short of breath before Null could respond and whimpered, "It can't be!"

"I'm sorry, I don't have your name, but is this little girl your daughter?"

"I want my daddy!" Jenna cried into the folds of his coat."

"My God." The woman cried. "Oh, my Jesus Christ!"

"I'm Null," he said quietly. "My name is Null. May we come in?"

The woman said nothing, so Null pushed past her carrying Jenna into what was a modestly furnished, clean and slightly Mediterranean tacky living room. He plopped the semi-sleeping Jenna in a gold trimmed yellow velour imitation Second Empire chair. The woman went over to Jenna and examined her closely.

"Can I go back to my daddy, please?" asked Jenna groggily.

"Shirley, sweetie, it's me, your mum. You remember me, honey?"

"Daddy says you and the other daddy are bad. I wanna go home."

"You are home, doll face!" And the woman bent down and embraced her while she sloppily struggled away from her mother's kiss. She left Shirley alone and rose coldly, staring at Null.

"What did you do to her, you son of a bitch?!"

"Take it easy Mrs.—? I don't know your name."

"It's Quinlan. And what the fuck did you do to my daughter? I'm phoning the cops."

"You might want to wait on that a little bit, Mrs. Quinlan, but sure, by all means, call them."

"What am I supposed to be waiting for, you pedophile fuck?"

"Just information, that's all. Maybe a little direction for you going forward. Nothing dire, I assure you."

"You're despicable, you cowardly shit."

"Mrs. Quinlan, please. It wasn't me. I didn't take her at all. I suppose you could say I rescued her, if you like that term. I prefer extraction. I extracted her from the pedophile operation that had her and brought her here."

"I don't understand—"

"You agree that that's your daughter?"

"Yes, didn't you know that?"

"I had to be sure, considering the world that I brought her out of."

"Oh, yeah, and what world is that?"

"You don't want to know.

"But yes, it's my Shirley. We—my soon-to-be-ex-husband and I—we thought she was dead. The cops gave up long ago."

"I don't doubt it."

"We had given up. I'm so confused! What are you? *Who* are you?"

"I'm the man who brought your little girl home."

"But why?"

"Because it had to be done. That's enough reason. It simply had to be."

"What do you want, Mr. Null? We—I don't have much money. The separation and divorce are costing us dearly. We're struggling—"

"I don't want any money. In fact, I'll check in and see if you need any money. I'll check in anyway."

"Check in why?"

"To make sure Shirley's alright."

"She seems good—she's clean. I can smell scented skin cream on her."

"I can assure you she's not good. No, not very good at all."

Shirley assented with breathy little snores that filled the short silences between them. There were no other sounds but the buzzing of the lights from a rheostat set on low.

"How long ago was she taken? How did they get her?"

"Six months ago. Taken right out of her bedroom window."

"Snatch and grab."

"Yeah. I blamed Irv because he never invested in an alarm system, said this neighborhood is safe."

"Nowhere is safe, Mrs. Quinlan. Nowhere at all."

"We know that now."

"Maybe having Shirley back will save your marriage. But I don't know about such things."

"What's broke sometimes can't be fixed."

"True, but it can be made into something new. Good or bad, I don't know."

"Just tell me what you want already, so I can put her to bed."

"Yes. What I want. Okay, Mrs. Quinlan, what you have to do is call the cops. Tell them a strange man you can't describe dropped your daughter off in the dead of night."

"You don't like the cops, do you?" She gave him a sly look.

"Not the point. Just leave me out of it."

"I can do that."

"Good. Tell the cops you're taking her to the nearest hospital. Newton/Wellesley isn't it?"

"That's the one."

"Have them meet you there."

"Why? Why not tomorrow?"

"Your little girl needs medical attention right away. She's been raped constantly since the time she was taken. Raped, sodomized, by we don't know how many men."

"Oh my fucking god!" She began quaking with rage and tears began to well in her drooping eyes.

"Hold it together, Mrs. Quinlan."

"She's six years old, for Christ's sake!"

"It's a dreadful thing." Null paused as if stuck, made a hesitant gesture to speak, then stopped. The buzzing of the lights and the little girl snoring seemed to envelop the small, white room. "They'll want to do a rape kit on her!" he blurted out. "Maybe give her something for the drugs they've been feeding her. Tonight, it's Thiopental, but we don't know what else she's been on. She's likely addicted to something—they'll need to start her on detox right away."

"I'll do it, Mr. Null. Like you said. Right away."

"Fine. Just leave me out of it, please."

"It's the least I can do."

"What you can do is take care of her. She's going to need a lot of help, probably a psychologist. Lots of therapy. I'll give you the money for that."

"I don't understand."

"It has to be done, Mrs. Quinlan. All you need to think about."

"How did you even know to come here? Did Shirley tell you?"

"No, the man who took her told me, very clearly. He memorized the address."

"I hope he dies a miserable death. What's his name, Mr. Null. I want to give it to the police."

"There's no need for that, Mrs. Quinlan."

"Why? Are you protecting that fucking monster?" She was wild-eyed in an instant, her hands strained to claws as the thought about coming at him, tearing out his throat, occurred.

Null hitched back his coat, slightly adjusting the guns and machete beneath. "There's no need for that, Mrs. Quinlan, because while Shirley was in a drugged sleep in the next room, I shot him twice, cut off his right hand then kept cutting him to pieces slowly until he stroked out and died. It might have been heart failure. I'm not really sure."

She recoiled. "You killed him?"

"Yes, Mrs. Quinlan. I killed him."

"Y-you're not going to kill me and Shirley, are you?"

"No. You're not the type of people I kill. But I don't want to come back and find that Shirley isn't being taken care of properly—isn't getting what she needs." He paused for a moment, wet his lips. "Or abused. Abused would be very bad. For *you.*"

"That would never, ever happen," she said, breathing hard and deep. "You said there may have been others. What about them? Do I get their names to give to the police?"

"No, Mrs. Quinlan. There's no need. I'll be taking care of them as well."

"What will you do?"

"Do I really have to explain?"

Her dead eyes livened with the knowledge.

Mrs. Quinlan gave Null her phone number, and he entered it quickly into his iPhone.

"What *are* you, Mr. Null?"

"Do you believe in God, Mrs. Quinlan?"

"Yeah, of course I do."

"Well, I don't. But to make it easy, look at it this way. When they took Shirley away, when they had her in hand and all hope was lost, and she fought back in any way she could, knowing it had to fail, well, she no doubt cried out to God for help, don't you think?"

"Jesus Christ, you think *you're* God?"

"No, Mrs. Quinlan. Not at all. You can look at it two ways. Either there is no God, and chaos just generates random, accidental order. Or there is a God—"

"And—?"

"He sent me as an answer."

Null turned and walked out cold into the night air as Mrs. Quinlan stood fixed at the door, watching him swallowed by the shadows into the flat black Ford Escort which left the drive in a slow and brooding way.

"Null," she repeated softly.

SEVEN

The next house was a cracker box ranch in Brockton, in Clifton Heights on North Quincy Street. Null got there in the late afternoon. The neighborhood was quiet and even conventionally suburban. The increasing urban rot and deterioration hadn't encroached yet, but it plainly—even starkly—defined the borders of the place. The house was a bilious yellow with white trim, faux wooden shutters decorated windows. Blinds were drawn and before he could think to ring the bell, Null heard noises coming from behind the door.

The door was oak and bolted securely from the inside.

The noise was plain.

Screams.

Girlish screams.

There were squeals that had nothing to do with pleasure.

The deep laughter of men.

Null was sure he had the right place.

He circled the house, the Heckler drawn and clasped tightly in his hand. He tried the windows. They had no give at all, so he went back and tried each again. One of the curtains moved as if by a breeze. Then he glimpsed it. The scene: a shaven headed, paunchy man bending a half-naked young woman over a couch, who was fighting and struggling awkwardly, ineffectually, screaming.

It wasn't just rough sex. Not from the look of the woman; there was something not quite right about her face he could see even through her squalling.

He kept it in mind.

Even through the filthy double windowpanes, Null could see it was a rape.

Null drew back a few feet and ran, throwing himself at the window feet first, landing awkwardly on a soiled carpet amid broken glass, protected by his long coat, weighed down by the Bushmaster, the Glock and machete. He sat there for a moment and blinked. What was it about the woman?

And what did this have to do with pedophilia? She was obviously a woman, not a little girl.

The shaven headed rapist let go the woman and jerked back. Another shaven headed man just like him entered the room just as Null landed.

"What the fuck is this?!" he hollered. Who the fuck is on the floor?!"

"We got a fucking break-in? Kill the son-of-a-bitch!"

Null sat, processing.

"Look at him! He's paralyzed!"

Sweaty and fastening his pants as the half-naked woman curled up on the couch, sobbing, the first shaven-headed man ordered, "Throw him a fucking beating then throw him out the fucking door!"

The second shaven-headed man in soiled tee shirt and sweats moved toward Null, who suddenly raised up the Heckler, silencer attached, and said, "I know what you are."

"Put the pop gun away, faggot, before I shove it up your ass!"

Null answered him with two quick Heckler rounds, one for each leg. He howled, going down to the filth-ridden rug.

The first shaven headed man eyed a Ruger 45 semi-automatic resting on an end-table. He lurched toward it, then stopped.

"If you go for that gun, I'm going to have to kill you. And I'm really not ready to do that yet. So, please back away from the gun, take the girl, get her dressed, and give me the tour."

"You want I should get her showered too?" he asked, thinking he was playing for time.

"No. They'll probably want to do a rape kit on her. Not that it'll make any difference."

"You a fucking cop?" he said, bewildered.

"No. You don't have to worry about that. It's not a problem."

"What about Aldo there on the floor?"

"We can let him bleed there for now. But get me his phone, and I'll take yours too."

"My goddamn life's in that phone. His too."

"Don't worry about that. Neither of you are going to need them."

He fished through his brother's bloody pants pockets for the phone, produced it, wiped his bloody hands on his pants, then grabbed his off the credenza, Null's eyes following him intently as he sat placidly amid a pile of broken glass on the rug. He tossed both phones at Null in an attempt to rattle him and make a move. Null didn't react, still pointing the Heckler straight at him. He feinted toward the Ruger.

"Don't do it. I'm not quite ready to shoot you yet, and I'm pretty sure you don't want to get shot and lie there bleeding like big brother over there on the rug."

The brother, who had been moaning throughout, began to whimper. It was a sound Null was accustomed to—the weak yielding to physical suffering.

"*Little* brother, you mean."

Null hoisted himself off the floor jerkily, somewhat unsteady on his feet. Despite this, he held the Heckler steady.

"Now," he said. "Show me around."

The shaven-headed man, whose name was Tony Spilotro, took the woman into the bathroom, washed her face, made sure her jeans were fastened and tee-shirt smoothed while Null supervised, grave. Something about the woman—whose name was Lisa (Spilotro couldn't give him a last name)—was very wrong. Null couldn't quite put his finger on it.

Her face is telling me something. What is it?

"That's fine," said Null. "Now sit her down somewhere and show me what I came to see."

Emerging from the bathroom, Tony pushed the woman away, making her lose her balance and almost fall over. Then he kicked open the nearest door at their end of the hall and another chunky man—this one with a full head of hair and a goatee—emerged holding an ancient shotgun.

"Let me show you this, motherfucker!" Tony screamed.

Null reflexively blasted the shotgun out of the new man's arm, blowing off several of his fingers before he could pump out a shot. The man curled up on floor, crying, "My hand, my hand!" over and over, blood saturating his pants and shirt. Null turned the Heckler on Tony.

"Another brother?"

"From another mother," said Tony carefully, adding, "Please don't kill me."

"Don't worry, Tony. The plan is not to kill you now." He paused, looking at him, the Heckler cocked and ready. Tony froze, not knowing when to move, the man with the goatee's sobs and whining filling out the silence. "We have some work to do."

"*Kill me later*?" asked Tony nervously.

"Let's go into that room your friend just came out of and see what's there."

Tony moved forward into the room, followed by Null, who kicked the sobbing man aside as he moved past him. There were two women who were approximately the same age as Lisa. They too were crying like scared toddlers, wrists and ankles zip-tied.

"What were your plans for these two, Tony?"

"Just the usual, boss. Nothing fancy."

"Cut the ties, Tony, then get me enough extras for you and the brethren.

"You're gonna tie us? What about Aldo and Seymour? They need to get to a hospital."

Something stopped Null like a hard punch to the chest.

He understood.

How could he have missed it?

Of course, the place was wired up for cameras. This strange foray wasn't a result of bad data but led to a verifiable playhouse. It was pedophilia alright, but of a more sinister and repulsive kind—the kind you don't whisper about, the kind that makes you feel ashamed just for being human, for having anything in common at all with the men who did this. Null processed it, but registered no emotion, no outrage, no hate, no anger.

His sense of purpose, however, had within him become somehow explosive.

Down syndrome.

They were raping and torturing Down syndrome developmentally disabled young women, as vulnerable and innocent and sloppy as toddlers.

They were serving this perversion up—putting it out pay-per-view on the deep dark web, streaming live, cameras in every room. They enjoyed their work for all to see, delighting in the abuse of presumably kidnapped, terrified young women who were barely more in thought, deed and personality than little, vulnerable, sensitive and frightened children. Toddlers, in fact.

This was like raping toddlers.

Null was cold.

"What am I doing again, boss?"

"Cut those girls loose and get me those ties."

"You can put the piece down. I'm doin' it!"

"The piece stays up and cocked. Better hope I don't slip and loose a few rounds by accident."

"Please don't hurt me!" cried one of the girls so pathetically it sounded like a parody of pathos.

"I want to go home," said the other.

"Shut the fuck up!" barked Tony.

"Be civil, Tony. Speak that way to the girls again and I'll put one in your brain."

"Okay, boss, okay. Calm down."

"I am calm."

"Please help me!" the first girl pleaded, bursting into tears.

Tony disappeared at the opposite end to get the ties and presumably to get something to cut the ties. He was out of sight and silence was disturbed by the girls crying zip-tied in the bedroom, not knowing what was going to happen to them.

"Try and hold court with me here, Tony, and you die on the spot."

"No worries, boss."

The screaming from the bedroom mixed with the sounds of despair from Seymore on the floor merged to become incomprehensible.

"Girls, I'm here to help you. I'm going to take you someplace and you'll be alright. You'll be safe."

"Mister, you promise me?"

"I scared!"

"I definitely promise you. It's all going to be okay. Just hang tight. The nice man will set you free."

"He's not nice!"

"No, he's not. But he'll do what I say. Right, Tony?"

"You got it, boss," he grunted, sidling by Null, feeling the solid edge of the suppressor as he did.

Tony cut the girls loose with pinking shears and they ran toward Null, huddling about him, frightened. Somewhat chubby women with little girl haircuts holding close to Null, if for no other reason than he was not one of the three that had kidnapped them.

Tony stood looking at Null holding the zip-ties, evaluating him for an opening to flip the situation to his advantage. His nostrils flared and acid sweat ran down the sides of his torso under his "Misfits" tee shirt. Null seemed encumbered by the women grabbing at his pant legs.

His attention must be divided. I could rush him now and get that gun.

"You're moving things ahead of schedule, Tony. Don't push it."

"Okay, boss. What next?"

"Bind up the brethren. And do it quick."

"But they're bleeding and in pain."

"Bind them or you'll join them bleeding and in pain."

Null patted each woman perfunctorily in a poor, insincere

imitation of comfort and helped them get up with one arm, training the Heckler on Tony with the other without a second's lapse. He brought them to the living room where a bleeding Aldo was rolling around on the rug. They sat down nervously next to Lisa on the debauched couch, clutching at each other in fear. Tony followed and bound his brother with the zip-ties as Null instructed.

"Don't be scared. You're going to be protected. You'll be okay."

"We wanna go home!" said Lisa.

The others assented.

"I wanna be p'tected!"

"I'll get you there. I promise."

Tony was creeping up on him, but Null had the Heckler on him pointed backwards without looking, so he stopped short.

"Now do Seymour."

Tony took his time complying, but did it, nonetheless, impeded by Seymore's flailing and crying.

"Get down on the floor, on your knees."

Null bound him quickly with the zip-ties, wrists to ankles.

"What's next, boss? My brother and Seymour there are gonna bleed to death. Get 'em to a hospital, turn us in to the cops, whatever you have to do, but *please*."

Null got up from the floor, turned, and spoke to the girls.

"Now ladies, we're going to go out for a ride and we won't ever be coming back here. That sounds good, doesn't it?"

They agreed it did and quickly they were all smiles, not so much actually being happy, but *hoping* to be happy. Their faces were all in a squint with smiles. It was as if nothing terrible had happened to them. Kindness, an errant joy, something you might even call sweetness, was in their expressions, all with that same, quasi-Asian seeming Down syndrome estampment. Their condition had deprived them of intellect but had left behind in each of them a base humanity that was not wild and bestial, greedy and fierce, but mild, nice and childlike—filled with innocent goodwill and a hope for goodness.

There was no meanness, spite, hatred, or distrust.

They were still trusting and there was a strangely powerful, eerie dignity to it.

Null recognized it, and it evoked a low memory in his brain.

"Young ladies, please, if you would close your eyes and please sing me a song, that would make me very happy. Can you do that for me?"

"Sure we can!"

"Let's sing *Frere Jacques*!"

"I don't know the words."

"Hum what you don't know, silly."

"That sounds good girls, why not do that one?"

"Are we girls or are we ladies?"

"You, my dear, are both. Now close your eyes and sing."

They did just that, sitting beside each other on the couch like dolls. "Louder, girls, with feeling!" Enthusiastically, they obliged him. Null pocketed the Ruger on the end table, which made his coat even more awkwardly weighty. When he was satisfied they were singing loud enough, Null nodded his approval, got down to Tony's level on the rug and beat him persistently with both fists until he fell unconscious.

Null led the three girls out of the house to the flat black Ford Escort parked just outside by the curb. It was bright mid-day. He coaxed them gently but firmly into the backseat, started the car and pulled off, his cellphone in his left hand.

Before he could dial it, Lisa asked from the backseat, "Can we stop for ice cream?"

"Yeah, we want ice cream!"

"I like Baskin-Robbins!"

"I like Baskin-Robbins too!"

"Okay girls, Baskin and Robbins it shall be."

He dialed Dapper O'Neil Shelter and Service Group on his cellphone.

"I like bubblegum flavor!"

"Chocolate!"

"Mrs. Coelacanth? Null. That's right. I have to tell you: Things have not gone exactly as planned."

EIGHT

"Mr. Null, I can't do anything with them. These are young ladies, not children. Why did you bring them?"

"I should have told you over the phone—"

"Well, they were singing. I could hardly hear you."

"Yes, but now that we're here, you can see the problem."

"But as I explained, Mr. Null. These are young women, not little children abused by child pornographers."

"What if I told you that they were, Mrs. Coelacanth? What if I could prove it? What then?"

"I honestly don't know. I don't even know where I could place them for the night—and then there are *three* of them."

The girls were singing and talking, sitting on a bench in the dilapidated, decaying plaster-walled waiting area. Null had told them to sit there and not move and so they wanted to impress him by being good girls, restless as they were and kicking their legs rhythmically.

"Mrs. Coelacanth, just go out there and talk with them for a few minutes. Look at them closely, then come back and tell me what you think."

Ruth Coelacanth sighed wearily and got up from her desk sagging with the weight of the day. And it was only two-thirds over. She went out to the waiting area and stood in front of the girls.

"Hello, ladies," she said with false briskness. "I'm Mrs. Coelacanth."

They said it together as they had been taught. "Good afternoon, Mrs. Coelacanth!" They were all smiles, with even an occasional giggle.

She saw it then, and the words stuck in her throat. She understood immediately.

The comprehension made her feel dirty, compromised.

A sickness rose up from her stomach and dominated her. She nearly lost her footing.

"Are you all right, Mrs. Coelacanth?" asked Sally.

She cleared her throat, fought for equilibrium and calm. "I'm fine, dear. What's your name?"

"Sally. And that's Lisa, and that's Jaqueline." She pointed to both with her thumb.

"I'm the prettiest," said Jaqueline. "Mr. Aldo told me so!"

"Are not!"

"Am too!"

"You're all so very pretty. If you could please just sit here a little longer, Mr. Null and I will take care of you."

"We like Mr. Null."

"Yeah—he took us for ice cream at Baskin-Robbins!"

"I got bubblegum!"

"You just stay right there." She turned on her heels, hiding her face which she knew then was flushed and lurched back into the office where Null waited unmoving in silence. Mrs. Coelacanth started to hyperventilate.

"This can't be true! Who would ever do such a thing to women—to women—"

"To women with Down syndrome?"

"It's monstrous and disgusting. I don't understand how anyone—how this could be—What kind of person would do this?"

"Don't ask me, Mrs. Coelacanth. I gave up on humanity long ago."

Mrs. Coelacanth leaned all of her weight on her desk, still hyperventilating. There were tears. "I can't—

really handle this. It's too much. I can't—"

"Listen to me carefully, Mrs. Coelacanth. These women were raped, beaten and abused on streaming video for a very special brand of dark web customer. Three grown men used them as sex toys for money, beat them bloody for fun, on a live streaming 24-hour camera feed. They enjoyed it and they intended to keep on doing it, until we had a little meeting."

"Oh, my God, it's too terrible. I don't know what to do—how to handle this!" she sobbed.

Lisa's voice chimed eerily far away: "Mrs. Coelacanth—we're waiting!"

"Yes, Mrs. Coelacanth. They're waiting. They're waiting for you."

She was full out crying and managed, "They have ligatures on their wrists! What kind of men—?!"

"Ordinary men. Below average men, Mrs. Coelacanth. Just men."

"It's beyond me!" she sobbed, red-faced and teary eyed. "I can't!" It appeared to Null that the weight of all she had to bear was crushing her. He had no way to stop it but with sober fact.

"Listen to me, Mrs. Coelacanth. I've done all I can do for them. There's nothing else I can do to help them. You are the only person who can help them now. These girls need you—they're depending on you. And you can do it. You have the expertise and the connections."

"I don't know—"

"But I know. This is what you do, Mrs. Coelacanth. This is why you do what you do. You have to get yourself together and think of the girls. Think of what has to be done. You're walking point on this—you're going to save them. And there is nobody else for them but you. So, breathe, calm down and focus on these poor girls who need you more than they have ever needed anyone in their unfortunate lives."

Mrs. Coelacanth straightened up, stopped leaning forward on the desk, went behind it and reached into a drawer for some tissues.

"You're right, Mr. Null. I forgot myself. It's just so terrible. I will help these girls—women. These *women*."

"You're right, Mrs. Coelacanth. They're young women and should be accorded that respect. They're so like girls, though, it can be confusing."

"So you stopped it, Mr. Null. Stopped it cold!"

"Right in the act."

"You didn't—um—"

"Kill them? No. There were three of them, Mrs. Coelacanth. And I can assure you they'll never do it again."

"I'll need to get a rape kit done and contact the law. See where these women were kidnapped from. Detox is an open question. They could be drugged."

"Yes, Mrs. Coelacanth. They were obviously kidnapped. It wouldn't be very hard with how trusting they are. A rape kit likely won't matter, but for appearances. Detox will, though. They probably are drugged, which is why they're so docile, easy to handle." He looked up at her with a dead expression. "You won't mention me when you talk to the police, though. Will you?"

"No. I won't. They wouldn't believe me anyway." She frowned and looked into Null's wide, shark-like eyes. "Why wouldn't a rape kit matter?" It dawned on her why, but she asked regardless. "Where are they now? These men."

"Trussed up in a dilapidated house in Brockton. They're not going anywhere."

She slammed her fist down hard on the desk.

"What are you going to do with them?"

"Do I have to tell you?"

"Will that really solve anything?"

"I think so, Mrs. Coelacanth. I think it'll address a number of issues. But you don't have to think of that, Mrs. Coelacanth. Just don't think about it." He checked his phone. "I don't have a lot of time to get back there and do what I have to do, and I have a few errands to run on the way."

"Alright, Mr. Null. Sure. Just go."

"Are we good, Mrs. Coelacanth?"

"Yes. We're good. I'll make damn sure these women get well taken care of, are placed and protected."

"I believe you." Null turned away to leave, hoping to move speedily past the women. He was on deadline. She stopped him.

"Mr. Null, before you go?"

He turned back to her. "Yes?"

"When you do what you have to do, will you do me a favor?"

"What favor might that be, Mrs. Coelacanth?"

"Make it *hurt.*"

Null's thin, scarred lips drew back to show clean, white teeth. His eyes opened wide and bore white, unblemished corneas in the fading light.

"My opening move," he said softly and left her sitting there in the gathering shadows.

———

The housepainter nonchalantly sitting in the silver Camry parked at the opposite curb across from the dilapidated cracker box house in Brockton was bored. His semi-automatic Smith and Wesson M&P Shield lay undisturbed in his lap. He was close to dozing. A figure appeared in silhouette quickly from nowhere, and asked him through the open driver side window, "Waiting long?" The housepainter jerked up and grabbed the M&P.

"Nope," said Null quietly. "Too late."

He took the Heckler and blew the housepainter's face away with a single shot. Then he waited for some other response to the shot. There was none.

Null crossed the street.

The second housepainter was standing at the door in topcoat and hat—a parody of Null's own appearance. He had missed the shot.

"Stop right there," said the housepainter. "Brockton police! Identify yourself before you go any further."

Null was faster with his Heckler than the housepainter was with whatever he was packing. He got off two shots into the man's neck before he could remove his piece from his coat. With great struggle, he managed to withdraw a Glock nine from his coat and hold it, which Null quickly kicked aside into the unkempt shrubbery.

"I really don't know what you've done, so this is you and your partner's lucky day."

The housepainter gurgled an inarticulate plea.

Null put two in his head.

"You get to die easy, no torture. But your friends inside, that's another story."

Null went back to the flat black Escort and removed a paper bag full of various items and a 12-pack of bottled water. He went back to the dilapidated house. The door was unlocked. He entered with the Heckler drawn and ready.

"No little extra friends to surprise me?"

"You're supposed to be dead!" squealed Tony.

"Some say I am dead," replied Null.

"I need a hospital!" Seymour moaned. "My arm's gone numb!"

"We can't have that," said Null studiously. "I think if I give it a little massage we can restore some sensation. It's important that your feelings remain intact."

Aldo made incomprehensible sonic eruptions from the floor where he still managed to flop about in a puddle of his own blood.

Null opened the door again and dragged the late housepainter inside, closing it softly.

He carefully removed his coat, still holding the Ruger, a Glock nine, and multiple phones in its pockets. Lastly, he took the Bushmaster semi-automatic rifle off his shoulder where it had hung from a strap, then gingerly put his hat on top. It had left a wide, red welt on Null's bony shoulder. The Heckler and suppressor went next to it. He removed the machete and lanyard from around his neck and leaned them up against a leg of the chair.

"Fuck, you got weaponry, boss!" whined Tony.

"Just prepared. Like a boy scout."

"But you ain't no boy scout!"

"A perfect tautology."

Null removed some cheap, blindingly white cotton coveralls from the paper bag and stepped into them, covering his clothes. He revealed himself clearly in the light as he changed, scars everywhere; emaciated, sunken looking, haggard. Not much of a threat at first appearance. But he was all muscle and sinew drawn taut and poised to spring at any time. He was a danger, camouflaged by the past evidence of injury, distress, and torment.

He was relentless; he would not stop.

Neither would Aldo and Seymour with their wretched noises. Null had to speak above them to communicate with the still-coherent Tony Spilotro.

"What—what the fuck are you doing?" asked Tony, struggling against the ties.

"Fucking cut me loose!" screamed Seymour.

Null quickly snapped face pictures of the three with his phone, placed it gently on top of his hat, and approached Tony, holding the machete and a bottle of water.

"You're fucking taking *selfies?*" Tony asked, incredulous.

"Just a memento mori," replied Null, kneeling down.

"What the fuck are you gonna do?"

"Where are the cameras, Tony?"

"Cut me loose and I'll show yez!"

"Just tell me."

"Two left-hand corners opposite each other on the ceilin'."

"Great. Mic's working okay?"

"They are. They saw and heard everything. You shoulda been dead by now. Front office sent the fucking housepainters for yez."

"I expected as much, as you can see."

"I can't see shit. You killed both of 'em?

Null ignored the question. "So, they can see and hear everything clearly at the user's end?"

"It's what the goofs are paying for."

"Just making sure."

"What the fuck's with the bottled water, for Christ's sake?"

"To lubricate your throat."

"What the fuck for?"

"You need to be able to scream."

"You're fucked!"

"That might more aptly be reversed here. Anyway, having you rendered mute might obscure my point. You should be able to scream out in agony as much as you can until you can't anymore. They need to hear as well as see. The Hebe people. Whoever's left."

"Are you out of your freakin' mind?"

"Clearly. But that's not really the question you should be asking."

Tony shouted defiantly: "They'll find ya, ya know! They'll get you, fuck you up good and proper—*kill* you, you stupid, motherfucking freak!" He was breathing hard.

"We'll see who finds whom first."

"You're gonna die, bitch!"

"So must we all. But I believe you're going first."

"Cut me loose, goddamn you!"

"Why'd they leave you tied up? You could've lent them a hand, you know. The housepainters."

"I guess they were using us as bait."

"I get it." Null paused and blinked—dead shark eyes aimed straight at Tony's face. "Did you ever hear of the expression, "to cut bait?"

"Ya. So?"

"Well, here's a new dimension to it."

At first, Tony had no time to scream.

Null swung up the newly sharpened machete and came down both hard and deep into Tony's torso. That was when his screaming began and did not stop.

Tony's screaming continued for hours—Null forcing his mouth open and pouring water down his throat, until it died down to nothing but a crackle and Null could finally get to the others.

They didn't last nearly as long.

NINE

"Martha, I need you to take a look at this video. The group sent it," said Steve Privilegiata, an early middle-aged man with close-cropped black hair and a dark tan dressed raffishly in a Lacoste jersey and khakis. That he was extremely nervous was plain. Little beads of sweat dotted his face, and especially his upper lip. He kept tapping the pad on the laptop as if it might change what he was looking at. It didn't.

"Why are they contacting us?" asked his wife. She was clean-scrubbed, blond with highlights, dressed in slacks and a blouse, wearing jewelry a bit too conspicuously. She was at the very beginning of being upset. "That's not right. We're supposed to be silent partners. What if this e-mail's a lead to track us? A way for investigators to find an in? What if we're compromised?"

"I don't think that's the problem right now. It was sent through an anonymizer and encrypted, so I don't think we need to worry."

"So then, why are you worried?"

"I think this is something our partners want us to worry about."

"Why can't Finnerty or the Comptroller take care of it?"

"Because according to the e-mail, they're no longer alive."

"What the fuck is happening?" she asked, disturbed, genuinely agitated.

"Just watch this clip with me."

Martha Privilegiata came up behind her seated husband and looked over his shoulder at the laptop screen. Her breathing was shallow.

"What the fuck is this?"

"Just watch. It's crazy. It's a taped feed from one of the playhouses. The one with the retards."

"Why are we getting this? No one from the group is supposed to contact us about anything but Finnerty or that little Jewish creep."

"The e-mail says they're dead."

"What? That just doesn't make any sense."

"Let me take the stream off pause here and I'll show you something that doesn't make any sense."

Steve took the media player plugin off pause with sweaty fingers and his wife breathed heatedly through her nostrils as she drew her face in closer over his shoulder to watch. Off pause, a picture clearly emerged of a high-angled view of the living room rug and some of the furniture in the main room of the Spilotro house in Brockton. A skeleton of a man with sunken cheekbones, hollow eyes wearing white painter's coveralls blemished with brilliant vermillion-saturated spots of fresh blood greeted them almost cheerily. The man was animated, swinging a machete. Lying at his feet was a bundle of gore barely distinguishable as a human being that had once been Tony Spilotro.

The little man spoke, clearly and evenly. Darker blood was visible in solid formations on the debased rug by his feet, which were sheathed in blood-soaked shoe covers for painting.

"I hope you can hear me clearly, since there really isn't any way for me to check the mics here to establish that they're working properly. I assume they must be, because, really, what value would your playhouse have otherwise? You should be getting all the moaning and crying and sobbing in the background, if things go right. For all you goofs, I just want you to know that if you log off and stop viewing this Hebe Group material, I won't be able to find you. I highly recommend it. Otherwise, you'll soon be on my list. But for you, Hebe Group employees, there really is no hope. Unless you kill me, which I have to say doesn't turn out to be as easy as it sounds. No, not so far."

"Anyway, you're going to die. I'm going to find every single one of you and do exactly to you what I did to this blob of mess right here by my feet—the late Tony Spilotro." He kicked the blob for emphasis. "I don't know if you saw the part of the feed where I slowly turned Mr. Spilotro into this pile of bloody gelatin," he kicked at the blob again, "but if you have, then perhaps you get the point. Not only am I going to kill you, but if time and circumstances permit, I'm going to torture you to death. You'll beg for me to kill you and I'll refuse. I'll keep hurting you and hurting you until you can no longer last. Of course, I'm a realist about things. If I'm hurried or there are just too many of you to see to all at once, I'll simply make do and kill you as quickly and painfully as I know how." He paused, unblinking, looking straight at the cameras. "And let me promise you right now: this is a subject about which I have a *lot* of knowhow!"

He moved his legs up and down for a moment, as if working them to bring back their circulation after having spent too much time in a bent over position.

"I'm sure you're thinking of coming after me. This, of course, is an impractical idea. Don't worry about trying to find me because I'm going to find you. You're going to see me, right up close, squeezing the light right out of your eyes until you die." He sighed and flopped his arm with the machete down by his side. "Still, you probably want to know who I am. That's easy enough. My name is Null. Call me Null. And if you want to try and call the police, which I think must be a funny idea even to you, I can tell you right off the bat that the punchline to that joke is that they think I'm dead. But when they find you, on the other hand, they'll *know* you're dead—that's if they can identify the corpse once I'm done with you."

Null shook his head, looked around the room toward the

background noises of sobbing and moaning delivered from Aldo and Seymour off-camera.

"If you didn't see the part of the feed that precedes my little speech, don't worry about it. I have two more to handle, just like the late Tony over there. Feel free to watch to your heart's content." Null went off-camera for a moment then reappeared, dragging the bloodied, bound and wounded Seymour into the frame. "Don't worry," said Null smoothly, as if in comfort, "this won't take long."

Seymour screamed, *"God help me!"*

Null went up, holding the machete high in both hands.

Then Null was suspended, stuck in time, the machete yet to come down.

Steve had put the recording back on pause.

Both he and his wife couldn't move for a moment—

they were frozen stock still. Steve forced himself to get up from the computer. His wife's eyes were welled with tears. Imperceptibly, she trembled.

"Marty, do you have the card?"

"What card?" she sniffled.

"You know the one."

"We're never supposed to call him. We're never supposed to call *anybody!*" she wailed.

"Yeah," Steve said, rubbing his hands. "Him. Legere. We need to call Legere."

"But he's street—we don't deal with *street* ever!" She was shrill, panicked.

"Well, my darling, it appears we do now."

———

An anonymous factory building off Cambridge Street in Allston set back from the street on a large acre of tar. Years ago, it was artists' work-live spaces when funding existed for such things. The impoverished artists moved in and bought lofts with friendly bank loans and state and federal underwriting. When real estate prices went up just before the last financial crisis, each and every struggling, starving, grants-saturated artist, adjunct professor of this or that sold their lofts out at a profit and moved off to the distant suburbs without a peep to the press, who ignored it regardless. After several failed attempts at adaptive reuse—

including an ambitious co-op initiative to turn it into an Ivan Illich-style alternative school—developers and investors abandoned the property altogether.

Fallen into disuse and disrepair (a rat-infested homeless squat for a time), it was picked up by an investment consortium for a song.

Now, it was a hive of activity.

Activity involving children.

Most businesses were closed, or at least shuttering their doors at this time of night in Allston. In the main office on the fourth level of the building, operations manager Benedict "Ben" Servus was wide awake, monitoring ongoing business on an array of screens set up in half moon formation with a wide Ford Executive Modern Desk set in the center. The screens all showed young children of various ages in sexual positions with an array of adults. He looked at the feed on these screens as dispassionately as if they were spread-sheets of numbers.

Servus was a short, paunchy man with a full head of salt-and-pepper hair, dressed in shirt-sleeves and dress pants, no jacket or tie. He was swarthy and large-pored with drooping, dark eyes. His posture was in a perpetual bit of a slouch. He thought for a moment he detected a disturbance at the second level on one of the screens. He used his dedicated walkie talkie to contact the employee nearest the disturbance. There was no answer. He left the office and went out to the catwalk, looking out over the various house-settings that were in plain view. Nothing. It was just a blip of activity on the screen, he decided. That sometimes happens. He shouldn't be so jumpy. His wife was right—he sorely needed to get some downtime and relax.

When he went back into his dimly lit office, he discovered a shape at his desk in the shadows. He kept his calm.

"I'm not alone in here anymore, am I?"

"Obviously," came the dead voice from the shadows.

"What do you want? I'm in no position to give you anything. There's nothing but petty cash on hand, and that's not even a thousand bucks. Sorry buddy, but you've come to a dry place. If you want, I can put you in touch with someone who can help you." He allowed his breathing to relax, told himself he was no longer in danger. What would be the point of his doing anything anyway? He wasn't even sure this guy was armed.

"The guy you want to put me in touch with—his name's Legere, right?"

"Yeah, that's him. How'd you know?"

"Everybody wants to put me in touch with Legere. Yet he doesn't seem to want to be very much in touch with me."

Ben Servus tensed. His back spasmed. He came to a sudden black and disastrous realization.

"You! You're him—you're—the crazy fuck on that tape of the feed."

"My reputation precedes me," said Null drily. "By the way, you should probably avoid calling certain people crazy fucks. You never know what they're liable to do."

Null got up from the desk and stepped into the light shining in from the long windows facing the catwalk. The Heckler was out and ready.

"Now me," he continued. "I'm easy. No doubt crazy, I'll give you that, but I'm far from unpredictable. With me, you always know what I'm going to do."

"Okay, whoever you are—"

"Null. You can call me Null."

"Okay, Mr. Null. I'm only the operations manager around here. I just keep things running smoothly and efficiently. Just tell me what you want, and I'll do my best to help you."

"Thanks, but I don't really want anything."

"You're the one put the faces of everyone you killed up on the landing page, didn't you? Twenty people?"

"On the nose. Good, you can count."

"High body count."

"Yes, it is."

"Isn't that enough? How many more are you going to kill?

And for what? It's not making you rich." His voice was trembling, breathing had become shallow and forced. He thought he was playing for time. He wasn't. Null was simply taking his time.

"I don't do it for money, not even for morality. I do it for ethics."

"Ethics? You think all these murders are *ethical?*"

"In context, yes, as a matter of fact I do."

"What are you going to do?"

"If you saw the feed, you wouldn't have to ask me."

"Please don't kill me?"

"Why not?"

"I'm a decent man, a family man—I have a wife—"

"And you have kids, no doubt. Nice, clean-scrubbed suburban kids."

"That's right. Two well-behaved sons, as a matter of fact."

"No rough life for them, was there? Nothing to make it hard. No privation or abuse."

"Not at all. Just good old American discipline."

"I see. You don't mind answering a question or two for me, do you?"

Servus thought it best to play for time. Security should be up there soon. He already had had the presence of mind to press the red call button on his walkie talkie that was now holstered and which he conspicuously made no move to touch.

"Of course not."

"Put the walkie on the desk."

"Sure thing."

"Slowly," intoned Null.

Servus did as he was told.

"It doesn't matter that you pressed the call button for security. They won't be coming."

"Wh-why not?" asked Servus, again playing for time.

"Because they're busy."

"Busy doing what?"

"They're busy being dead," replied Null.

"Wh-what are you going to do?"

"I'll get to that. But first, the questions I wanted to ask you."

Servus fidgeted, shifted his weight from foot to foot. "G-go ahead."

"Why do your children get to grow up safe and protected and the ones downstairs wind up raped, abused, tricked out and used up and — if they survive to get old enough — outright sold to rich perverts as slaves?"

Servus took a deep breath and explained, doing his best to pitch it hard like a sale. "Luck of the draw," he said. "These children are cast-offs anyway, thrown-away items, no parents, no relatives, no prospects, foster homes couldn't cope with them, juvenile facilities too overcrowded and down-sized to take them. They're casualties of the modern economy — like little animals, feral wild things. We take care of them, feed them, house them, get them medical attention —"

"Treatment for venereal diseases? Herpes, hepatitis?"

"Of course. All of that."

"So, it's really okay that they're anally raped and used as human sex dolls? Just the luck of the draw?"

"It's how they sing for their supper, as the saying goes. They grow to like it, the physical affection."

Null didn't blink.

"You're at ease with what you do?"

"I am. Taking the great pay, job security and medical into account, you get used to it. You can get used to anything. They're just a commodity, like loaves of bread. Get 'em in get 'em out, and that's that."

"Bernie said the same thing, about loaves of bread."

"Well, he's right. The expression fits."

"That's it?"

"That's it."

Null checked his phone. "It seems we still have plenty of time. And I intend to use it."

"What are you going to do?"

"Fair question. You have a good style. And you're right. To me, you're just a commodity. Get 'em in, get 'em out and that's that. Excellent phrasing, by the way."

Servus inched toward the door backward.

"Oh, and you were doing so well," said Null.

"What are you going to do?!" Servus screamed.

"You deserve an answer," Null replied softly. "And I'll give you one."

"Okay," Servus said distractedly, eyeing the door, sweating and trembling.

"I'm going to fire two rounds from this pistol straight into your belly. Then, with the machete I have hanging from a lanyard around my neck under my coat, I'm going to chop you into pieces, see how long you last before either one kills you."

Servus smiled and laughed in nervous relief, wiped his sweaty brow with the back of his hand. "For a moment, I thought you were serious. But you're joking, right?"

"No, I'm really not."

Null showed him, fired two shots into Servus' copious gut from the Heckler, then maneuvered the machete out from under his coat.

Servus screamed for a very long time.

TEN

Null was spotted with blood, and it was unsightly, he knew. He reminded himself to find a dry cleaner that could get it out for the most part. Clothes shopping was something he was totally unskilled at doing. Maybe he could delegate Do-rag to do it for him. Nothing complex, just a trip to Marshall's or Target. At least his hat was unscathed.

"How many dead, Do-rag?"

Do-rag, sporting his namesake in red, wearing a down jacket and the usual baggy, sagging jeans, shuffled in place nervously. He was always nervous when facing Null.

He turned to the other members of the Gangsta Boyz crew, standing pat behind him sporting various manner of assault weapons. None of them had the slightest interest in looking the seemingly benign, inoffensive Null in the eye.

"Do-rag, it's a simple question."

"The security fuckers—they be gone."

Voices of assent coming from behind.

"And the rest?"

A lone voice from behind articulated for the group. Null couldn't see who it was.

"We don't know what the fuck to do with them perverts and the kiddies, yo."

"I promised you good pay, did I not?"

"Yo, man. Fuckin' A."

"Gave you a packet of cash up front, did I not?"

They assented in a collective grumble.

"Then I need you to go to each setting where these men and women are cowering. I need you to secure the kid without injury, no matter how hard the child resists, begs and cries, and then shoot the malefactor. Kill the pervs, in other words. Points of appreciation will be given to anyone who makes them die suffering."

"But what if they come, boss?"

"Who's they?"

"Anyone. Cops, reinforcements. This is a dope set up. They gots the cheddar!"

"True enough. Even I realize we're on the clock, so we'd better get to it. The question is, are you ready, Gangsta Boyz?"

"Ya, man. We down!"

They muttered assent in unison.

"But what about the kiddies?" Again, the voice of slightest dissent.

Null made a face, targeted the owner of that voice. "And you are?"

"Shadow, man."

"Well, Mr. Shadow—and all of you. Think of this as a rescue mission, an extraction. We're going to get those kids out of here in one piece."

"We need to get that money, nigga!"

"Then get to killing these fucking pieces of shit, if you please."

As they prepared to scatter and comb all the floors, Null reminded them: "And take a picture of their faces and send them to the email address I gave you. Don't forget."

"A'ight, 730 mofo!"

They scattered fast. Null proceeded slowly behind them, carrying his Bushmaster fully loaded and primed.

It was appalling just on the mezzanine, which was where it all started—a straight shotgun row of scene stations, each with a maximum of two adults and one child in various stages of undress. Lacking Null's commitment, the Gangsta Boyz simply aimed for kill shots at the adults and grabbed each screaming child, fighting to restrain him or her, found clothes for them, then collected them at the building lobby for Null to decide what to do with them.

Null surveyed three floors of damage, corpses of adult abusers littered across varied scenes of schoolrooms, Toyland, nurseries, fun houses—each one a box-like playhouse all its own, all wired up for sight and sound and live streaming treats for driven goofs paying with everything from debit cards to Bitcoin. The array of corpses satisfied Null, until he came to a candy store setting with a naked, dead, fat man draped over the counter and an unhappy big-eyed Gangsta Boy huddling in the corner with a small girl dressed in a jumper cradled limp in his arms. From the gaping wound in her head, it was reasonable to assume she was dead.

"Yo, boss—I fucked up. Hit the kid merkin' the perv!" He looked panicked, trapped.

"I see that," Null said calmly.

"Accidents happen."

"Did you send out the photo of the face?"

"Ya, man—the Internet guy gots it."

"Good," said Null, then nonchalantly nailed him in face, neck and torso with the Bushmaster. He slumped back dead, still cradling the child. Null grabbed the small corpse, looking hard for something, squinting his eyes. He found it. The camera lens. He spoke directly to the corpse of the dead Gangsta Boy first, as if he could hear him. "Chaos accepts all different kinds of input."

He then faced the camera lens, holding up the child.

"However quickly you get here, it won't be fast enough. Do you see this dead child? This raped and tortured, murdered child? This is on you, and all of you will pay in blood and pain. And you goofs, if you're still watching, if I get your ISP, I'll come for you too. If you think I'll stop or that you're in any way safe, put it out of your mind. I'm coming for you. And when I get there, you'll have wished you had killed yourself before I got there, and before I let you die."

Null threw the corpse against the wall, leaving a red smear on the white paint.

"I'm coming for you! I am *coming!*"

Null joined the Gangsta Boyz and a cluster of unruly children surrounding them like little predators in a swarm, like piranhas at their legs.

"Yo, where's Alphonse?"

"He's been terminated. No severance I'm afraid."

"Just askin'."

"Ask away. Let me ask you—have you got the thermite charges?"

"Yeah, we ready fo' all dat."

"Deploy them and let's get the fuck out of here."

"True dat." Four Gangsta Boys scampered off, one of them carrying a book bag holding the charges and fuses, leaving Null to contend with the children.

"Come on kids, we're going outside cause we've got a bus to catch!"

It was worse than herding cats, and clothing had to be sought out from the various stage sets for the small ones who were still naked. No child there was over the age of thirteen, Null assessed, and he knew he was lucky they were drugged. He and two remaining Gangsta Boyz led the children out into the cold, black night air, keeping them together a few hundred feet away from the squat and stunted, soot-dappled, refurbished brick factory building. The three Gangsta Boyz who set the charges on each floor of that building came running toward them fast, snorting mist from their noses in the cold night air.

"That fuckin' thing'll melt to hell when timers go off."

"Let's hope they do," Null replied, and checked his cell phone for the time. "Do a head count for me?"

"We gots twenty-three kiddies here."

"It makes a dent," said Null.

"What we waitin' here in the cold for?" asked Shadow, lighting a cigarette.

"A bus," said Null drily. "We're waiting for a bus."

———

The smartly rehabbed factory building, sparsely lit on its acre of tar, was now blossoming into a bright and beautiful bloom of orange. The children were distracted by its strange beauty, the quiet of a terrible conflagration whose heat warmed their faces like a warm summer day as they watched, dismayed and frightened enough not to speak. Null waved down the eighty-six bus at a stop set at an intersection by the acre of tar.

The bus stopped and Null stepped up and in. He greeted the driver pleasantly.

"Move to the back, please!" the driver drawled.

"Mr. Driver, I'd like you to put this bus in park and tell all the passengers to get out now. This bus is going out of service, and so are you."

"What the fuck? That ain't gonna happen, nevah! Now get the fuck off my bus!"

Null brought up the Bushmaster and fired a few rounds into the ceiling.

"*Au contraire.* I beg to differ."

The bus driver was trembling and stuck in position, breathing heavy, eyes wide.

"Come on now, Mr. Driver. You can do this." Null patted him on the shoulder stiffly. The driver used the half-broken PA system to announce that the bus was going out of service and that another would come on schedule to finish the route. He opened both doors and the passengers—of which there were more than a few—

piled out.

Without a word, the Gangsta Boyz and the children piled in.

"Do-rag, which one of your buddies is the MBTA dropout?"

A short, slender Gangsta Boy timidly raised his hand.

"What's your name, kid?"

"It's Jo-jo, yo."

"Well, Jo-jo, it's your chance to shine. Take your seat at the front of the bus."

Jo-jo did so and didn't have to be told to start the bus and put it in gear.

"Where we headed, boss?"

"Dapper O'Neil Shelter and Service Group on University Place in Brookline."

"I find it, boss."

"Extra money for you, Jo-jo, if you get us there extra-fast!"

"I'm up on this bitch!"

The bus jerked and sped off clumsily from the curb.

The kids cheered rowdily, feeling a momentary rush of freedom.

Null dialed Mrs. Coelacanth, who answered, annoyed.

"Mrs. Coelacanth, you'd better get down to the Dapper O'Neil Shelter and Service Group pronto. We have a situation. No, Mrs. Coelacanth, these are children, actual children. A bunch of them, and we're on our way!" Null was speaking loudly to be heard over the din of the rickety, rumbling bus and the rowdy release of the children. They picked up on what he said and one small boy repeated it as loud as he could, as if drunk:

"We're on our way!"

"That's right, kids," Null announced. "We're finally on our way!"

ELEVEN

The wrong bus in the wrong town on the wrong street flew down University Place in Brookline going the wrong way. It parked illegally but neatly right in front of Dapper O' Neil. Twenty-three screaming kids, all amped-up despite being drugged and ready to party jumped off the bus, collecting on the sidewalk of an empty quiet street in front of a bland, gray building locked up for the night. Null and the remaining Gangsta Boyz struggled to keep the kids from running off, waiting by the parked bus in the cold. The entrance to Dapper O'Neil was tar black behind the locked glass door. It never occurred to Null at all to break into it.

Mrs. Coelacanth pulled up in her magenta Nissan Sentra, honking the horn frantically. She also parked illegally, got out of the car and headed straight for Null, indignant and enraged.

"Do you have any idea at all about what you're doing, Mr. Null?"

"Yes, Mrs. Coelacanth. I'm honoring our agreement. I hereby present you with twenty-three children rescued from a kiddie porn factory off Cambridge Street."

"In Allston?"

"That's the one."

"What am I supposed to do with twenty-three abused and damaged kids at nine-thirty at night? Couldn't this have waited until at least business hours?"

"No, I'm afraid this was the best time for extracting twenty-three kids, murdering twenty-five guilty adults, blowing the place up and hijacking a city bus to get them here just for you. No other time seemed likely."

"Murdering?"

"After all this time, Mrs. Coelacanth, do we really have to play that game?"

"I'd like to keep a semblance of sanity here, if you please."

"Whatever it takes."

"Who are these young gentlemen, Mr. Null?"

"This is my crew, Mrs. Coelacanth. They're Gangsta Boyz—anyway they were when I took over. I found no good reason to change the name."

"They don't care that you're white?"

Null faced the crew, still awkwardly wrangling tots.

"Gentlemen, does it bother you that I'm white?"

All cowed, knowing full well that Null was insane, but also insanely profitable, all volunteered several kinds of negatives. With the meth lab set up in Methuen pumping hard run by BU dropout Riley and Gangsta Boyz associates slinging meth wildly in the streets where even the cops didn't care or venture to go, money was rolling in. One good thing about Null that every Gangsta Boy knew: he wasn't greedy. He only took an equal share out of any score, like everyone else. He wasn't stingy with the cheddar. They didn't like him. They thought he could blow at a moment's notice and knew for a fact he had no compunctions about killing. They knew that long before Alphonse left them only an hour or so ago. They had witnessed it. They didn't understand him. They knew he didn't care about money—it seemed he didn't care about anything. This made him dangerous. Yet, he was fair. So, they accepted him as lead until something happened.

They knew that sometime something would happen and Null would be out and probably dead.

"Race relations aside, Mrs. Coelacanth, where do we go from here?"

"You mean you hadn't thought that out?

85

"That's where you fit into the picture. Past the point of extraction is a little out of my league."

"You have an illegal bus parked illegally in front of my place. It has to go."

"I thought you might need it as further transport for the kids."

"That's a thought, but no, not this time. I don't know what we'll do any other time." She paused and eyed Null warily. "And I suppose there will be other times."

"I plan on that, yes."

"Well, I'm not planning on it, Mr. Null, but I don't think I can scare up the facilities to handle this kind of volume of children."

"You're going to have to try, Mrs. Coelacanth. It's what you agreed to. I always keep to my agreements. I'm holding up my end." He paused and narrowed his eyes. "This is yours."

Mrs. Coelacanth let it process through her mind that what she was dealing with here was very possibly a psychopath—an admitted killer. She was picking an argument with a murderer. Not the best idea from any angle. No, not at all. She removed a jangle of keys from her coat pocket, hands shaking imperceptibly.

"They can't just stand out in the cold. Let's bring everybody inside."

Mrs. Coelacanth unlocked the security and entry doors, pressed in codes on a keypad to disarm the alarm system and turned on all the lights on the first floor. She went over to an ancient thermostat and turned up the heat.

"Just watch the kids out here in the big front room," Mrs. Coelacanth directed to nobody in particular. "We'll be back in a few minutes." She led Null into her office.

"Are you out of your mind?"

"I thought we settled that issue."

"We haven't settled anything."

"We're settling these kids, I think. And we'd better do it now."

"Twenty-three of them?"

"That's right. And you're on point again. You're the only thing between them and disaster. I told you this is what would happen. I was straightforward."

"I didn't believe you."

"I wasn't asking for faith. I simply wanted the benefit of the doubt. Maybe you believe me now."

"I do. And now I don't know what to do."

"You're going to start by making some phone calls. You're going to start by bedding down the kids in this place until morning. Then you can start working on placing them. Either way you're going to start. And start now."

"How do I avoid dealing with local police about all this?"

"You don't. Go through all the channels you need to. There's too much work here for even a task force to wade through. A thoroughly coordinated police effort still wouldn't be able to get through it all. Red tape notwithstanding, the devil's in the details and the details will swallow them up."

"Meanwhile, more kids are coming?"

"Exactly. I think we've got two hundred more to go, give or take, or so the laptop that once belonged to the CEO of kiddie porn told me."

"Give or take? You mean you don't know?"

"Well, there's been a casualty tonight, unfortunately. It's not out of the question that there'll be more."

"I have to know about this?!"

"I don't see any way around it, Mrs. Coelacanth."

"I'm complicit."

"Yes, Mrs. Coelacanth. Complicit in doing something right."

"That remains to be seen."

"For you it does. But it's too late to back out. You're in it now."

"Yes. I am." She removed her glasses and rubbed her eyes for a moment, then squeezed the temples of her head to massage away pain before giving up completely. "Get rid of your Gangsta Boys or whatever they are. Have them make themselves scarce. Ditch the bus. It's illegal six ways to Sunday. The cops no doubt are hunting it up already and it won't be hard to find, parked where it is."

"I'll have Jo-jo take care of it. What about your illegally parked car?"

"I'll move it now. We don't want your friends in the police to get here any sooner than they have to."

"Yes, I'll make myself scarce as well. Would money help?"

"When doesn't it?"

"I'll have someone make an anonymous donation. Help grease the wheels."

"Drug money."

"Do you really care at this point?"

"No, I suppose not."

Mrs. Coelacanth got up from her desk wearily holding a different jangle of keys. She went into the big front room with Null and sighed. "So, you mentioned the CEO of kiddie porn a few minutes ago."

"I did, in fact."

"You have his laptop."

"I do."

"You killed him, didn't you?"

"I did. With a pencil."

"A *pencil*?" she asked with dull-eyed confusion and disbelief, stopping dead in her tracks before facing the children and their reluctant attendant Gangsta Boyz.

"Yes, Mrs. Coelacanth. I killed him with a pencil." He looked at her coldly. "As you well know," he added with near reverence, "sometimes in this life, you have to improvise."

TWELVE

Null was on yet another bus, this time heading to Dudley station in Roxbury going back to the squat in Mattapan. He boarded by Johnson gate in Harvard Square, going unnoticed except perhaps as being somewhat overdressed for the mild weather of the day. It wasn't unusual for people in New England to either be over or underdressed for the weather, being that it was so changeably quirky. It was the usual diverse crowd of students, visible alcoholics, mental patients, old ladies and even a few businessmen clambering up into the bus.

Null was lucky to find a seat.

Despite being crowded in by an elderly woman with shopping bags in his dual seat, the blood that had stained his overcoat and hat went unnoticed. It occurred to him that his body was sending him messages he would have preferred not to receive. It was hard to move. His equilibrium was off. Phosphenes, like little colored ghosts, played before his eyes.

He realized this all amounted to being overtired.

He hadn't slept for a few days, nor had he eaten. It was beginning to catch up with him.

Null determined that he actually felt fine—as much as could feel anything.

The sensations were there, however, but he simply had no mental connection to them.

He was great in his brain—it's just that his body had a whole list of opposing ideas.

Despite the jerking, weighty stop-and-start of the bus in its hesitant progress toward Dudley Station, Null was swallowed by an enormous black shadow, far too big to fend off. It wasn't painful, and it wasn't pleasant; it was simply present, insistent, implacable and all-consuming. Null went with it, having no further choice to make.

Null's chin dropped, shoulders slumped down, giving in to the weight of the Bushmaster, Heckler, Glock, machete and phone beneath his overcoat. He began snoring gently, his chest heaving, now heavy in sleep.

His slumber was dreamless, empty, as much a death as oblivion could approximate.

Null awoke to his hat being placed squarely on his head by sensitive hands.

A woman had put it there.

She wore no make-up, agate-eyed, strawberry blonde, dressed down to almost unisex in yoga pants and hooded sweat-shirt, though her fully feminine shape was easily detectable beneath. She had a bright, clean smile. She sat down right next to Null in a curiously empty seat, as the bus was still fairly crowded. He noticed, blinking to clear his vision, that the bus had less than half the passengers it had when he boarded.

"Sorry to wake you up, mister, but you dropped your hat. I didn't want to see it get messed up." She had to shout a bit to be heard over passenger din and grumbling of the beleaguered bus.

"Thank you," said Null.

"You must be very tired, Mr.—?"

"Null. They call me Null."

"*They* call you? What do *you* call you?"

"Null is fine."

"My name's Janis."

"Thank you, Janis."

"Well, this is my stop. Why not get off with me, unless you have other plans?"

"Not any that won't keep."

"Get off with me then, Mr. Null. You look all in and a bus is nowhere to sleep."

"I think I need to sleep. More than I would have thought. It just didn't occur to me."

"Too much work, not enough play."

"You could say that in one sense, then the reverse in another."

"You're a philosopher, I see." The bus jerked as if to leave and she dragged him clumsily up, surprised by the uneven heft of the weaponry beneath his coat. "Let's get off before he pulls away."

"Fine," agreed Null, awkwardly rising. The cumbersome settling of the weapons beneath his coat made him almost fall over. Janis grabbed him before he did.

"You're really under the weather," observed Janis as they descended the steps, leaving the still somewhat crowded bus.

"That could very well be," replied Null. His footing was still unsteady and Janis took his arm to steady him as they walked off from the bus stop.

"My place is a block away. Maybe you'll come up for a while?"

"You always invite strange men you meet on busses to visit your apartment?"

Janis laughed. "You're not so strange, besides, you're falling asleep on your feet. You don't look too dangerous or threatening to me. Just worn out."

"Again, you're probably right."

"What are you going to do? Slash me with a machete or something?"

"No, of course not. Absurd."

"You're not kidding it's absurd. Now come with me. I won't take no for an answer. You can have a bite to eat and take a little rest while you're at it."

"I'm not really hungry."

"That's not what your stomach says. I can hear the thing rumbling from here without having to strain."

"Maybe that's not a bad idea then."

"No, Mr. Null, it certainly isn't."

Null actually had trouble managing the stairs to Janice's walkup apartment in the South End off Clarendon Street, weighed down by the weaponry under his coat and immense fatigue. She grabbed him, uncertain as to whether he could handle the stairs without him, her arm around his slender waist, feeling the barrel of the Bushmaster.

The apartment was a comfortable, down-market affair with familiar furnishings from Pier One Imports and some odds and ends from Crate and Barrel. Without troubling him to remove his coat and hat, she sat him down at a table in the big center room of the place and served him a sandwich from the kitchenette, which was off to the side.

"It's Italian cold cuts," she said. "I was going to eat it myself, but you need it more than I do."

"I shouldn't be taking your food." Deadpan. No reaction. This strangely didn't affect how Janis dealt with him in the slightest. She was smiling.

"No biggie. I can make myself another one later. Go ahead, it won't bite you."

"No, I didn't think it would."

He wolfed down the sandwich, which was entirely gone in under five minutes.

"All I have to drink is Diet Coke. Is that all right?"

"Fine. They say it tricks your body into craving sugar, so the diet effect is mitigated. I always thought the phenylalanine was more of a concern. Anxiety and hypomania. But everything kills you no matter what you do, so a glass of that won't amount to much harm I think."

"Are you a scientist?"

"No, just an amateur researcher of sorts."

"Research into what, may I ask?"

"Into human depravity."

"Sounds messy."

"It actually is."

He downed the entire glass in a single gulp.

Null's eyes began to lose focus. Shadows encroached on the center of his vision. He wavered in his chair.

"I think you're due for that nap," said Janis brightly.

"I think you're right," Null replied, slurring his speech.

Janis ushered him into her bedroom, whereupon he threw himself across the bed in a spastic motion and fell asleep instantly.

Janis stood over him and laughed, shaking her head.

———

"Get the fuck up, shitstain!"

"Rise and shine, fuckstick!"

Null sat up, seemingly unaffected by events that brought him there. He felt himself for his coat and the weaponry that had been beneath it, not panicking that both were gone or even displaying dull surprise.

Three large goons fit awkwardly into the modest bedroom, hulking over Null on the bed. They all wore heavy topcoats, looked to be in their early forties, gray-faced, stubbled, bleary-eyed, exuding deliberate menace.

"Stand, piece of shit."

"Sure. Looks like this is supposed to be my comeuppance."

"Some very influential people want you dead, fucker."

"My name is Null. Call me Null."

"I'll call you dead."

"Many people have called me that—they weren't wrong."

"We're going to make them right."

All three had pistols of various kinds. Null identified a Glock and a Sig Sauer. The other was a revolver, maybe Smith & Wesson. It was an academic point. The reality he was facing was certain death.

"You're working with that lesbian bitch from Boston PD. No other explanation. What's the matter with her She didn't quite get the message with what we did to the kid?"

"Oh, she got the message all right. Which one of you is Legere?"

"He ain't here. I don't think you're ever going to meet him."

"That's a pity," Null said, stretching as he stood before the three goons, defenseless, outmanned and outgunned. "People in your group were so eager to have me meet him."

"This is as close as you get, shitstain. You've fucked with the wrong people. Now they're fucking you back. But good."

"Are you going to kiss me before you fuck me?"

"Antoine, Gustav. Tune this motherfucker up."

Two of the goons socked their pistols away in coat pockets. The biggest of the three put Null in a full nelson from behind and his cohort hammered away at his face, chest, and midsection. Null didn't utter a sound, not even a grunt of pain. They all saw Null go limp. The lead lit a cigarette and checked his watch. It was a long time before he ordered the two to stop.

Null was slack in the big man's grip, obviously unconscious.

The lead pocketed his pistol, checked Null for signs of consciousness and found none. "All right, so that's that. Let's take the fucker back to the dump so we can finish up."

Janis appeared at the door. The lead turned and noticed her, irritated. "What the fuck are still doing here? You finished your end. You were paid."

She had shucked the loose clothes and was now wearing makeup, a black cocktail dress and some modest jewelry. "I just wanted to look in on you and see how you were progressing."

"Like we need you to check on us or something? Get the fuck lost. Our business with you is concluded. Take a fucking hike."

"Sure. I will eventually. But in the meantime, let the mook loose!" She raised up Null's Bushmaster 90291 semi-automatic rifle, primed and loaded. "It's one of the pieces I took off him. Guy comes prepared. I reloaded the clip myself. He even carries extra rounds in his coat."

The lead went for his coat pocket and Janis fired a burst by his feet.

"Go for your gun again and I'll cut you in two. I think I'm probably better at handling ordnance than you are, Buster Brown."

"Are you fucking high, you stupid bitch? What the fuck do you think you're doing?"

"What I'm doing is setting this Null fuck free. What you're doing is cooperating."

"Pound sand, bitch. We're going to grease this little prick and there's nothing you can do to stop it."

"I think putting some of this clip in your belly will stop it. And I have enough rounds here for both of your friends as well. So, big boy, just how do you want to play it?"

"Antoine, Gustav, go fling that piece of shit at the bitch."

They obliged and tossed Null at her like a bean bag. Or tried to, for when they released him he opened his eyes and stiffened up, fully conscious, despite the obvious damage his now swollen, bloodied, scarred face reflected.

"You're conscious," said Janis, nonplussed and a little unsettled.

"I always was. This was no big deal. Drop in the bucket."

"How about saving your ass? Was that a big deal?"

"You could say that it was."

"You could say thank you."

"I could. You're right. Thank you."

"As you say, it was nothing."

"All right, lovebirds, what's next in this comedy of errors?"

Null grabbed the Bushmaster from Janis, who smoothly produced a nickel plated twenty-two from her purse. "It's a small gun," she said wryly, "but there are those who love it."

"Been to Dartmouth?" asked Null.

"Made it to junior year, but life intervened."

"It always does. Better than death."

"Okay, you two, what's it gonna be?"

"I think I'll be leaving that up to Mr. Null."

Antoine and Gustav were heaving with silent anger behind the lead at the door. While Null stood there holding the Bushmaster on them, Janis slipped the machete lanyard around his neck, the topcoat about his shoulders and the porkpie hat atop his head.

"You're probably going to need some first-aid for that face," Janis observed.

"Probably too late for that. Doesn't matter—just more scars."

"You're a tough nut, Mr. Null."

"He's a fucking nut," observed the lead. "And he's destined for the grave."

"Aren't we all," said Null. He turned his head toward Janis, the Bushmaster still well aimed at the three goons. "This your place?"

"Are you kidding? I outgrew that kind of thing long ago. No, it's just a pied-a-terre for company use. God knows what shit's gone down within these walls."

"Well, more of it's going to go down very soon."

"Listen, you fucking cunt," shouted the lead. "You welshed. People who sent me aren't gonna be too happy they paid you a chunk a change for nothin'."

"But it wasn't for nothing," Janis replied brightly. "I was paid to deliver you Null, which I did. That's it. There was nothing in the agreement that said I had to allow you to keep him."

"We'll be coming for you next, chickadee, you better bank on that!" The lead just about growled that statement.

"I'll take that bet. Because I think you're on your last errand right here and now."

"So, you're good if I do what I have to do here, Janis?"

"That's right, Mr. Null. I'm out of here."

"Got a hot date?"

"No, you might say he's a cold one."

"You better think twice about what you're doing, bitch."

Null cooled the lead quickly with a burst from the Bushmaster right to the gut. Then he obliterated the hand that came up with the pistol, which thudded to the hardwood floor.

"Seems to me she's thought it through already."

"That's my exit cue, Mr. Null. I put my card in your coat pocket along with the cell phone and the Glock. Call me sometime. You're an interesting guy."

"I may not be your type, Janis."

"You're a tough goddamn motherfucker, which is exactly my type, scars be damned. Gives you character."

"Pretty that you think so. Paraphrasing Hemingway."

The lead was writhing in a gathering pool of blood on the floor.

"You'll get yours you traitorous fucking bitch!"

"Maybe, but you're getting yours now. I know what you assholes are involved in. I know what your disgusting business is. I may have suspect morals, but I draw the line at what you do. No, I won't stand for that. I know what Null is doing. He's eradicating the filthy infestation that you are. Frankly, I'm on the side of that. You have to be stopped."

Gustav screamed, "You're done in this town, you fucking cunt. Nobody'll hire your ass ever again!"

"Maybe, but it's such a pretty ass I may get away with it."

"You're on the side of a goddamn mass murderer!"

"I am. And I'm proud of it. Maybe by the time Null's done, there won't be enough of you left to fuck with me. Either way, I'll take my chances."

"See you in fucking hell!" screamed Antoine, whose hands were held up in the same way Gustav's were.

"Could be," said Janis with a shrug.

"I think I can handle things from here, Janis."

"Sure thing, Mr. Null. I have no doubt you can. But before I go, let me tell you something."

"Tell me what?"

"No matter what anybody says, no matter how they come after you, I think you should know. I'm pretty sure you're actually one of the good guys."

"I don't really abide by good and evil. Just ethics, situational dynamics."

"Doesn't matter, Mr. Null. You're still one of the good guys in my book."

"Okay. But I really need to turn my attention to the three stooges here."

"See you around, Mr. Null."

"It's a possibility," said Null.

Janis left and didn't lock the door behind her.

"Now, gentlemen, we're going to have a little discussion about the meaning of child abuse and how it affects our lives."

"It doesn't fucking affect my life, shitstain!" boasted Gustav, whose face was dotted with beads of sweat, rivulets of which cascaded down his high forehead. Antoine looked seasick, his rough stubbled face having gone pale.

"Well," said Null equably, "it may not affect your life. But I guarantee it'll affect your death."

THIRTEEN

"I fucking hate you."

"I understand — you've had enough of love. None of that ever worked out, so hatred would logically be the next thing. I admit I'm quite hate-able. No argument there."

"Just fuck off, Null. I don't need to see you."

"I disagree. You need to see me. You really do."

"You're wrong. I haven't had enough of love. Rudy hadn't had enough. There was never enough." Boyd, hair unkempt, void of makeup, slouched back in her chair at the table opposite Null and shakily lit a cigarette.

"Nobody ever has enough. The nature of the beast."

"You think love is a beast?" She released gouts of smoke without coughing.

"Of a kind."

"You don't know anything."

"Arguable. I do know this, however: You've been through hell. You're angry, and you want to show the fuckers that murdered Rudy and stopped your investigation cold just what hell feels like."

"They don't already know? They manufacture hell!" she shouted, getting the attention of one of the milieu therapists. The therapist, a prim woman in casual dress wearing a purple cashmere sweater stopped when she saw the scarred, wounded, and swollen face of Null. She walked off, suspiciously eyeing them both.

"Maybe we can teach them."

"*We* can teach them? Are you out of your fucking *mind*?"

"I thought that was settled long ago. And maybe you're forgetting your surroundings. They committed you, you know. Court ordered, in fact."

"So, you're saying *I'm* out of my mind?"

"It's a matter of legal record. What do you want to do about it?"

"Nothing I can do. I admit I'm fucked up."

"We're all fucked up. The price of life in civilization."

"I don't know what you want, Null. I don't know what's on your fucked-up agenda." She stood up hard and pounded the table harder with both fists. "What do you want? Just what the fuck do you actually *want*?" She sat down, spent and nearly in tears from that one moment of fulmination. The milieu therapist began prowling back to them. Null stood up and took a few steps forward, presenting a barrier against her progress. The therapist saw something in the eyes set so deep within the scarred and blotchy face—something that made her walk away.

"If I could want anything, and if you know anything, you know I can't—I would want revenge."

"You know what they say about revenge—that by the time you're done, you'll have to dig two graves."

"That must be funny, I think, because I surpassed two graves quite a while ago."

"It's a high body count alright. I stopped the count at about forty."

"You saw the web page—resolved it on your phone?"

"You sent me the address. You wanted me to see it."

"I intended for you to see it. It was meant to make you feel better. Did it?"

Boyd stubbed out her cigarette in a paper foil ashtray, hung her head, and mumbled, "I guess it did."

"You guess? You're not sure?"

"I said it fucking made me feel better!" Trembling now with wide, bloodshot eyes, her hair sticking out wild and to the sides.

"Revenge then, digging optional?"

"No, justice. It felt just somehow and right."

"Really. You don't think they were treated unfairly? Deprived of their day in court?"

"I decided on that. No, it was fair enough. If they wanted to face the law, they could have given themselves up. They could have surrendered and had full access to the justice system, if they wanted it. They didn't."

"Exactly. They didn't want it. But I think some of them may want it now."

"You have something in mind."

"I do, and I suspect so do you. And you know you can get out of this cracker factory whenever you want. *If* you submit a three-day letter to hospital administration."

"Yeah. So what."

"I could use your help.

"You're talking a partnership?"

"I am."

"Tell me how."

"It's not hard to dope out."

"Pretend I'm from Mars."

"I think I bit off more than I can chew with my initial approach. Killing and torturing the KP professionals. There are just too many of them to do it efficiently. Even with help, it's a problem."

"And by help you mean those warm and cuddly Gangsta Boyz of yours."

"You're being funny again, I think. They're cold customers, the Gangsta Boyz. Cold but useful. I'm not really sure I can control them for much longer. Something's always brewing with them."

"You're not thinking of having me arrest them, are you?"

"The Gangsta Boyz?"

"No, the fucking perverts."

"I am. You can give them the option. You can prevent me

101

from killing them all—stop the bloodbath. That agrees with you, doesn't it? Your sense of justice?"

Boyd brightened up. "You have all the names and addresses —you know where all the playhouses are, don't you, you fuck?" Null stood silent. She laughed. "You're unreal, you are!"

"Very real. I killed a couple of upper-level men to get the data. They needed killing, badly."

"Good cop, bad cop, then?"

"No, not at all." He paused, thinking of how to put it, then spoke offhandedly, "Bad cop—*murderous psychopath*."

———

"He's got their goddamn faces up on our server on the goddamn dark web, for Christ's sake!"

"This is just one guy?"

"We don't know how many, but we only got one on tape. He seems to be the main guy."

"I know. We all saw the tapes."

"Digital camera recordings. Not really tape."

"Figure of speech."

It was a conference room dead center Boston at the top of One Beacon Street—huge imposing and corporate. The conference room was lit by broad windows with an expansive view of the city in fading winter light. They were seated at the long table, each with a laptop computer in front of them. Several of them were smoking. There were six of them and three were smoking using emptied Starbuck's coffee cups as ashtrays as the offices of the law firm Chattels and Pelf were non-smoking. They didn't care. Each one of the participants was agitated. The unhappiness was palpable.

"We have a madman on our hands," observed Steve Privilegiata. "He's killing profits and ratcheting up expenses." He looked as if he were dressed for a tennis match.

An older man in khakis, tan cable-knit sweater stood and proclaimed, "Fuck killing profits, sonny—he's killing *people*. We're being targeted by a mass murdering nut job!"

"Where's Legere? He's the one that called this meeting!" announced a portly gray-haired woman still wearing her down jacket, despite the more than adequate heating of the law offices. "What's he doing about this?"

"We don't know anything about Legere. He's a shadow that lives amongst the shadows," offered Martha Privilegiata. "We don't know anything and what's worse, we're not *supposed* to know anything. Aren't we all silent partners? Investors who have nothing to do with day-to-day operations, never mind street. Legere should take care of this—*he's* street. We're not street. We don't know anything about it and it was supposed to be kept that way. All I have to do with this Hebe Group shit is collecting my monthly dividend checks, and that's it. How can we handle something like this? We can't. We have got to pull out and cut our losses!" Her chest was heaving, and she was close to hyperventilating. Her husband grabbed her hand to comfort her, and she jerkily sat back down.

"Marty's right," said Steve Privilegiata authoritatively.

"We can't, and you should know that by now," said the older man in the cable knit sweater, stubbing out his cigarette. "So, go ahead and tell me you don't know—that the rest of us don't know. Go ahead."

"I don't know. This is a very quiet side financial investment. We just end our minimal involvement, whatever few strands there are remaining, eat the loss of our investment and go on our merry way. Other than the loss, I don't see the problem."

An older woman in a hoodie and sweatpants dragging feverishly on her cigarette with a drawn and wizened face stated the case: "I saw the tapes. Whoever this cocksucker is, he knows who we are and where we live. And he basically intends to torture and kill us all."

"Well, he can't just go out and do that. Let's be realistic." This from a mousy forty-something woman with thick glasses, a puffy face and stringy hair. "You're fucked in the head, Beatrice."

"No, the guy that's coming after us is the one who's fucked in the head. And it doesn't seem that he's *so* fucked in the head that he can't do what he claims on the tapes he's obviously setting out to do, which is fucking why we're here!" Beatrice screamed back.

"Why don't we have anyone from management here, taking charge of this situation?" asked cable-knit sweater.

Martha Privilegiata slammed her fist down on the table, startling everyone sitting down at it with a tiny simultaneous jump.

"Legere says they're all dead!" volunteered Martha. "We all got the same e-mail with the link back to the site of the dead faces, didn't we? Didn't *you?* You didn't recognize anyone, for god's sake?"

They all asserted that they did.

"Someone has to be in charge, otherwise we'll just lose everything we put into this fucking enterprise!" said Steve Privilegiata.

"Maybe if we could just abandon the whole thing and let it fall is exactly what this shitbird wants to leave us the fuck alone!" Beatrice, the wizened woman, offered.

"I think," said Steve, "from the tape I saw, this sonofabitch is coming for every single one of us no matter what we do."

"So, you're saying what?" offered cable-knit sweater.

"I'm saying we have to get somebody to kill this rat bastard while we still can!"

"We already have Legere for that."

"We do. And he's supposed to be very capable, from what I understand. Still, I like to hedge my bets. So, to be on the safe side, we're going to need someone else who's—even more *capable.*"

"Who are we going to get to do that? Do you have any idea how many people from the group this mook killed already?"

"About forty, right?"

"Give or take. And don't forget the fun factory in Allston. Jesus Christ, he not only torched it, but melted steel and brick right down to the fucking *ground.*"

"It's true. He's become our fucking problem, Hal. No joke."

"Him and his people, whoever he is. Ya. No joke there."

"Well," said Steve Privilegiata, as if pondering the issue. "I think I have somebody in mind to take care of this fuckwad."

"We don't even know who he is," complained Beatrice, the woman with the wizened face.

"We don't have to. When we find him, we can ask him his name right before we blow his fucking brains out."

"He mentioned his name on the tape," answered Martha Privilegiata in a questioning tone. "Called himself 'Null,' said we didn't have to worry about finding him—that he was going to find us first."

"Good to know," replied Steve. "Let's make sure he finds somebody else along the way too, yes?"

"And who do you have in mind for that?" The slim man bent over in his chair with a caved-in chest, obviously bald and wearing a cap to hide it, sat up and spoke up. "Just who's gonna handle a thing like this if it isn't Manny Legere, whom none of us has ever met or even freakin' seen?"

"I've got a guy in mind—a truly warped, sick and twisted fuck. A fuck to end all fucks, in fact."

"So, who the fuck is he already?"

"I don't have a name, really. Just an email and a nickname. It's what other people call him. According to them, he doesn't call himself anything at all."

"Yeah, so what's that?"

Steve Privilegiata stood up and rubbed his forehead to answer. "They call him 'The Expert.' I think you can guess why."

"Well, I can't guess, Steve, and I've never heard of this guy before," Martha Privilegiata said sullenly.

"Nobody has, Marty. But from how the rumors go, he's the best at what he does. I think we can retain him at a price."

"Good money after bad."

"Maybe. But with luck we can off Null, take what's left of Hebe and get it back on track, fix the site and shore up the remaining play-houses. We may not have to sit back and watch it fall at all. In fact, we may not have any further financial need of

Mr. Legere either. From what I understand off the PDF files of the books, he's pricey enough."

"I'm with ya, kid," said Hal, the older guy in the maroon cable-knit sweater. "So, what does this guy do that he's so expert at?"

"Pest control. He kills bugs dead, as the expression goes."

"Like Raid, for god's sake?"

"So, he's an ace hitter, you're saying."

"No, I'm saying it's like fighting fire with fire."

Hal was irritable and fidgeted in place. "Yeah, okay, so tell me how's that?"

"Simple. We're simply going to send in one fucked up dude to put an end to another."

FOURTEEN

The next playhouse was in Squantum, a bedroom community by the sea, an inlet on the bay. A subset of the town of Quincy well-enough off to have an industrialized waterfront and boasting more than its fair share of clean beaches, redolent of Mass-achusetts nautical history boasting a seaside and shipping feel. The house was a nice, white two-story Federalist type—a clap-board deal never meant to become as exorbitant as skewed and ruined real-estate demand had made it. The place wasn't well maintained, was in dire need of a paint job and the grass in the front yard was wildly overgrown. Boyd noticed the exterior drabness of the house like a warning sign to stay away: No one is wanted here.

The gulls were crying and the smell of the salt air in the cold of the late winter day was keen. It should have been spring, but anyone who lived in Boston and environs knew the season for the region was strictly a myth. Winter often lingered on right into May; sometimes through it. Boyd hitched up her black pleather jacket and used the salt-spotted, corroded brass knocker on the weather-beaten door with some force. There was no answer. She had to kick the door a couple of times before somebody answered.

"What do you want?" asked a slightly stooped older man with white hair and wire-rimmed glasses. He wasn't welcoming.

"Detective Lieutenant Kay Boyd, Boston P.D." She flipped him the badge in its leather wallet and he grabbed it hard, which made Boyd want to punch him in the face, but she refrained. She yanked it back and pocketed it.

"I suppose you'll be wanting to come in then."

"If you don't mind, Mr. Eldritch."

"Do it then." He shrugged and drew back from the doorway, leading her into the kitchen through a musty, dust-ridden den that hadn't seen daylight in years walking in a hunch. He led Boyd through the living room, where light had obviously been blocked by heavy dust- and cobweb-clotted maroon drapes for years to a kitchen brightly lit by the light struggling in from bare, albeit dirty windows. Eldritch had already sat himself down at the classic gold-speckled Formica table as if he expected something. Boyd continued standing, despite his gesture for her to sit.

"You have kids. Where are they?"

"They're playing in the back."

"They are? I didn't hear a sound when I knocked on your door."

"My wife and I have taught 'em how to behave quietly. They wouldn't be disobedient."

"They wouldn't? And why wouldn't they?"

"They know discipline. It's important for children to respect their elders, know their place, to know *discipline.*"

"I see," said Boyd, sizing Eldritch up. Sizing up the house in the bargain and getting nowhere. "You made them afraid."

"Sure, fear is good for children. Teaches them respect. You don't respect what you don't fear. And they respect me and my wife. Totally."

"I can see that."

"You can't see shit. Tell me what you want and get the fuck out. In fact, I didn't have to invite you in at all. I could've just slammed the door in your face and there'd be nothing to be done about it. I'm getting stupid in my old age."

"That's true. But you invited me in, and since that happened, I can look around."

"You can, but you can only use what you find in plain sight.

And you can't go upstairs—no, no you'd need a warrant for that and obviously you ain't got one. So, take a look at what's available to ya on the first floor, which ain't gonna be nothin', and then go screw yourself."

"I don't need to take a look around here, Mr. Eldritch. I already know what you and your wife Mildred are doing. I assume all the outfitting, the props, the cameras, and the hard drugs are all on the second floor?"

"Don't matter what's up there, missy, 'cause you ain't goin'."

"You do know why I'm here, don't you?"

"Haven't a clue."

"Let me clue you in, then. You and your wife and your four foster kids are streaming live hardcore kiddie porn over the dark web from the upstairs bedroom. Some bondage and light S-and-M play for the niche market. I'm sure you have floggers and ball gags and paddles and all the accoutrements we could confiscate. And even an actual cage, I understand." She seemed bored and unconcerned. She wasn't.

"Fuck what you understand. You can't touch a thing. I'm calling my lawyer. Maybe he can get you to leave."

"Oh, I'll be going, alright. Don't worry."

"You're not going to arrest me?"

"Well, that was the plan."

Eldritch's face went slack with perplexity; gray wattles, long deep creases dragged down to the Formica table, distorting him like a cartoon. "*That* was your plan? And you were going to arrest me off *what?* No warrant, no evidence, no back up? Tell me how the fuck you planned to arrest me!"

"Well, not just you. Mildred too. And then we'd be getting the kids out of here into some sort of residential therapy. We have an accomplished social worker on our side who does some pretty amazing things."

"Miracles, to be sure." He removed a mostly empty half pint bottle of Jim Beam from the side pocket of his khakis. "So how do you think this will go down? Just how are you intending to arrest us?" He slammed the empty bottle down on the table with a delighted gasp.

"I thought you and Mildred would just confess and let me take you in, after arranging for a sitter first, of course, until DYS gets here."

"Are you blind high on molly or something? No shit, Detective Boyd, but you are off your bloody fucking rocker!" He cackled at her in a superior way, proving that someone could actually do that convincingly. Eldritch was ready to make short work of Boyd.

Boyd shook her head. "Stone cold sober. Unlike you."

"Ain't a crime to take a taste in your own goddamn house, is it?"

"No, not at all."

"I'm not confessing to any of your bullshit and neither is Mildred, who's upstairs napping, by the way. And I'm not even going to wake her to tell her you were here. My confessing and your arresting me is a pipedream, and you can shove that pipe right up your ass."

"No, Eldritch. If you don't leave here with me in cuffs and your wife too, *all* of it will be shoved right up both your withered asses!" Her temper was rising.

"Take your best shot, you smug, fat little bitch!"

"Fat? Really?" Boyd felt her torso with her hands theatrically over her pleather jacket. "This is Boston, and we all wear bulky clothes this time of year."

"Yeah, well, Quincy ain't Boston, so, don't let the door hit you in your fat ass on the way out, bitch!" Eldritch belched.

Boyd smacked him hard with an open hand hard across his weathered face, so it turned pink quickly. Eldritch cradled his cheek and moaned like a wounded calf.

"Listen up, you stupid pervert. It plays this way: Either I place you under arrest and you and your wife confess, or some dreadful fucker much, much worse than you is going to pay you and your wife a visit and torture you both to death."

"What the fuck?"

"You haven't heard about all the deaths of all your perverted little cohorts down at Hebe Group being murdered? I know it hasn't made the papers, because nobody but me has made the kiddie porn connection between all these new torture murders—about forty of them, I'd say. Mutilated corpses. But I bet your nifty paychecks or Bitcoin blockchains from Hebe Group have been suffering some miscalculation and delay lately, no?"

Eldritch turned even more white than before and then went ashen. "How the fuck did you know that? It's like nobody's running the show over there, for Christ's sake."

"So, you're confessing?"

"I never said anything of the kind. Besides, if you know this bozo is coming, you have to protect me. You're a goddamn policewoman."

"But I don't know that's true, Mr. Eldritch, at least not officially. No one's investigating this torture killer. And those who know about it don't give a rat's ass because he's preying exclusively on scumbags just like you."

"Well, if that's so detective fat-ass, why don't you protect me? Post a detail outside the shanty and prevent this boogieman from causing me and mine bodily harm! Christ almighty!"

"Can't do that, Eldritch. There's no investigation open on the torture murderer. Could be he's just a folk myth, an urban legend. But I heard tell he sent some cam-corded messages distributed to assholes like you. Didn't you get the memo? Links to the streaming video?"

"I don't always read my emails. Usually nothing but junk. I open the ones that talk about payment and that's about it."

"You should go back a few days and read some. Might clear your head."

Eldritch slammed a flat hand on the table. "If you know some jamoke is coming here to do us harm, you're obligated to prevent it." He screwed up his face and raised one eyebrow over one open eye, the other frozen in a wink. "You're fucking law enforcement, ain't ya, bitch?"

"Sure. But we enforce the law *after* it's been broken, not before. All I have here involving you is an unconfirmed suspicion of child abuse, rape and kiddie porn distribution. I got nothing on any attempted murder on you and wifey. Nada. I'm offering you a chance at cooperation, so I can arrest you."

"So, you'll do nothing then?"

"Come on, Eldritch, be an adult. When have you ever known of any policemen to actually *prevent* a crime? Like never. We don't prevent anything. We execute law enforcement after the crime is committed, not before."

"But me and my wife may need protection!"

"Well, I can protect you once I arrest you. Otherwise, no."

"Fuck off then. We'll take our chances. I think your talk about a torture killer boogieman, whatever, is a good goddamned fairy story."

Boyd sighed, put her hands in her pockets. "Alrighty then, I'll just go. You have a nice day, Mr. Eldritch. Enjoy it, because it's going to be your last."

"Ah, bullshit!" Eldritch didn't get up to escort her out.

As Boyd made her way through the dim, dusty living room toward the front door, she turned and called back to him: "You had your chance, Mr. Eldritch. Good luck to you."

"You stupid cow! You think confessing to felonies and getting arrested by you is any kind of a chance? Blow it out your generous ass, why don't you!" He laughed a harsh, dry and mirthless laugh.

"You'd think it wouldn't be, and normally you'd be right on the money, but in this situation, it really was your last, best hope and now it's gone. Just like me."

"Good riddance then!"

"You're right, Eldritch. I'll be saying that myself pretty soon."

"In a pig's eye!"

Boyd shrugged and let both the hard and weathered wood door with the corroded knocker on it and the bent, spotted aluminum storm door in front of it slam tight behind her with a high-pitched bang. She gave a crisp little nod of satisfaction to herself and walked briskly back to her car, mindful of the cold.

———

They were in full swing.

The Eldritches using the disciplined foster children—everyone naked. Mildred dancing around her breasts flopping about, a ten-year-old sandy-haired boy hands behind his back tied to a sawhorse taking blows from her multi-tressed flogger in the well-carpeted expanse of the second floor of the house in Squantum; Eldritch coupling with a 7-year-old girl with a bright orange ball gag in her mouth, making muffled noises. Screams, pleas, sobs and whimpers, muffled. The boy's back was welted to bleeding. Eldritch whooping loud and hard. A digital camera on a tripod recording. Cameras set in each corner of the ceiling narrow-casted the scene on the dark web to a new Hebe Group server. Two other children, a boy and a girl, both redheads, were tied and gagged and stashed in a back corner, presumably waiting their turn. Old rock music from the sixties played loud and distorted.

"Inna Gadda Da Vida" was screaming.

Null crashed in through the center bay window that had a blanket tacked over it. He landed on the floor on his back amid shards of glass and splinters of wood. He had swung in on a corded nylon tether anchored to the roof, freed himself quickly with a panic snap. When he got up, a screaming nude Mildred wearing harlequin glasses faced him with a shotgun. She couldn't be heard over the music.

"This stops now!" shouted Null, barely audible.

"This will go on forever!" countered Mildred, shrieking, and resolutely pumped both barrels into Null's chest, putting him back on his back on the plush rug, flopping about.

She strode away and hit a button on a wall console that killed the music.

"Fred!" she screamed, as if the music was still on. "Look what I caught!"

Genitals glistening, Eldritch approached Null, who was struggling and coughing flat on his back. He was flopping pathetically like a goldfish whose bowl had been smashed.

Eldritch was beside himself with glee.

"Well, lookee here! We got the goddamned boogie man that

fucking police cunt threatened us with. Ain't that somethin'. I am so *scared!*"

He produced an excited laugh that sounded like *"ee-hee-hee."*

"We'll bury him out back in the yard—nobody's going to miss this fucker." Mildred chuckled and blew on the empty holes of both barrels of the shotgun by her side for emphasis.

"What the fuck was he thinking?"

"I don't know what kind of game they were runnin', but pretty much it was a stupid one. Probably nothin' to do with the law, fake badge and all."

The children were quiet, all but the girl with the ball gag in her mouth, who had sat down in the middle of carpet, weeping so furiously that the sound could be discerned clearly for what it was in spite of the gag. It was both sloppy and frustrated.

"Even if it was the legitimate law, they couldn't do shit. They need warrants and subpoenas up the wazoo we could always beat. We're on the good list with Norfolk County judges. Not that the real cops would ever even suspect a nice foster family like us."

"Then how'd these freaks know?"

"Maybe they got lucky."

"Maybe we got careless."

"Doesn't matter for right now. Be a doll and get me two more rounds from the nightstand by the bed, would you? I need to finish this fucker off."

"Okay. I'll get to cleanin' up the blood in the morning. First, we'll have to take him out back, bury the bastard."

The sobbing of the young girl was a keening muffle. The sound was like that of a dying gull.

Then another sound startled them both.

They heard the click.

They froze, rattled.

Null was standing there in front of them, breathing hard.

He spoke evenly, seemingly unaffected by having taken two full shotgun blasts in the chest.

"You didn't get lucky, and you didn't get careless. You were targeted. By me." Null glowered before them, the Heckler drawn and cocked.

"How the fuck—?" clucked Eldritch.

"Flak jacket," replied Null softly. "I thought, in view of the last playhouse I visited, that it would be prudent to wear one. Forewarned is forearmed, although I think I may have broken a rib. Maybe two." He blinked.

Mildred, holding the now empty shotgun, decided to turn on the charm. "I can fix that for you, handsome, if you *let* me."

Null's response was four quick rounds from the Heckler, two in each of their stomachs.

Both Eldritches collapsed to the rug, moaning and wailing simultaneously.

"Yes," said Null approvingly. "It hurts like hell, but it won't kill you right away. I have no intention of letting you die quickly. No, not at all."

"Listen!" gasped Eldritch in sincere remorse. "Get the Boyd bitch on the blower for me. Tell her we'll take the deal she offered. We'll confess, take the arrest. We'll even name names for you, you fucking son-of-a-bitch!"

"No need. I have all the names that are necessary. And as you can see, I already had yours."

Null walked about surveying the room, eying the children, trying to decide whether to untie them or leave them as they were until he was finished. There was sobbing and a breathy child's plea to a nonexistent god.

Both Eldritches began to make considerable noise. He went over to them again and fired one more round each in the belly, then knelt down and explained himself in a gentle seeming tone. "That's right, you won't be going anywhere, but go ahead and try to get out of this. Crawl in your own blood, making for an escape. Slither if you have to. I salute your tenacity. You can go. But you won't get far—you'll just bleed out all the faster. Or stay in one place and slow down the inevitable, if you like. Either way, I'll get back to you. Either way, we're going to have a little talk about the importance and value of children in the world, and how they should be treated."

"We know how the little bastards should be treated!" coughed Eldritch defiantly.

"They earn their keep!" spat Mildred.

"And now you'll earn yours. If you don't know how children should be treated, you'll die trying to know. In fact, I guarantee, you'll die anyway."

He left them there, struggling and bleeding, casually adding, "Ignorance is no excuse."

Null went to the small naked girl now lying on the rug, her hands zip-tied and the ball gag still in her mouth. He released her, lifted her up, smoothed her hair. He took a tissue from his pocket, dabbed away tears.

The girl was shaking, having trouble standing. Null steadied her.

"It's going to be okay, kid. I know it doesn't quite look that way now, but it will. What's your name?

"I'm Robin," she said in a rasping whisper and burrowed into Null's coat for safety.

"'A robin redbreast in a cage. Puts all heaven in a rage.'"

"What?"

Null took her gently by her shoulders, put his face close to hers. "Okay, kid. I'm going to need you to be a very big girl and help me. Can you find everybody's clothes while I get them untied? Can you do that for me?"

"Yeah," Robin said in a small voice. "Sure."

"You go get dressed and get their clothes on them and I'll take care of everything else. You're okay, aren't you? You're a big girl—you can do it."

Robin sniffled. "Yeah. I'm okay. I can do it." She broke away from Null with surprising energy and turned to look at him as he cut her brother's zip ties with a buck knife. "Mister, are you gonna kill ma and pa?"

Null looked at her analytically.

"You know they're not really your ma and pa, don't you?"

"Yeah, I do. Are you gonna kill 'em?

"Well, do you think I should?"

Robin cast her eyes to the rug and mumbled to herself, but perceptibly enough to be heard: "Yeah. I think you oughtta."

"Well," said Null, "you and I are two minds that are very much alike."

"We are?"

"Yeah, because I think so too."

·

FIFTEEN

"What I know is you're getting your revenge for that thing that happened with the foster kid, right?"

"If that were true, the department wouldn't let me make the collars." Boyd gritted her teeth with suppressed irritation, which was her usual response to Homicide Detective Byron Wurdalaka.

"I have to tell you, Boyd, we can't figure out how you're doing it.

"There's no big secret, Wurdalaka."

"Don't hand me no bullshit about good police work. You got some sort of hincty inside deal going, don't ya?"

"Nope. No inside deal. I just bumped into the right CI, is all there is to it."

"Well, fuck all, I hope you're paying that shitbird some decent money, so he keeps coming across with the goods."

"I do my best to keep him happy, if happiness were even a thing with him, which it isn't."

"You're fuckin' him, right?"

"Don't be an ass."

"I feel you, LT, he's a doper though for sure, right? You're passin' him baggies of skag from the evidence locker, ain't you, you fuckin' hot ticket?"

"You know I shouldn't say."

"Aww, c'mon, LT, just between you and me. I gotta know."

"I'm not gonna let you steal my goddamn, CI, Byron."

"Alright, but still, it's righteous *amazing* what this guy, if it even is a guy, gave up. What, five solid kiddie porn busts in, what, two weeks' time? Each one an uncontested confession, no question of undue duress, no brutality complaint. No surveillance, no nothin'. They just open up the freakin' door, you walk right in, they confess right off the bat, then let you cuff 'em, Mirandize 'em, walk 'em right out the freaking door with you like zombies and then they confess again, no trouble at all, write everything down, everything they did, gave up the kids, payments, cam feeds—fuckin' beautiful! You know you got one stone bonnaroo CI, and that's no joke. What the fuck did you do —sell your soul to the devil or somethin'? It's freakin' eerie."

"You don't know the half of it."

"Do I even wanna know?"

"You're the one asking the questions, Byron."

"Okay, okay, I get it. So. what brings ya down to homicide? Miss my pretty face, did ya?"

"Only so I could get close enough to kick it with my boot," she replied with an unforced smile. "Maybe I could ram one of these steel toes squarely up your ass too, while I'm at it."

Wurdalaka chuckled at this, with a thin slit of a grin bisecting his crinkled-up face. "Funny stuff. What's funnier is if they actually certified you as fit for duty there, Mary freakin' sunshine." The grin evaporated.

"Ya, genius. Like I made those collars on my own time."

"What if I double check that recertification?"

"What if I choke you out on the floor?"

"You are a testy—"

"Don't call me a bitch, Byron."

"Fine. But you are."

"Sure, but don't call me that."

"Fuck all, Boyd, if you're still out on medical, what the fuck are you doing here bugging me for? Don't you have a few more classes to audit at the laughing academy or something?"

"No, you fucktard. I'm *not* out on medical. Those five busts were goddamn righteous. Just ask any one of the ADA puppies prosecuting down at Suffolk. They'll probably piss up your leg with enthusiasm."

"Ouch, LT, you really know how to hurt a guy who's got nothin' but good intentions on ya." Wurdalaka took it down a notch. Let the grin be a smile that split his face. "So, you wanna introduce me to this mutt, or what?"

"You wanna fuck off and die, or what?"

"Okay, okay, so tell me what it is already."

"What *what* is?"

"Just spit it the fuck out, LT!"

Boyd cleared her throat, adjusted her posture while Wurdalaka slouched leaning against a gray, gunmetal desk. "I'm here to ask you about some unsolved homicides. Anything you got in the files recently stick out for being maybe a bit odd—hincty as you say—no evidence onsite you could run, no witnesses, strange victimology?" She paused for a moment, watching the wheels turn in Wurdalaka's head. "Like maybe a bunch of 'em, maybe?"

"Seriously, LT, for once you ain't asking such a stupid question. We got a few in the backlog of cold cases, nothing new except just one that fits your bill exactly.

"Just one. That's it?"

"Yeah, but it's a big it."

"How big?"

"Mass murder."

"Come again?"

"One of those high mucky muck city officials with an office on the same floor as the mayor's. The whole division's working it and we ain't got diddley yet."

"Really? Who was it?"

"You know Joe Finnerty? Code Enforcement?"

"Never heard of him."

"Well, some professional hitter took him out a few weeks back. Killed him and his entire security down at One Boston. A fucking bloodbath."

"Why do you think it was professional?"

"Fucker didn't miss a trick. Came in light, went out heavy.

Whacked the principal, then exited in broad daylight, taking out every man on security and maintenance without a thought, no misses—used some freakin' fancy German sidearm on the exit. Ballistics had it as a hack something."

Boyd's expression brightened for a moment. Her face was a little bloated, and rum blossoms were beginning to show about the nose. "Heckler and Koch P7, maybe?"

"Yeah, that's the one. Registered to Finnerty it turns out, so he got it off him. You a gun freak too, LT? In addition to being a freak?"

"No, Byron—I'm just that savvy."

"Sure you are, LT and I fart nickels."

"I hate that expression."

"I saved it especially for you."

"You're sure it's even a guy?"

"We at least got that. The witnesses who saw the mope leave down in the lobby also watched him pop the brains out of some stockbroker. They all swear up and down it was a little guy with a funny walk, overcoat and hat hiding his features. Walked right by the uniforms coming to nab him and they didn't even notice – funny walk and all."

A limp, thought Boyd with a chill of realization. *Fucking Null.*

"Security tape showed that, too. Sound familiar to you, LT?"

"No, not at all. So, what do you figure?"

"You wanna try and steal my case while I'm trying to steal your CI? Too fucking much!"

"You can have it, I just wanted to know—

"I fuckin' *know* what you want to know, lady, right goddamn now. And I wonder just why it is that you want to know it so bad."

Boyd stayed calm, went with it. "So then, is it true or not?"

"Yeah, it's fucking true. You knew it before you crossed the threshold."

"I wasn't sure."

"You're a pain in the ass, LT, no denying, but you got good instincts."

"I don't think I can link it to my five KP busts."

"It's just a rumor. But I made cases before on rumors less good." Wurdalaka sighed. "We came up empty at the scene, and it was his private office, not the one at city hall. Should have been a fucking treasure trove. Too many prints, most of them smudged, and the ones that weren't were nobodies who never even hit the system."

"Not even one?"

"Why? You were hoping for someone?"

"I never hope. It was a pro hitter, right?"

"Well, it wasn't no fucking jealous girlfriend, that's for sure."

"So maybe you're thinking it's related to my collars after all and want to horn in."

"Why would you say that?"

Boyd poked Wurdalaka hard at the collarbone. He made a slight wince of discomfort. "Because you didn't mention that the laptop was missing, and it would have to be missing because that's where all the evidence of KP would be, wouldn't it?"

Wurdalaka gently seized Boyd's hand and put it aside. "We didn't find no ledger either."

"There wouldn't be one. It's all on the missing laptop."

"You're still running this down?"

"Fuckin' A, Byron."

"The Captain on board?"

"For once, he loves something. A gang of KP collars gets good ink. So, I'm good."

"When are you coming home to OC? Once this CI runs dry or gives himself a hotshot, whichever comes first?"

Boyd smirked. "I think he prefers meth."

"That makes him a dead bang short timer, then."

"Probably, but as for OC, I'm still doing that. I haven't left but for my, umm—"

"You mean your *period of adjustment*?"

"Yeah. Exactly that."

"Fuck, you actually think this fucking thing—this CI even— is part of an organized ring? A network of dark web KP goofs?"

"That could very well be."

Wurdalaka stood up straight and hitched his pants, kicking the toe of his boot against a stout leg of the gunmetal desk. "Borrow me in on it, then, LT. I'm useful. Never mind stealing your CI. I want in. Tell Parseeman you need him to mandate me in."

"You're serious."

"Deadly, baby."

"You can dream it, but you sure as shit can't be it."

"You're saying no?"

"I'm putting my foot down."

"So, it's still that way?"

"It's never going to be any other way, Byron."

Boyd started to draw away from the homicide detective, but he stopped her. "Just wait a fucking second LT, think about it. And while you're thinking about it, I got a little tidbit for you for free. A gesture of good will—a olive branch maybe." The face-bisecting grin reappeared.

She moved yet further away down the hall from where Wurdalaka stood by the door, turning her head. "Yeah? Whaddaya got?"

"A whacko missing persons down in Southie."

"Why whacko?"

"Nobody in homicide can make heads nor tails out of it."

"Hit me."

"Some company, a sub-chapter S Corp. called Tiresias or somethin', just disappeared. No other filings on it, no paperwork or permitting anywhere—all aliases if anything at all, and all pointing back to the company address which is as vacant as the president's brain. The place was obviously cleaned, not even a single desk in sight."

"Blood evidence?"

"Bleached clean. Whatever happened, it was another pro job —or just a fluke—but pretty fucking crazy."

"Okay, so?"

"So, this, LT. Fifteen human beings seem to have disappeared right along with the company—no blood, no bodies, no debris, no nothing. And get this. None of their cars are anywhere to be found, even the ones with Lo-Jack. Poof —*gone*."

"Disappeared?"

"Gone as in loved ones calling up all *verklempt* gone."

"And who's workin' it? Who's the primary?"

"Nobody. Missing persons kicked it up to us after the fifteen reports were filed, all saying the exact same thing, and they couldn't get nothin' from it. They figured, anyone disappears like that, they must all be dead. So, they gave it to us and we put it in cold case. There wasn't nothin' for us to work. No witnesses, no blood evidence, no corpses, no nothin'—nada! Fuckin odd, wouldn't ya say?"

"I would. You givin' this one to me?"

"Shit yeah, LT, take it if you want. It's all yours. Maybe your C-I knows somethin' about this too—tie it in neatly with all them easy kiddie porn bust leads."

"Sure, I'll take it off your hands, if you want." She moved down the hall toward her own office, but not too fast. She could feel there was more coming. And there was.

"Hey, LT, your CI ain't really that zombie fuck Null, is it?"

Boyd froze. Swallowed hard.

"Of course not. He's dead."

"Great. Maybe he can look up the missing fifteen while he's down there visiting hell."

Boyd turned to face him, seething. "Maybe he'll visit you too, while he's at it!"

Wurdalaka crossed his arms over his heart, cast slit eyes skyward, clearly mocking her. Then he intoned it like a holy chant:

"*Oh babe—lemme tell ya somethin'. I'm counting on it!*

SIXTEEN

"How do you like being dead?"

"I was going to ask you that question."

"Bit of a reversal for you, Mr. Null?"

"I can't say it was unexpected, since I expect exactly nothing."

"Then nothing I do is going to disappoint you."

"I am never disappointed."

"Want some light?"

"I really don't care."

"Light then."

The space burst into view.

It was a sparse, gray concrete basement it the bottom of a building somewhere in greater Boston; ancient but sandblasted clean. Null couldn't see who was talking to him—the light in his eyes was blinding. He didn't squint, but all he could see was a hot, yellow, distorted star.

"Better now?" A self-satisfied voice—high, thin and reedy.

"Compared to what? I can't see you and I can't make out much about this room with the light in my eyes."

"That's a shame. Too bad. I like it that way, so we'll keep it that way."

"I have no choice since I can't make out where I am, and you have me strapped down."

"I heard it wasn't a good idea to leave too much to chance with you."

"You heard right."

"Want to know why you're not dead?"

"I thought I was dead already."

"For a dead man, you're droll in your own way, aren't you, Mr. Null?"

"I'm not really known for my sense of humor."

"Funny, yet true!" The voice was almost gleeful.

"I only do one thing—just one thing." Cool, unexcited, breathing easily despite open cuts on his scarred face, bruises, contusions—a deep purple hematoma on his left ribcage.

"Perhaps I can teach you some new tricks?"

"I don't think so. My one trick will do. It's all I need, if I ever needed anything at all."

"You don't sound like any of this bothers you at all."

"It doesn't."

"I don't believe it."

"Try me."

"If you don't mind."

"You should get to the point whether I mind or not—either kill me or let me go. Otherwise, this is a waste of your time and mine."

"Since you don't mind, it doesn't matter, does it? I can use my time anyway I like."

"You can. So what?"

"So *this*, Mr. Null!"

There was a period of silence interrupted solely by the sound of a rattling from Null's throat followed by gurgling. Labored breathing soon replaced that.

"How was that, Mr. Null?" The high, reedy, smug voice echoed.

Null spat. "How was *what?*"

"You're joking."

"I really don't know what's funny or not anymore. I have to depend on others for that. You found it funny?

"You're a problem, Mr. Null, *not* a solution."

"That's my starting position, Mr.—you have me at a disadvantage."

"I don't understand it. I was sure it was just a myth."

"People tell stories for amusement. They exaggerate the fine details."

"Amusement. I like that."

In response, Null started coughing, and heaving, bucking up in place from the board onto which he was strapped down spread eagled by leather and steel. His chest was bare and electric lead wires coiled out from nearly every region of his body and his pantlegs. He involuntarily arched his back up hard, so that his ribcage shone, sweaty and defined. Foam gathered from his mouth and dolloped down to the floor. A network of purple, red and purple scars swelled in high relief in the extreme lighting.

When his eyes were finally able to focus, Null saw a tall man dressed in black shirt and khakis with a paunch and a slack jaw, middle-aged with jet black hair obviously dyed, adjusting horn-rimmed glasses. The man stood before Null, eying him critically.

He ran a finger over Null's chest.

"Looks pretty much like you've been tortured before. Quite a bit, it seems. Doesn't really seem to have done any good, does it?"

Null was still panting but was otherwise calm and unfazed. "No, I suppose it didn't."

"Funny to the end."

"I always seem to be the last one to get the joke."

"I suppose if I took another finger, maybe took your testicles, hamstrung your other leg, stuck a drill in parts of you, it wouldn't really much matter, would it?"

"You're welcome to try, but I doubt it would do either of us any good."

"I can see that. You took quite a bit of voltage, but it doesn't seem to have bothered you even a little bit."

"Not that I noticed."

"If I gave you more, it would've stopped your heart and that would be that."

"Why didn't you? Obviously, you're going to kill me."

"Obviously."

"It's a good thing I don't get bored."

"Don't you want to know why?"

"I know why. By the way, I never got your name."

"And you'll never get it. They call me "The Expert." That's all you need to know."

"Well, so-called Expert, you failed completely."

The man threw up his hands and yelled, "I know it! It's so obvious and it's a god damned tragedy!"

"It can't be the first time."

"It might as well be."

"Whatever you say. You might as well go ahead and kill me now."

"Fuck! I can't do that now! Not yet."

"A dilemma, isn't it?"

"You think you're fucking smart, don't you?"

"I don't have to think it."

The Expert sat down cross-legged on the floor in front of him, holding his chin in his hand. His face was drawn, and his glasses were crooked.

"Mr. Null, a lot of people want you dead."

"You're obviously a people pleaser, So go ahead and kill me then." Spoken in a monotone, zero ironic inflection.

"You know I can't do that."

"I do. I think that might actually be funny, but I don't really have enough of a sense of humor to produce a laugh."

"You may not be smart, but you have a smart mouth."

"You're the Expert—you ought to know."

"You've cost some powerful people a great deal of money, not to mention putting their livelihood in jeopardy. They got your cute little messages, and they took them to heart."

"I thought I killed them all."

The Expert glared at him, his pallid cheeks reddening. "You'll never kill them all."

"We'll see about that."

"You're not listening, Mr. Null. A consortium of investors—

the principals, if you want to call them that—paid me a shitload of money to take care of you."

"Do you ever get to the point?"

The Expert popped up abruptly from the dusty concrete floor and slapped Null across the face open handed. Null retained a stone-faced blankness to his expression.

"You're an annoying fuck, do you know that?"

"Perhaps that's why I don't have many friends."

The Expert took a deep breath, gathering his patience. "We're being recorded. This whole thing is going to get streamed to the entire consortium of Hebe Group, and I'm not showing them what they need to see."

"Can I guess what this is?"

"Just shut the fuck up!" the Expert shouted shrilly. "The need to see you die in agony—you have to be tortured up pretty, be presented in agony beyond description. They want you begging for death, which I would deny you as I continued to inflict more pain. Finally, after I convince you that I'll let you live and your torment is at an end, I blow your face off with my Magnum— one careful round should do the job." The Expert paused and swallowed hard so that his Adam's apple bobbed up and down. "That's not going to happen, is it?"

"Not a chance."

"You wouldn't just play along with me, would you? Fake it for me."

"What do you think?"

The Expert began to pace, massaging his chin with his hand as he did. "If I used your machete to chop you up into pieces, body part by body part—no anesthetic of course—you wouldn't break a sweat, would you?"

"They still owe you the money, don't they? You just got a taste up front, but the balance has yet to be remitted, hasn't it? You need the confirmation of torture and my corpse to seal the deal, and you just can't provide it."

"I could kill you and fake it."

"Lots of time and trouble with no guarantee of a result."

"I should just kill you for pleasure."

"Sure. Except that we both know the pleasure that you get is from the money at the end, not the killing itself."

The Expert kicked his boot toe at the dust on the concrete basement floor. "God damn it!" he cried in near falsetto. "I'm going to get fucked this time." He then spoke *sotto voce* as if only addressing himself: "This has never happened before—this just never happens. How am I going to get my fucking money?"

"Okay, Expert, where do we go from here? You going to keep me here all day, kill me or what? Because this conversation seems nothing more than another one of your failed attempts at torture."

The Expert made a face and ignored that question. "So, it's true what they say on the street. You don't care about anything. Nothing and no one. I can't even go after someone you love or care about because you love and care about no one and nothing. Maybe you care something about the little kiddies, but there's really no opening for me there either. Hebe Group is already torturing and killing them."

Null's breathing became more labored and his eyes narrowed at that remark, but the expert didn't notice.

"And physical pain just doesn't hack it at all. You've been tortured so much you don't even feel it or if you do, you do a brilliant job of hiding it. You didn't even piss or shit yourself the two times I nearly electrocuted you. The other times you literally slept through it. I don't know how you did that, and I'm deadly smart."

"So where do we go from here, Mr. Expert?"

The Expert adopted a thoughtful expression, gazed upwards. "It seems killing you won't get me to my financial goal. This is true because you still have value. Perhaps the niggers in your little gang, the Gangsta Boyz, will pay heavy to have their leader returned to them intact?"

"You have a better chance asking them to help you kill me. Maybe they'll pay you something for that. It won't be much, though. Stingy bastards."

"No honor among thieves?"

"What's honor got to do with anything?"

"Okay, so you're pretty adept at killing. You have a high body count to your credit and no legal prosecutions pending." He clasped a hand on Null's shoulder. "You could come work for me. Between the two of us, we could clean up. Who cares about the petty fucking job?"

"Do you really think I need the money?"

"That's another valid point. You don't. That meth business you've got going is putting you knee deep in the cheddar, isn't it? Not too hard to manage either, since it allows you plenty of time to go off on the little escapades that brought you here."

"I'm not complaining."

Steely-eyed with a saturnine expression on his face, the Expert spoke as if delivering a body blow. "I want half."

"You might as well kill me and take it all, if you can."

"But you know I can't without your help. You die and it all falls apart. I don't see the Gangsta Boyz working for me."

"I don't see that either."

The expert leveled a hard punch directly into Null's abdomen, which produced a quick jag of coughing and gagging and then nothing at all.

"What am I going to do with you, Zombie fuck? You're not even worth anything dead."

"Let me loose, and I'll solve all your problems."

"Yeah, I just bet you would."

"I only do one thing, Expert, just one thing."

"I've heard that about you, Mr. Null. Just one thing. Well, you're not doing it now, but you can be sure it'll be done to you later."

"So what if it is?"

"You don't care?"

"Dead is dead."

"Yeah, you took about two hundred volts. Twice. You should be dead, or at least fucked up."

Null stared at him, eyes as dead and empty as those of a shark.

"Okay, so you're fucked up. But you don't seem much more

fucked up than you were when me and my friends first zapped you back at the playhouse. Even then, you went down hard. Took a few knocks on the head and a pentothal shot in the neck to get you to be all compliant."

"I don't remember getting here, and I don't know where here is."

The Expert chuckled. "You're a piece of work, Mr. Null. You know you're going to die, but you want to focus on all the niceties. It's hard to believe you caused these Hebe people so much grief."

"They're almost gone, Expert. I took out some key personnel, from the top down."

"You forgot sideways, because that's where it's all going. Who do you think was going to pay me for this shit job you just fucked up for me?"

"I assumed it was Hebe's head muscle, Legere."

"I've heard the name. Never met the gentleman. Maybe he knows about our little soiree here today, maybe he doesn't. Anyway, they farmed it out to me—wanted you done extra-sick, which is *entirely* my jam. I just have to figure a way to do it."

"Just like life, even the dead can surprise you."

The Expert smiled and shook his head, produced a shiny new switchblade from his pocket, popped the blade and waved it before Null, who didn't even blink. "It relaxes me to do a little cutting while I think about ways to totally mess with a subject, Mr. Null. I take it you won't even scream for me. Yes?"

"I can hum you a tune, if it'll make you feel any better about it."

"Brazen to the end. You're a ballsy fuck, I'll give you that."

"Not yours to give or take, Expert. When you're done with me, someone else will simply take my place. It's inevitable. I'm the destiny of hatred and abuse—period. By trying to escape me, you just wind up confronted by me. I'm your appointment in Samarra."

"An old wives' tale, Mr. Null, and you're not death."

"But I'll do until the real thing comes along."

"Sure, you will, Mr. Null," he chortled, grinning. "I guess you're just going to have to be more fun than profit. At least I can kill you. I'll get some money out of the deal yet."

With a failed effort at grace, the Expert sliced an X neatly and deeply into Null's chest. The blood immediately trickled down. His breathing was calm and even. The sound of it echoed through the basement.

The Expert admired this, shook his head and clicked his tongue against the roof of his mouth a few times. "Oh, Mr. Null," he said quietly.

Null's eyes widened enough so the Expert took notice. "What a surprise," he said flatly. "You really have to believe me when I tell you how nice it is to see you, Janis."

The Expert put the knife away, clapped his hands thrice. "Bravo! Really, Mr. Null, isn't that just a bit cliché? Trying to make me think there's someone behind me? And when I turn to look, what then? Going to fire bullets at me with your mind? Those restraints are good and tight, pally. You won't be getting out by distracting me. And I'm *not* distracted."

"But *I* could always distract you," said Janis, blasé and cheerless, who was, in fact, standing behind him. The Expert spun about, made a bird-like sound at the sight of her and was stopped cold, zooming in on her Pico Lavender Beretta, modified at the barrel to take thirty-two caliber shots. She didn't cock it. She didn't have to—one fine squeeze of the trigger and the Expert would be rendered defunct.

"How the fuck—?"

"You *replaced* me, genius, that's how the fuck."

"Nifty little semi-automatic you have there. Cute." The Expert was bucking himself up, realizing he was trembling and sweating bullets at the brow.

"Cute enough to make your chest a memory and split your head wide open while I'm at it."

"No need to be surly."

"Mr. Null," she said with a sigh, "you do have a knack for getting yourself into some compromising situations, don't you?"

"And you seem to have a knack for getting me out of them."
"Someone has to look out for your scrawny ass."
"Like I said, Expert, even the dead can surprise you."

SEVENTEEN

"Just take it easy with that cute piece there, Janis, alright?"

"Take him down, Expert," she ordered.

"Let's discuss it first."

"You don't know his real name?" Null asked.

"That's all this fuck goes by," she replied. "Nobody ever wanted to get close enough to find out more."

"All I know is that he's an expert at boredom."

"You know, for a dead man, you got a mouth," the Expert sneered.

"Is that a compliment? I'm not sure," Null said, perplexed and no longer breathing very hard. He seemed relaxed.

"You're siding with a corpse, Janis, when you should be making a deal with me," the Expert whined.

"What kind of deal?"

"How to squeeze money out of a dead man."

"You think that'll happen?"

"We can fix it to make it happen."

"You're live streaming this, genius. How the fuck do you think you can fix that?" she taunted.

The Expert sighed and slouched a little. "Yeah, you have a point."

"Like I said, cut him loose."

"But I like him that way, and maybe I can still make a go of torturing him before I get tired of it and just whack him out. Maybe if I throw you in as a bonus, that'll make up for the lack of suffering. You're not really showing yourself to be very loyal to the cause here, you know. I don't think Hebe Group will consider hiring you again after this feed."

"Fuck the feed."

"We could do that."

"You're stalling."

"You gonna shoot me?"

"You know I will."

The Expert shrugged. "Yeah. I know you will." He slowly raised his hands up, and Janis suddenly fell to the concrete basement floor twitching.

Lead wires were extending out of the Expert's pants pockets and he produced a giddy laugh, watching Janis helpless on the floor. The leads were now attached to her.

"It's amazing what a nine-volt battery can do. Multiple transformers and components in the little doohickey boost the voltage in the circuit to at least 20,000 volts and reduces the amperage. Could go up to about one-hundred-fifty thousand, if you like. What do you think?"

Janis made choking noises.

The Expert set the mini-taser down, the leads still connected to Janis, and turned his attention to Null. "It's a puzzle, I admit," he said, rubbing his chin and looking thoughtful. "Just what to do with it. Shrugging his shoulders again, The Expert reached into his capacious khaki pockets and produced the switchblade again. It made a curt "snick" sound opening.

"I guess I'll just have to wing the torture part. At least they can't say I didn't try."

"Forgive me if I fall asleep."

"A wit to the end, aren't we?"

"Who's we?"

"I'll show you."

In a clumsy move meant to show insouciant grace, the Expert slashed a line across Null's stomach.

"Jesus, you didn't even fucking flinch. What the fuck is the matter with you? Don't you know how to suffer?"

"They broke me of the habit, The Family. I repaid the debt. I broke them of the habit of being alive."

"You're going to require some work," the Expert replied.

"You won't."

"Spoken like a man who doesn't realize he's going to die— the dead man walking actually becoming a true corpse."

"No. Spoken like a man who doesn't give a shit."

"I don't understand."

"You'd better see to Janis before her heart stops."

The Expert grunted. "Fine." He saw to Janis quickly, kneeling down, powering off the unit, removing the leads and pocketing the Pico Lavender Beretta. Janis just lay there panting and twitching every few minutes.

"Back to you, Mr. Null. Where were we?"

"You were about to slice me up for the benefit of the continuous dark web stream."

"It's for a torrent, Mr. Null. You know what a torrent is, don't you? To be downloaded, viewed and enjoyed later by all involved."

"More illegal sharing software."

"Yes, and this will be quite illegal. But you don't really care about that, do you?"

"I'm beyond caring."

"Try and make it look good, Mr. Null. Give us a scream or two, some writhing maybe. At least *pretend* you're engaged and in the moment, please."

"Sorry, you'll have to take me as I am."

The Expert shrugged.

"It'll have to do then."

"What was that?"

"What was what, Mr. Null? I didn't hear anything."

"It sounded like a shot."

"If you don't care, Mr. Null, then why the corny dodge? It's all just so disappointing."

As the Expert raised his arm to slash at Null again, he stopped mid-motion.

"Fuck. I heard *that*."

"Two shots now, I think."

The Expert turned, blocking Null's vision, but he recognized the voice.

"Make another move, fuck-o, and the next bullet goes in your head."

"Who the fuck are you?"

Null gave an uninflected answer. "Chaos gets the better of us all."

"What the fuck is that supposed to mean?" The Expert cried in exasperated frustration.

Null's response lacked humor. "It means that Lieutenant Detective Kay Boyd of the Boston PD Organized Crime Task Force has you square in the sights of her non-regulation Sig-Sauer. She's a pretty fair shot even with a Kalashnikov KR9. Actually, I remember her hitting a target a fair distance away once upon a time on George's Island."

"Don't you ever shut up?"

"He likes to talk, or haven't you realized that by now?" sneered Boyd. "Now take that nice purple Beretta Pico out of your pocket and toss it on the floor or I'll shoot your eyes out. Slowly, please."

The Expert grudgingly obliged, moving carefully. He cleared his throat.

"So, are you really going to arrest me now? Really?"

"You have any alternative ideas?

"I have an external drive on my laptop. Take it and go and let me finish up with numbnuts here."

"And why would I ever do that—Expert is it? That's the alias you go by?"

"Hey, it's my work ID, okay? This is business. Just take the fucking drive and go."

"Why, what's on it?"

"It houses my Bitcoin wallet. I have enough blockchains stored to translate to a tidy sum on any one of a number of exchanges. Virtually untraceable, it's the perfect dark web payout. Nobody knows from nothin'."

"I heard it's volatile. Goes up, down and sideways. Hither, thither and yon."

"Whatever. It still has value so you should hurry and cash it in though, before the next big drop in the market."

"No, I think I'll just kill you now and take the drive anyway."

"You don't know where it is."

"After I kill you, I can take my time finding it, though, can't I?"

"You don't really want to kill him, Boyd, do you?" Null asked placidly.

"Great. This guy just won't shut up!"

"Don't make me fire the Sig again, Expert. I might not miss."

"Can I put my arms down at least? They're getting tired."

"Keep them up till I say otherwise, fuck-o."

"Fuck!"

"No, Null, I suppose I really don't want to kill him. Not really."

"I thought not. That's okay."

"Why is that okay? Why is anything about this okay?" the Expert whined.

"It's okay because we're both live streaming and being recorded for widely distributed torrent downloads."

"So? They'll use it to blackmail me or something?"

"I doubt it."

"Will you two just get a room already? Jesus!" the Expert shouted.

"It would be tempting to shoot him."

"I can understand that. But it wouldn't be the best idea to be recorded doing that."

"I see your point."

Janis began moaning from the floor, slowly coming around.

"You should help Janis get up and have her release me while you keep the Expert in line with the Sig.

With that, Janis made more noises, forcing herself up into a seated position on the dusty concrete, looking dazed.

"Okay. *Then* what? Since we're live streaming and being recorded for torrent downloads, whatever the fuck that is."

"Well, everybody in Boston knows about me, even if they claim *not* to know about me."

"So? What does that have to do with the price of tea in China?"

"I don't think I'll be surprising anybody, do you?"

"I think you're always a surprise."

"Jesus, you two!"

"Shut up, Expert. You'll speak when I tell you to."

He nodded shakily, squinting his eyes as the wheels of his mind began spinning. He was calculating a way out of the situation all too obviously. He looked feral with a smoldering anger.

"As I said, it'll come as no surprise."

"I'll bite. What will?"

"When I kill the Expert, live streaming and stored for torrent downloads to get a message to Hebe Group and, more importantly, to a man named Legere."

"Who the fuck is he?"

"He's my kiddie porn counterpart who wants us both dead."

EIGHTEEN

They were at the S&S Restaurant at Inman Square, Cambridge by late afternoon—all three of them. It was a New York-style coffee shop-deli, both modern and bright, sparkling clean in shades of light brown wood and turquoise booth padding. The light poured in through generous windows, providing a good view of Hampshire Street traffic and the whole place exuded an atmosphere of urban *gemütlichkeit*. A prim costumed waitress or casually formal waiter could serve you kosher and they could serve you *goyisher*, meaning you could get a corned beef and tongue sandwich as easily as you could off the same menu that boasted barbecued pork ribs.

The two women at the table didn't seem out of place, but Null did.

Null was always out of place, even when he managed to blend in, not really resembling his surroundings, but being so unprepossessing of appearance, his face shaded by a porkpie hat and his body cloaked in a slightly oversized topcoat, both shades of an uncertain brown or blue closest to black, he was easy to ignore. Janis and Boyd were somewhat mussed, maybe a bit ruffled. Null was wearing his hat and coat, marked by dust and in some derangement, dappled unevenly with the rust color of dried blood. Janis and Boyd sat in chairs next to each other while Null had a booth side seat to himself.

"I can't believe what you did," said Janis tremulously. "I just can't. I've seen some things. I've done some things. Nothing like that."

"It's not like it is in the movies, is it?" Boyd said wearily.

"You can actually look at what they show you in the movies, but you couldn't look at that. Nobody could look at that. And I did. Look."

Null spoke in a blasé tone, or maybe no tone at all, but context provided inflection. "It's nothing any trauma surgeon hasn't seen. And it was just as necessary."

"You don't get the picture, do you, Janis? Null is different."

"I got that from the jump. But this is ridiculous."

"I'd tell you that Null was ridiculous, but he defies even that."

"Jesus, after that, how can you even eat?"

Null sat silent and unblinking. He hadn't picked up the menu to decide on what to order yet, though Boyd and Janus had both opened theirs and already seemed to know.

"How can I not? It's been a long time since I had food, and I think that might be wearing me down." He cleared his throat. "I have work to finish, and you two are going to join me."

"How can you even say that? I mean, I helped you before—it was no trick to let you put a few slugs in those clowns I served you up to in the South End, but what do you think you're getting me into?"

"I did a little more than just put a few slugs into them," Null stated dully.

Janis' lower lip trembled.

"You're already in it," Boyd sighed. "And so am I. Null has that knack. He drags you into whatever crap he's up to."

"Not me."

"You have no choice, Janis." Null finally blinked. "You women seem ready to order, what should I eat?"

"Jesus, Null, you can't order? What do you like?"

"Janis, you haven't gotten it yet. And now you're going to." Boyd smirked, shook her head.

"I'll eat anything. Just tell me what. Something nourishing

on the high calorie side with protein and carbohydrates. It doesn't matter."

"Food doesn't matter?"

"It keeps me going, so it matters. Beyond that, no."

"I dig your strangeness, Null, and that's a fact. But I don't know what to do with it."

"Janis, you're going to figure that out soon and Null knows it. And even I know you're in this, whether you opt out or don't."

"The live streaming—"

"That's right, Janis. Legere hired you and he knows you. And now he's going to see you standing around looking queasy in the stream hanging out with a policewoman while I did what had to be done to the Expert. He's going to see all of it, and so are the people who hired him, who run Hebe Group. They'll get my message. And they're going to get yours as well."

"It's not hard to see where he's going.'

"Nope. I'm there. If I don't come after them, they're guaranteed to come after me. That's about it."

"What should I order?"

"A corned beef on rye and a French onion soup in the crock," Janis replied off the top of her head.

Null didn't miss a beat. "That'll do. Then."

"I guess I'm just calling you Null now, not "Mr. Null" anymore."

"That'll do also."

"Okay, Null. But you didn't really have to do—what you did. Nobody had to do that. Ever," Boyd said.

"But they do it all over the world in places you think have no civilization, even though they think themselves civilized. And you think you're civilized when you have to blow a man's brains out with your lavender Beretta, don't you? You're paid to do it, leveraged to do it, your life depends on your doing it. You even did it for me."

"I thought you were different then."

"I am different."

"No argument there."

"They have to die that way. Whether there's a god or not, heaven and hell or not, they'll leave this life in an agony of consequences for their crimes."

"But you're a criminal too, aren't you?"

"That's what it takes to give the lesson."

"They can't learn anything when they're dead."

"They'll learn it on the way out the door."

"Door to nothing."

"We can only assume. Odds are you're correct."

"This is going to go nowhere, Janis. You know that, right?" Boyd was getting edgy, fidgeting a bit in her seat, nipping at her glass of ice water.

"I want to know. What crime is so bad you need to mutilate and torture people? What's the difference? Plus, it puts you in jeopardy, the extra time it takes. Doing what you do."

"Cutting them up, you mean," said Boyd coolly. "Mutilating them."

In a soft and even voice just above a mumble, this is how Null replied. "My ass is my own to risk, such as it is. What's so bad? Why do they have to die that way? Listen, this is a crime-ridden, corrupt, bent and twisted world. To live in it, you have to be a criminal of some kind, even if you're just profiting off someone else's crime. All well and good. There are very few virtues in this world, but one of them is clear. Children. The small children, even the bigger children. They embody hope. They are hope. They are the only thing that can turn the foul world back upon its axis into something else. They're the agents of change, as I'm an agent of change. If you murder that hope, trick it out like a whore, corrupt it, fuck it to death, squeeze it dead to the husk for a buck, then you're a different kind of criminal. The kind that can't be allowed to live. The kind that has to suffer. The kind that dies in bloody pieces by my hand."

"Is he fucking for real, Lieutenant?"

"Too real to suit me, Janis. That's a fact."

"I'm having trouble believing any of this is real."

"That'll fade," Boyd replied glumly.

"The Expert wasn't really one of them, Null. He was just a hired gun, like me. He was no baby-raper."

Null stared fixedly at Janis. His lips hardly moved. "You know he had to die, just like I know he had to die. All of them have to do die. And do so badly."

"And what about me? They hired me to get rid of you. Do I have to die?"

"But you didn't, did you? You went the opposite way, instead. So, now, just like me, you have to kill them to stay alive. Your account has been zeroed out."

"What account?"

"It's one of his many colorful metaphors," said Boyd.

"Colorful," Janis repeated snidely. "Right."

"You said you thought I was one of the good guys. Still think that now?

"I don't know what to think."

The waitress returned to the table and asked with brisk professionalism: "So, what's everybody having?"

"Me and my friend here aren't eating." Boyd indicated a somewhat revolted Janis with her thumb, then indicated Null with a sweep of her hand. "Ask him."

"And for you, sir?"

"A corned beef on rye and a French onion soup in the crock, please."

"Very good. And you know the soup is going to be extra-hot, because it's baked in the oven to melt the cheese? You don't want to burn yourself."

"That's alright. I won't really notice the difference anyway."

———

Kenmore Towers in Kenmore Square is a fifty-year-old architectural post-modern dinosaur of icy edges and spartan stature now just an overpriced dump, as are many of the Boston luxury apartment buildings of yore, like the West-End-obliterating sprawl of Charles River Park. Janis had a two-bedroom condo tricked out in the kind of mousey, arid décor favored by

Museum of Fine Arts/Boston Symphony Hall donors, of which she happened to be one.

The building had the warmth of a defunct investment and the quaint charm of a trauma center as the three of them took the elevator up to Janis's apartment.

"Nice digs," said Null, plopping down hard on the Castro Convertible sofa when they entered the living room.

"It's amazing that I live so close to Kenmore Square, really just a walk. But this building seems so remote and detached from civilization," Janis replied.

"Boston isn't much of a city. Start anywhere you like and you can just walk off into the wilderness," Null opined.

"What are we doing, Null? I have no idea where this is going. Still think you're wiping out all Beantown KP? Even after what you just did?" Boyd asked glumly.

"He had it coming. They all have it coming."

"I'm done doing business with them."

"They're not done doing business with you, Janis."

"I know. What does that mean?"

"It means you had better move, and soon, Janis. You can assume Legere and his friends are coming here to find you. You don't want them to find you."

"No, you're right. Anyone want a drink?"

"I do, but I'm not going to have one."

"You always do, Kay. Good idea not to have one."

Janis went over to the credenza and retrieved a bottle of Crown Royal and a tumbler. She poured herself four fingers and downed it with the surprising quickness of any character in any TV show or movie drinking to drive home a dramatic point. She drove one home straight at Null.

"Give me the bottle, please," asked Null politely.

"Why? Can you even *get* drunk?"

"He probably can but wouldn't notice it if he did." Boyd had nowhere to go with her exasperation.

Janis handed the bottle to Null, who opened the front of his topcoat then the front of his shirt and poured the whisky onto the wounds of his chest. Janis jumped back as if wounded herself.

"Shit, Null, you're ruining my sofa!"

"It shouldn't make a stain. Most of it went where it was needed to go."

"Couldn't you just use isopropyl alcohol in the bathroom like a normal person?"

Null slugged from the bottle, then put it on the floor by his feet. He wiped his mouth with his sleeve.

"I'd be nervous too, Janis. I'm not, but I probably should be."

"You kicked a fucking hornet's nest, Null, your usual M.O.," observed Boyd bitterly. "You're a freakin' menace no matter what you do."

"Yet you feel better since I broke you out of the happy hotel, though. Right?"

"Yeah. What of it? Doesn't make you any less of a walking catastrophe."

"I have no freaking idea what to do here. Am I stuck in this annihilation vendetta of yours against KP, or can I walk, because I positively *have* to earn? This condo won't pay for itself, you know. I'm just a working woman."

"You're stuck, Janis. Null planned it that way. He knew after you pulled your rescue back at the South End that you'd come looking for me. And we'd come looking for him, which we did."

"So what. Every mook on the street knows you've been running the zombie Null fuck as your CI. Big deal. You can't say he planned it."

"Sure I can. Because he did. It's what he does."

"I went looking for you to find out for sure what he was up to. I didn't want to get caught up in no police sting."

"You bet on that, didn't you? Zombie Null fuck?"

"Sounds like a title."

"It is," said Janis. "What they call you on the street, when they feel brave enough to do it. They think you're some monster like Dracula."

"No, I'm nothing like that."

"You didn't plan your escape from the Expert, though. That's just bullshit."

GARY S. KADET

"Is it? I lack the gut instinct for that sort of thing. So, I don't know that. But I *do* know how to improvise, and you, Janis, were part of my improvisation. A panic snap, you could say. In that capacity, you worked out nicely."

"He improvises, he says," leveled Boyd witheringly, wishing she had accepted the offer of a drink. She needed one. Bad.

"And you're telling me you felt absolutely nothing butchering the Expert like a hog with your fucking machete?"

"Not a thing. And a hog is possessed of much more decency than the Expert ever considered having. It was nothing to take care of him. And it will be as nothing to take care of the rest of them."

"You mean the ones who don't accept our deal, remember?"

"Absolutely. The ones who don't confess and let you arrest them will still be left to me. And I will take care of them. As slowly as possible."

"And what about me?" asked Janis, pouring herself another drink. "Are you going to take care of me, too?"

"Of course, Janis. But I'm not going to kill you." Null paused, looking hypnotized for a moment, licked his lips and added, "You need to stay with Boyd until we end this contretemps."

"Oh, that might not be the best idea. Don't you think they'll come gunning for me, too?"

"They already have. You're the reason this all came about. They murdered Rudy with all the fanfare and panache of taking out the garbage. Gave you a video on a data stick, sent you straight to the laughing factory. Why? Because you were after them. You were getting close. You made them an OC deal, put Hebe Group on the radar."

"I did that. And what did I get? The corpse of a child who never had a break. A broken, discarded doll."

"They used him up and threw him away. And how many others get the same treatment?"

"I haven't counted," Boyd sighed.

"I have. According to Hebe Group's comptroller—"

"Who you shot in the back of the head. Didn't really take your time with him, did you?"

"He cooperated nicely, so I did him quick. That's the best they're going to get from me."

"So what. It landed us all in a jam."

"No, you did, Boyd. I merely joined in and recruited Janis for good measure. I've had to make some alterations."

"Alterations like what?"

"Like I'm not really sure I can kill my way down anymore. It looks like I'll have to go sideways."

"This whole thing is going sideways. I never asked for this."

"Maybe not. Either way, you're in it now."

"I know. Thanks to you."

"You're welcome."

"Fuck you, Null," Boyd snarled.

"You started it and now we'll finish it." Null gave her the hardest of his already hardened looks. "No matter what you think, they're not coming after us. We're coming after them."

"You think they won't try for us both in my apartment? Are you brain damaged?"

"Possibly. But that's neither here nor there. No, since their attack on you through Rudy, which paid off in my involvement and the addition of their contract hitter, Janis, they won't come after you again directly. You're a cop. They don't want Boston PD to finally get off its collective lazy ass and come after them. No, they'll reach for you in the shadows instead, maybe politically through friendly payments sent to the right players in the Boston bureaucracy. You remember the Director of Boston's Code Enforcement Division was head honcho. He was a connected guy, on the city since day one. No doubt he infected the hierarchy somehow. So, watch for that in the coming days."

"Yeah. I remember. Finnerty. A crony from way back. And you stuck a pencil through his heart."

"Once again, an improvisation. You have to do that now and again when you're killing your way through the ranks of a kiddie porn operation."

"You know Null," offered Janis, feeling the effects of the

whiskey, "thinking about all that's gone on since I met you, I think I was right in the first place."

"Right about what?"

"In your own strange way, you *are* one of the good guys."

"High praise coming from a contract hitter."

"Hey, I'm good at what I do."

"Despite a sensitive stomach."

"Yeah? So, what. We all have our faults. The main point for me is that I have to earn. How am I going to do that when I'm involved in this shitshow?"

"How much do you get for a run-of-the mill job?"

Janis cited an inflated number just as Null knew she would.

"I can match that. There could be upwards of a million in Bitcoin on the external drive we took from the Expert. That might do."

"I wouldn't know what to do with it."

"You sell it on one of the online exchanges."

"I don't have any clue as to how to do that."

"One of the Gangsta Boyz does my IT. He's already posting the Expert's face on our little rogue's gallery on one of Hebe Group's defunct web sites. He'll take care of it."

"How long will that take?"

"Weeks if he does it right."

"I can't wait that long. I've already spent Legere's money, and I was expecting to get more work from him."

"You can expect something else from him now."

"So, what's your solution? You said you were going to take care of me."

"I did and I will." Null clicked his tongue more from the dryness of the whisky than from intent, his eyes wide and unblinking. "I have some extra cash lying around all neatly shrink-wrapped in plastic, waterproof packs. I'll have one of the boys deliver you one."

"Boys? Isn't that just a little bit racist?"

"Not if you're in a group calling itself the Gangsta Boyz. That's boys with a Z. But I don't intend to sound racist. A person is a person to me. My only real point of discrimination is separating the living from the dead, and the very soon to *be* dead."

"You going to deliver me that amount? In cash? And where the fuck is all this money coming from?" Janis was still incredulous and light-headed from the whiskey. She realized she should have ordered lunch at the S&S, but at the time, it being so close to the sickening demise of the Expert, she just couldn't.

"It's drug money, Janis. Didn't you know I'm the meth king of Boston?"

"By proxy," chimed Boyd.

"Yes. By proxy. The boys are doing an excellent job in not fucking me over yet, though I'm sure the time is coming. In any event, you'll still have to launder it. It's dirty drug money. That work for you?"

"Yeah. It works fine."

The song "No Headstone for My Grave" by Charlie Rich played out loudly from underneath Null's topcoat. "I have to take this." He cut off the ring tone and spoke into the phone, making no effort to conceal what he said. "Are you certain that's what happened? Yes, it was a mistake. No, it's not on you—it's on them and for them it's not really going to be an issue anymore." Without so much as a goodbye, Null pocketed the phone again. When he did, he removed a small plastic baggie from his inside coat pocket full of greenish powder. He laid some of it out on the glass top of the coffee table, separated it into discernable lines using a credit card from his wallet. He also took out a dollar bill and rolled it up.

"Jesus Christ, Null, you're doing *lines* now?"

"That's another fucked up thing he does," Boyd commented glumly.

"Yes. Do you ladies care to join me?"

"No!" they both said, almost together.

"Just as well," replied Null before leaning over the table and snorting up two lines quickly and neatly with no semblance of a response.

"Is that your solution to the problem? Getting high?"

"It's part of the solution, yes. But I really don't get high. This just keeps me going when I haven't slept, and I need to keep going because now there's even more work to do."

"What do you mean "more work?" We didn't have enough work from before?"

"We had enough. Now we have more. You noticed the call I just received?"

"Sure. What about it? Something about your meth operation in Methuen?"

"Not exactly. But it was one of the Gangsta Boyz. They don't usually call me. They know not to. But Do-rag, who just called me, had a very good reason to do it."

"And what was that, pray tell?" Janis drawled.

"Hebe Group sent me a message. They wanted me to understand it loud and clear."

"Jesus, Null, what kind of message would they possibly send you?"

"A death letter of sorts."

"What the hell is that?"

"They detonated a bomb at the Gangsta Boyz club house on Tremont. Probably a pipe bomb, knowing them, to cast suspicion aside. The intent was not to look too professional, cast the blame on some other gang bangers. Obviously Legere's work."

"Shit!" replied Boyd, reaching into her purse for her cell phone, which had just vibrated and buzzed loudly as Null spoke. "I'm getting a text about that now. All hell's broken loose down on Tremont!"

"Yes. I foresaw this, and I suggested to all the Gangsta Boyz that they steer clear of the clubhouse for the time being. Two Gangsta Boyz, however, disobeyed me and went back to play video games. They shouldn't have disobeyed me, but I suppose they learned their lesson the hard way. All for a game of *Grand Theft Auto*. Or was it *Halo*?"

"Fucking Christ, Null! How can you just sit there calm and stone out on meth? What the fuck is wrong with you?"

"It's too much to explain, Janis. Take it from me, that, for him, it's normal."

"Yes. Normal. Okay, well, I received that message. I understand where they're coming from." Null was deadpan, cool down to zero.

"And where are they coming from?" asked Janis, somewhat haughtily.

"From the pit of hell," replied Null starkly. "Where I'm going to bury each and every one of them. Permanently."

NINETEEN

The sun was bleeding it seemed, as the day faltered into dusk. Screaming fire trucks and their shouting personnel blocked off Tremont Street with pizza wagons, squad cars and a hullabaloo of official uniformed action, confused, unfocused, but most importantly overbearing. Uniforms kept the bombed out, blasted façade of what was once the Gangsta Boyz clubhouse clear of onlookers.

Homicide Detective third grade Byron Wurdalaka in his shabby trench coat that hung off him like rags barely concealing a mismatched blue and brown suit beneath, wearing a peaky worker's cap on his matted hair, squinted at the sun, his stubble looking prickly and like conductive filaments in its light. Boyd cast a long shadow over him as she approached.

A fireman in full turnout and bunker gear—helmet and protective coat, Black Diamond yellow and black boots—was idly hosing down the last of the flames and smoldering wreckage of the once Gangsta Boyz clubhouse. Wurdalaka didn't bother to look at Boyd when he spoke.

"You're late to the party," he drawled, or perhaps honked. He pronounced the last word *"Pah-*ty."

"I didn't know it was in my honor."

"It isn't. But it's still your party and I'll cry if I want to."

"This is gang territory, or so the text said that brought me here."

"This is *your* territory now, LT. The pundits at One Schroeder want to bundle the Gang taskforce into the OC task force for budgetary reasons. We also never really *had* a Gang task force, if you don't count four half-in-the-bag pension palookas, so it makes us look good on the news to show we have one when we say we have one. You know this shit's gang related, right?"

"Do I? Exactly how do I know that? I just got here, for Christ's sake. Is it even a homicide crime scene yet?"

"Yup, we got two barbecued Gangsta Boyz gettin' loaded up into the pizza wagon as we speak for a berth down at Southern Mortuary. Your buddy with the knitted yarmulke bobby-pinned to his scalp is getting them ready now for their final journey."

"Yonah Shimmel."

"Yeah. That little faggot."

"He's not gay."

"You know what I mean."

"How do you know they were even Gangsta Boyz? And how the fuck many of them got deep fried?"

"Two so far."

"C'mon Byron. Small turnout for a gang retribution. Only two mutts got cooked when the bomb went off."

"Gang members, for sure."

"So how do you know they're Gangsta Boyz? They carry cards in their wallets?"

"So freakin' funny. Nope, we know it because one of my CI's claims this is the Gangsta Boyz dugout."

"Dugout? They playin' baseball?"

"Video games," said a gray-templed Battalion Chief in full turnout gear, intruding on the conversation with the usual pushy fireman's aplomb. "One of the mutts died holding one o' those doohickeys clutched in his hand—a game controller they call it."

Boyd turned to face the man, squinting. "And you are?"

"Battalion Chief Haggerty. I'm in charge of the scene here."

"I thought I was," sneered Wurdalaka, picking his teeth.

"You just said I was, Byron, for fuck's sake."

"Well, if you want to hereby take on this clusterfuck for yerselves, you're welcome to it. You don't even have to ask. I don't think we're gonna need a full forensic arson investigation to type out this piece of shit."

"And why is that, Mr. Battalion?"

"Call me Sean. Mrs."

"It's Ms."

"Whatever. Even the greenest rookie could detect the malodorous scent of a fucking pipe bomb here, strictly gang related, I am sure."

"What if it was someone just aping a gang, to put us all off the scent?"

"Haggerty's right, LT. Why even bother? What pro-outfit would ever want to concern itself over these petty crime *negroes?*

"Don't you have any black friends working homicide with you?"

"Sure as fuck do, LT, and they use the term nigger a helluva lot more than I do. In fact, Charlie Turner was offered this plum little homicide detail, but said he'd rather work the unsolved mass murder case we got that went down there in Southie."

"He refused to investigate what might actually *be* a hate crime? Really?"

"I didn't take that angle and neither did he."

"Alright yez lovebirds, I'm going to close up shop since the scene's contained and my report's already half-written in me head. You might wanna catch up with your pet kike, Shimmel, though, before the Post-Toasties take their final ride in the pizza wagon."

"What did he tell you, Haggerty?"

"Who knows what the little prick's got in his *Yiddisher kopf?* The whole fuckin' domicile was a tinderbox anyway—no sprinklers, no smoke alarms, those damn abo's involved in who the fuck *knows* what petty crimes got it and got it but *good.* This don't seem too complicated to me."

"I look forward to your report."

"You can get it from your captain, not that I don't have respect for youse lesbians or anything."

"Not that you don't. I'm not a lesbian, Haggerty."

"Whatever floats yer boat, *Madame* Lieutenant. I'm not judgy. I'm the live and let live kind, if you take my meaning."

"We all take your meaning," Wurdalaka sneered.

"What was the bomb made of, if I can ask before you scurry off to your commode?"

"You have a flair for poetry, I think."

"And you have a flair for evasion. What was in the freakin' bomb. Match heads?"

"Would that that were true, milady. But no. That weren't no match head pipe bomb. Those fuckers went full Timothy McVeigh on the shitty little thing."

"Fertilizer?"

"Ammonium nitrate/fuel oil combo most likely—just killer-diller when packed in a tightly compressed lead pipe, which this one was. Good bang for the buck, though, if you want to look at it that way."

"And I don't."

"I'll bet you don't. So, if that's everything, me and the crew is out of here. You can secure the scene any way youse like, darlin'. I'm turnin' it all over to you as of right now."

"Gee, fucking thanks."

Haggerty grinned and his perpetually youthful face crinkled into a nest of dimples. "You're fucking welcome, Ms. Lieutenant. Now if you'll excuse me, I'll go get on me horse and ride."

"Yeah, great," Boyd muttered, adding softly, "*fuck you and the horse you rode in on.*"

Wurdalaka burst into a laughing jag. "*Jesus H.*, LT, next time, just say it right to the cocksucker's face. You'll feel better, I promise."

"Well, at least you got your jollies."

"Exactly, LT. Sometimes you just gotta grab what you can get. Short life o' trouble, ya know."

"Yeah. It was that way for the Gangsta Boyz."

"But only two, which presents a troubling question: Just who the fuck tipped off the rest of them, and were those who were not at the exalted clubhouse actually themselves the doers?"

Boyd sighed, accepting the inevitable. "Fine. Go ahead and round up the rest of them and see what we get."

"Well, if you're ordering me to do it, LT, I don't see how I could properly refuse."

"Fucking A, Byron, you know you were going to do that anyway."

Wurdalaka tipped his peaky cap to her, saying with a responsive laugh, "That's right: fucking A indeed!"

———

Null stood watching the bombed-out scene, looking disheveled, unshaved, scarred and derelict several blocks down from the action on Tremont street. A short, distraught and visibly nervous Do-rag was waving his hands while talking to the impassive Null, who didn't so much as nod. The red bandana tied around Do-rag's head flapped in the breeze.

"How did you know, boss? How'd you get the nod for those fireworks?"

"It doesn't matter. What mattered at the time was minimizing losses."

"We gots two of 'em fried extra-crispy, homes!" Do-rag shifted his weight from one foot to the other.

"They have families?"

"Got some I s'pose."

"I'm promoting you to fixer. Can you fix this for me?"

"What you want? Somethin' heavy?"

"Pretty heavy."

"I'll do it. I always do what you say. We make massive mooga doin' what you say. All of us."

"You like that, the cash."

"Shit, everybody like that. Fuckin' universal."

"So, the rest of the boys are waiting to kill me only when the cash runs dry."

"No, no, homes—we got real loyalty. We *stickin'* wit' you."

"You ever see that before?"

"Maybe. I think it's possible. We look after each other—that's sumpm!"

"Do you though?"

"Just tell me what you want."

"I don't know where the boys are holed up. That's not good. I don't know who's slinging the gak. And who the fuck is watching the storage locker in Watertown where all my packets of cash are at?"

"Don't worry."

"I never worry. And is my lab producing?"

"Same as always, boss. You know Brother Ray is doing his IT thing, hackin' the dark web 'n' shit."

"Posting my photos."

"Yeah, boss. Posting your photos, and they ain't too pretty."

"They're not supposed to be."

"You postin' up Edgar 'n' Howard?"

"No. They deserve privacy."

Do-rag ticked it off with his fingers, trembling slightly. "The lab in Methuen is rockin' hard. Riley the chemist is cookin' and Ronald's runnin' the sling. Jo-jo and alls slingin' so hard, they stayin' far away from the crib, like you wanted." He held up his hand. "No schools, just like you say. You and me gots the only keys to the stash in Watertown. Nobody knows but you, me and Jo-jo, who drove the bus, and he ain't gonna spill. He's seen you close up. *Everybody* knows what you'll do if anything fucks up. Nobody wants to fuck up with you, not no how."

"It's not failure tolerant, our business, is it?"

"Shit, homes. Alphonse didn't know that and he mother-fuckin' *dead.*"

"Good lesson there. They want to kill me, though, don't they? You can be honest."

"I'm not gonna argue with that, boss. But with all that wallpaper comin' in and you sportin' so much hardware and takin' you down not bein' no easy thing, I say we pretty good for right now."

"You'll let me know when we're not pretty good?"

"Course, dawg. Course."

"Maybe when they come for me, you'll be the one holding the gun, don't you think?"

Do-rag's hands shot up fast, fearful of Null raising up one of the fancy guns he carried, like that Heckler he kept mentioning. "Won't be me if that happens, homes. I'm not made that way. I don't play with no gats. Ever. I don't know who's even the one to do it—they dig you runnin' shit. You make shit and all happen. And you're a scary fuck, too."

Null narrowed his eyes and thought about that statement. Do-rag started to get visibly jittery.

"No, no, I meant that in a *good* way, boss. You the shot caller!"

"You turn my head with praise."

"Just facts, boss. You scare the shit out of me. Ever since that day you blipped off Cheese."

"How could I forget?"

"Fuck. I can't. So, what's the heavy deal you need me to do? Don't ask me to kill no one—*please*." He was sweating for having been so forward with the man he made long ago for a hair-trigger psycho, a pathological killer. Null looked calm alright, maybe even a little sick, but Do-rag knew not to trust it. He had seen Null up-close move way too fast to clock."

"So, you want the job of fixer?"

"Yeah, man. I'm all about it."

"Good. It's yours. Go down to the Watertown stash, get two medium-sized shrink-wrapped packages of cash and one of the smalls."

"Y-you mean the forty k ones? The small one's twenty k, right?"

"That's right. You know who got burned today?"

"Edgar and Howard. Guess they did the Dutch." He shook his head. "Fuckin' X-Box."

"You know where their families are, whoever was closest. The next of kin?"

"I can find out."

"Don't make me regret trusting you."

"No, boss, I'm on it. Who's the twenty for?"

Null hunted in his coat for a slip of paper, found it, fished it out and passed it to Do-rag.

"Take the small package to the woman on the slip—the address is on there too. She'll be expecting you. Just say I sent you when she pushes the intercom."

"Yeah, I be on fleek wit' dat."

"As you guessed, I want you to take the bigger packs to the families of the ones that died in the fire."

"Edgar and Howard. You cleanin' it, too?"

"No, I'm not laundering it for them. They'll have to figure that out for themselves."

"I can do that. They won't be too unhappy about it."

"Everybody loves money, except me, even though I need to keep it comin' in. That I do."

"Price o' doin' business, boss."

"Don't I know it."

"You want me to get that thing done now?"

"I do, but one other thing." Do-rag automatically started feeling nervous again.

"What you got, boss?"

"I need you to group text all the fellas and tell them that we're all going to meet up tomorrow night. At 8:00 p.m. Sharp."

"Where you wanna do it?"

"Who's the one with the two-bedroom near Geneva Avenue at the Warren Gardens?"

"Desi, man. Desi live there."

"We'll meet at his place and tell them to think back and remember "Bloody April.""

"Fuck! We *alls* know about that one, boss. Surprised you do – but I guess not really." A street feud less than a decade ago with Latin Kings and Gangster Disciples wannabes lining up gun-shot bodies all along Geneva Avenue. Who could forget that? Do-rag couldn't.

"April is the cruelest month, some poet said."

"Yeah, boss, and we in it now for sure."

"Do-rag, you couldn't be more right."

———

"What the hell are you still doing here?" Boyd asked, annoyed. Do you want one of the boys to make you and hold you for questioning? I'm in charge of the scene now, thanks to you."

"No thanks needed. Just marking time, waiting for a phone call." Null barely spoke above a whisper.

"You have a mobile. You can wait for that anywhere."

"True. I thought it was appropriate to wait here, where my guys died. I thought I owed them that."

"Think you might have owed them anything else?"

"I do. About eighty K, I think. For the families, whoever Boston hasn't swallowed up yet."

"You threw that much cash at the survivors?"

"It wasn't much, I know, but I have to be frugal. Keep reserves for when the Gangsta Boyz turn on me."

"How do you even know that?"

"It's inevitable and I expect no less."

"Wurdalaka's going to round up the Gangsta Boyz for a little *tete-a-tete*."

"If he can find them. My hunch is no, he won't."

"He's not as stupid as he looks."

"I believe you. But the boys have gone to ground, out on the sling. Good luck hunting them. Maybe if he cruises up and down tornado alley, he'll have a shot. Where's Janis, by the way?"

"She's hunkered down in at my place streaming Netflix. Waiting for her money."

"She'll get it. I have my fixer on the case. He'll get it done."

"She's more nervous about that than getting whacked out by this Legere creep."

"People often have funny, topsy-turvy priorities when it comes to money."

Null's phone rang out its mournful song. He dragged it out from his pocket and held it in his hand looking at the screen, counting the seconds before answering.

"Is that your guy?"

"Should be. And he's a little late."

"Put it on speaker?"

"Why not? There's nothing to hide at this point."

"That you, Null fuck?" The voice was thick; it sounded like whoever was on the other end was speaking through dough.

"You know it's me, Legere."

"How do you know it's Legere?"

"If it's not, I can just hang up."

"Fine. It's me. Get my little message?"

"I did. Finally, you answered all the messages I sent you. Took you long enough."

"You're a little hard of hearing."

"My hearing is acute. Your message is dull."

"I think I made my point today."

"You did. I intend on making a few to counter it."

"Big talk from a little guy."

"Size is not necessarily relative to efficacy."

"They're gonna stop as of today."

"Because you say so?"

"Because you're gonna be dead."

"Really. Triangulating the signal from my cell on GPS— some marauder in a passing car gonna do a drive by on me? Right by the scene of the crime? I think I like my odds."

"Your odds suck."

"They do? Now why would that be? Oh, yes, you want to arrange a meet so you can whack me out standing in front of you? Everybody says we should meet, you know. It's the hottest ticket in town."

"You can't hide forever."

"I'm not hiding. I'm disassembling Hebe Group piece-by-piece, house-by-house, mutt-by-mutt. I've got a scheduled raid on a special youth hostel you guys are running up there near Brighton. Should hold a special message for you."

"You think you're pretty fuckin' slick, don't you, you little prick?"

"No, but what's left of Hebe Group does. I'm not going to argue the point."

"You're a dead man, Null."

"There's another point I won't argue. It's awfully hard to kill the dead, you know."

"We'll find you, kill you and everyone you love."

"If you knew me, you'd realize just how absurd that statement really is."

"You think you're funny—you're a funny guy, fuckstick."

"Everybody says that, even though I completely lack a sense of humor. I just state facts."

"We're gonna do Boyd, just like we did that little piece of chicken Rudy. We'll do her hard, get it all on video, sell it on the dark web, then we're gonna do you—extra hard. You can't run and you can't hide. It's inevitable."

Null might have been commenting on the weather when he responded to the threat.

"Oh, well, if it's inevitable, I don't see any reason to put it off, do you?"

Meanwhile, Boyd had been giving Null desperate hand signals to control the conversation, mouthing words for him to take note of and echo, but he ignored her. She became furious with suppressed rage and a need to shout with a desperation that she had to either stifle or blow the call. To the casual observer, it looked as if she were doing an Indian rain dance while Null spoke calmly on the phone next to her as if she weren't there.

"What the fuck?"

"Sure, yes, okay, let's meet, talk it over like men. You know, face to face."

"Now you're being half-smart."

"Only half?"

"If that."

"I'll make it easy, Legere. I'll text you a location and you can meet me there. Then we'll have a discussion."

"You're coming alone?"

"I think you know both of us are going to bring some of our very dear friends along for the ride."

"You don't have any friends."

"You'd be surprised."

"Tell you what, fuckstick, I'll text you *the time and location. You can meet me there and we can settle it out. And I mean out."*

"I was counting on you. I'll hang up, so you can do that. But, before I do, for the record: as far as settling it out? That won't happen even when I'm done with you. Oh, no. That'll only happen when the last one of your group dies, screaming in agony by my hand. Then the account will be settled. Only then and not until."

Null didn't hear the click on the other end, just the cooing sound of the lost connection when Legere ended the exchange. Boyd looked at him wide-eyed, silently hysterical in utter incomprehension, not really quite sure as to how to respond to the call. Null looked back at her, also somewhat puzzled.

"That's just great. Super! Do you know what you've just done? Have you seriously lost your fucking mind?"

"Oh, that was sometime ago, if you remember. Psychosurgery down at Mass General. Right?"

"Never mind that. How do you think this is really going to go down? Just what do you think is going to happen?"

"I think the next phase of our program can be summed up in one word: ambuscade."

"If that's anything like an ambush, I'd say we're fucked."

"You're right about one thing. That's exactly what it is."

TWENTY

"You're late," said the dark figure smoking a cigarette, his face obscured by shadows defined by the glowing red end of the cigarette. He was tall, athletically built and this could be seen even under the topcoat that no doubt concealed weapons and maybe even a flak jacket as Null's did.

He had been waiting for Null by Paulie's Deli on Broad Street at the bottom of the financial district, close by Faneuil Hall, Federal and Franklin Streets, sticking to the shadows, avoiding the light. Squat gray buildings defined both sides of the street, Null neither looked up nor did he even look directly at the man who had been waiting for him. He had the appearance of a burned-out case, maybe half a step up from a wino, his sunken, stubbled face impassive with scars.

"I had to make preparations."

"Won't matter if you did."

"I'm a boy-scout of a kind—always prepared. Maybe an eagle scout."

"You're a boil on my ass, and that's a fact."

"So, you're the famous Legere."

"Not too famous. Anyone who knows about me shouldn't. Call me Manny."

"Make your pitch, Manny."

"I need to make *you* a pitch? You got chutzpah, I'll say that for you."

"Say something of value, so I'm not standing here for nothing."

"You're done Null, finished."

"I've heard that before. Hasn't proved true yet."

"It will tonight. You'll see."

"If I had known meeting you had entertainment value, I'd have brought some popcorn."

"You like popcorn, do ya?"

"You look a little nervous there, Manny. You're sweating."

"I said you're goddamn finished already!" Legere had gotten loud and his eyes were darting about, but at that moment he and Null were the only two figures on Broad Street.

"Make your move, Legere, or I'll make mine."

"You don't have to do a thing—just walk away is all. That's it."

"You're telling me that if I do, all is forgiven?"

"That's what I'm saying."

"So where's my walkin' away money, then?"

"You don't get any. You get to live. That's it. That's all there is."

"And if I decline your generous offer, what happens?"

Legere cleared his throat. "Then we'll be coming for you, full court press!" By now, he was shouting.

"Why not just take care of it here and now and spare Hebe Group the trouble and expense?"

"I'm tellin' ya, back off!" Loud again.

Null said nothing, but quick as a dying whisper he worked his way around Legere, had his arm creasing his windpipe, the Heckler and Koch making an impression on the side of his head.

"That was a little too easy, don't you think, *Legere?*"

"You'll get yours, you zombie fuck! You're a dead man!"

"I get that a lot, Manny. In some ways, it's true and in some ways not."

Null released his hold on Legere, pushed him away then

patted him down, paying special attention to hips, chest and even ankles. Null pushed him again, hard enough so that he almost lost his balance. He cocked the Heckler and aimed it straight at him.

"Strange you're not packin', *Legere*. You want to tell me what your deal is now?"

"I, uh, I honestly don't know."

Null put the Heckler back in his coat pocket. "They didn't give you a very good script, did they?"

"No." His face was drained of color and in the intermittent streetlight looked young, callow, unblemished in the shadows.

"How was it supposed to go down?"

"The-they didn't tell me."

"If you try to run, I'll make a kill-shot right to your head. My accuracy's improved with all the additional corpses. I think I can make the shot."

"What do you want me to do?"

"Nothing. Just stand there."

"Listen, I—"

"Shut up or I'll plug you now just to be on the safe side."

A female figure approached both of them out of the shadows from further down the street. Even at a distance, her feminine figure was obvious. Her high heels made a clacking sound that echoed.

"Where's the other one?" Null called to her.

"She's still up there, getting some answers."

"Your guy all done?"

"Yeah, but not permanently. He'll be out for a while, and I shot him in the leg to boot."

Janis appeared relaxed and expressionless in the streetlight. She seemed neither friendly nor affectionate, matching Null.

"His rifle's down a shute to the basement, I'm guessing. What have we got here?"

"I don't really know. A faux Legere at the very least."

Janis went over to the man and stuck her lavender Beretta in his ribs. "Tell us all about yourself, you fuckin' mook!" she ordered.

"I think that's a good idea. Tell me what you are and do it quick or you're apt to become a corpse of convenience."

"Save the long story, stretch. You're a paid actor doing this as a gig right?"

"I don't have to say anything."

Null lowered the Heckler, stared quizzically at the man. "You do if you want to live."

The man shrugged and sat down on the curb with no one stopping him, rested his head in his hands, "What are you both so angry at me for? I was just following the script the way I was paid to. When I got to the cue 'You're done Null, finished," the other actors were supposed to enter the scene. This was supposed to be a demo short film for some wannabe college kid director. I was supposed to get my SAG-AFTRA card out of this."

"That was you I spoke to on the phone?"

"Yeah. That was all me. Convincing, right?"

"You went downhill from there."

"Everybody's a critic."

"*Your* performance needs work, Null, while we're on the subject," Janis jeered.

"It probably would, if I were acting." He kicked the actor to get his attention, who then looked up at Null with confusion.

"What do you know about Hebe Group?"

Another woman approached from the shadows, not quite as shapely as the first, but definitely feminine. "He doesn't know jack shit about anything, Null, up to and including acting."

"I was put on the wait list for Yale Drama, you know," he said petulantly.

Null knelt down and put the Heckler and Koch to the actor's temple. He half-whispered when he spoke. "Tell me what you do with little children. Tell me what they have on you."

"Listen, man, I swear, I don't know nothing about kids. Hell, I don't even like them. This was just an acting gig with good money, that's all."

"Tell me about Legere."

"He's just a character, nothing else. No one real. Some woman named Phyllis something gave me the script, told me the director would be hiding, and we'd have to get as much as we could in a single take. I had to get off book fast. She also told me I'd have to do some improv when I met up with the other actors—paid me half up front in cash. Said I'd get the rest when the shoot was completed. It was a good gig. I could even use it on my resume."

"Who was the woman?"

"I have her card." He withdrew it from his coat pocket and shakily handed it to Null, who stood up as he took it.

"She give you that costume?"

"She just told me what to wear and I put it together myself."

"Cut him loose," said Boyd, looking both tired and exasperated. "He's a citizen, knows nothing."

Null nodded, bent down, dragged the actor up from the curb and nailed him directly in the face with a single hard punch. Then the man went down again, sagging back to the curb, hands to his face to stanch the flow of blood.

"Tell me again you don't know anything about Hebe Group. I want to hear this again."

"You broke my fucking nose!"

"No, I didn't. I didn't hit you hard enough."

"Felt like you did."

"Listen, Null, there's nothing coming from this guy. He doesn't even know what you're talking about."

"He's an actor. He could be acting."

"Do you really think he's that good?"

"You have a point there."

"Jeeze, you punch me in the face and then you attack my art. Fuck! *Admit* I had you going!"

"Maybe we should make ourselves scarce before the two snipers wake up and start figuring things out."

"If your guy wakes up at all, you mean. Besides, how far is he really going to get with a Beretta slug in his thigh?"

"You got a point, Null."

"With luck, it won't have killed him," added Boyd.

"Would it really matter if it did?"

"It would to me."

"What about your guy, Boyd? Did you wax him or what?" Janis seemed calm, her fidgety left hand betraying her.

"I cooled him out." She produced a small though weighty-looking sap from her handbag, where she also kept her non-police issue Sig-Sauer. She lightly hit it into the palm of her hand, not hard. Her point was made with the sound of a sharp smack. "He'll live, but he's not moving anytime soon."

"Gun went down the chimney?"

"Where else?"

"Hey, I'm still sitting here listening to all of this. Do I need to hear more, or can I just fucking go?"

"Get up," ordered Null, and the actor did so, his face stained with blood.

"What, you're gonna *shoot* me now?"

"I don't see any reason for that. Here, take this." He handed the actor a wrinkled yet clean handkerchief from his pocket.

"Thanks." He dabbed at his face with it. It didn't help much.

"Okay, Daniel Day Lewis, just in case you're not too bright, let me break it down for you. You're not getting paid for finishing this job. Try connecting with this Phyllis woman again and you'll probably end up method-acting as a corpse next time. Hebe Group doesn't appear to like loose ends. Not that I do either, but I flatter myself that I'm a bit more ethical." Null plunged his hand into a pocket of his coat that already seemed to be threatening to burst at the seams, took out a full up money clip and peeled off three one hundred-dollar bills, which he held out toward the actor.

"Go ahead. It's clean money."

He took it from Null shakily.

"You want my card too, just in case—"

"There won't *be* any case. I don't need to know who you are and, believe me, you really don't *want* me to know who you are."

"I believe that."

"Consider that your final payment, and also for one small extra service."

"Um. W-What is it?"

"Don't get tense."

"Okay."

"Forget about this gig. Don't contact Phyllis again. Forget about me and the two women with me. We never met—this never happened. Delete any emails you have about this when you get home. Do we have a deal or don't we?"

"We do."

"Then, kindly get the fuck out of here!"

The actor obliged, walking away pell-mell down Broad in the direction of South Station, presumably to catch the Red Line back to Cambridge.

"Okay, Null. You're in charge of this shit show now," Janis sighed. "Where to next?"

"You shouldn't even have to ask that," said Boyd in hollow tones. "It's sort of obvious."

"Who knows what goes on in this motherfucker's head?"

"He gets predictable now and then, in his own unpredictable way," Boyd said, almost sadly.

"I think we'll be paying Phyllis a visit next. And when we finish with her, we'll have a house to visit."

"What's in the house?" asked Janis tentatively.

Null smacked dry lips, lit a cigarette and blew a smoke ring in robotic fashion, broke it with his index finger.

"What do you think?"

TWENTY-ONE

She was a woman who might have just seemed matronly if it weren't for her flirtatiously sly, oddly open air of welcome. She wore a red blouse, a dark skirt, stockings and lipstick that matched the blouse—all somehow both salacious and prim. She answered the door of her suburban Waltham home quickly after Null used the weather-beaten brass knocker to announce his presence. She was all smiles and seemed to recognize the trio upon opening the door.

"You're Phyllis?"

"Oh, you must be Mr. Null. Yes, I'm Phyllis Goldstone. Do you want to come in, and your friends as well?"

"If it's not any trouble."

"No trouble at all. Come on in."

Upon entering, Null's Heckler was drawn and cocked. He pivoted about the room in an incidental dance. Boyd had hold of her Sig-Sauer and Janis also drew her Beretta.

"You don't have to worry, Mr. Null. Manny's not here. You can put your gun away. You too dear." And she winked at Janis. "Who might you be, honey? Go ahead, take a seat at the table. I was just about to take the cookies out of the oven. You couldn't have picked a better time to get here. You too, Detective Boyd. It looks like you and Mr. Null have had a very long day indeed.

You should sit down too, dear. What did you say your name was?"

"I didn't."

They all sat down at the table and Null shoved the Heckler back in his coat.

Phyllis waved her red-lacquer-finger-nailed hand foppishly. "Oh, that's all right, dear. You don't have to tell me. Now, do you like milk or tonic with your cookies? I only have diet, though."

"Listen, Phyllis, why we're here—"

"No need to tell me, Mr. Null. I know why you're here. Some vendetta against the Hebe Group. It's all silly, Mr. Null. You seem reasonable to me. I'm sure it can be explained to you just what a decent and fine set of people Hebe Group is if you only take the time to listen with an open mind.

"My mind is as open as a casket."

"Okay, everybody, how about some cookies?"

"You can stop that, Phyllis."

"Why, Mr. Null, I was only being hospitable."

"No, you were following out a plan."

"Nonsense, Mr. Null. I really wasn't expecting you."

"Sure you were. You were told to. Legere set it up as a fall-back position. It's good in a way since he's obviously too scared to confront me. Show's me he knows what he's doing. It's an intelligent idea not to confront me."

"I'll go get those cookies and the milk and tonic."

"No you won't, Phyllis. You'll stay put." Null reached into his coat, pulled out the Hecker and Koch from its strained pocket and rested it in his lap.

"You're not going to shoot me, Mr. Null. I'm just a harmless old lady. I'm the den mother for all the children I can fit into my schedule. I'm not a bad person, and Manny said you'd be reasonable when you got here, so, surprise! Here you all are." Phyllis smiled beatifically, nodding her head.

"I am nothing if not reasonable."

"Phyllis, you might want to be careful here."

"Janis, this is going to go how it's going to go. Null isn't reasonable. Ever."

"Wouldn't you all like some cookies, tonic or maybe milk?"

"We don't want anything you have to offer, Phyllis, except information."

"Oh, I don't think I know anything that can help you, Mr. Null. May I sit down?"

Null aimed the Hecker straight at her face.

"Keep standing, Phyllis."

"Detective Boyd, will you stop this please?"

"Hell no. I want to see where Null is going with this. He's dangerous and unpredictable, sure. Stupid? Not on your life."

"I suspect it's going to be on her life," said Janis. "This time I *know* where he's going."

"I'll bet you were a looker back in the day, right, Phyllis?" Null seemed ingenuous.

"Real men used to think so." She smoothed her hands like red taloned claws down the front of her blouse—a sphinx with a bee-hive hairdo. "You're a real man, aren't you, Mr. Null?" She smirked.

"That's a debatable point."

"Why can't I sit down?"

"Because I'm holding the gun."

"What about the cookies that I—"

"You mean that you made special for us? Sorry, Phyllis, but your cookies aren't so special, are they?"

"Well, it's true. I make them for the kids. Batches and batches of them."

"Yes, batches and batches of cookies laced with heroin and horse tranquilizer. Doesn't really break down and degrade with the heat so much, does it?"

Phyllis pouted and frowned. "Fentanyl was cheaper, but it didn't work. Harder to handle."

"And the drinks?"

"Nembutal. Pretty easy to dose out. But listen, I'm not in charge of anything, and I really don't know anything. I just do what I'm told, that's all." Phyllis was overtly nervous, breathing hard. "I'm really nice to the children. They think of me as a second grandmother."

"I'll bet they do, after those cookies," said Boyd.

Null stared at her, blunt and dull as a lizard. He didn't blink.

"Often, I'm their first grandmother, really. I'm kind to them. I sing to them, read them to sleep, going from house to house to do it, tirelessly. It's kind of my role. My—*contribution, even.*"

"You do this for all the children?"

"Well, not for the ones old enough—"

"Old enough for what?"

"To be shipped off. But I do all the rest."

"That's a high body count."

"I wouldn't put it that way."

"No, of course you wouldn't," Null said with a nod. "You get them ready. You prepare them."

"Prepare them? I don't understand."

"For where they're going. For what's going to happen to them."

"Well, yes. Certainly, but can't you see it's just a business? They're well-taken care of, the little lambs, all nourished, groomed, their dental and medical paid for and provided, nothing to worry about, ever. You know what their only real alternative without us would be? A quick death out on the street. That's what."

"I understand."

"You know, you can't get sentimental about the little darlings. They're like a commodity like—"

"Like bread someone once told me. Like little loaves of bread."

Phyllis beamed and breathed a sigh of relief. The crow's feet around her eyes took on a life of their own. "That's right. What's the harm? I'm really good to them, honest I am."

"I believe you."

Null shot her three times with the Heckler, hardly moving a muscle. He cut a line across her midsection. It looked like she was laughing as she fell to the floor. She wasn't.

"Would you believe I saw that coming?"

"We both did, Janis," Boyd said, lighting a cigarette. "It was almost predictable."

"Why almost?"

"Because if she'd have just shut up, it might've gone the other way."

"I'm glad she's talkative. I have questions to ask her, and she's going to answer every one of them before she passes out completely." He paused thoughtfully. "Or dies."

———

They were in Janis's black Altima, heading back to Boyd's condo in the Fens. When they were stopped at a red light, she banged her hands on the steering wheel and screamed, "Holy shit, I just can't believe you went and did it again!"

"And he'll continue doing it again and again, until he's done," said Boyd, sitting next to her in the front seat. Null was quiet in the back, staring blankly ahead with his classic fish-eye.

She went back to driving when the light changed and sped onto Storrow Drive. "I don't know if he'll ever be done with this gang. Kiddie porn is fucking huge. You know, Null, do you care that I'm probably going to lose half my income due to this vendetta of yours?"

"You should have thought about that when you stepped in and helped me take care of those gunsels."

"I know. But I have to agree. Hebe Group is slimy and awful and thinking about what they do is like thinking about what they do to animals at a slaughterhouse, to livestock on a farm—"

"Well, isn't that what they are, Janis? Livestock on a farm?"

"Yeah," she said vacantly, maneuvering in traffic. "Kids."

"Don't ask him, Janis. Just. *Don't.*"

"Why are you doing this, Null? Why bother? You're not going to stop it. It's too big for you to stop, no matter what you do."

"Here we go. Once again, you get what you ask for."

Null said nothing at first. Sat immobile in the shadows of the backseat. Boyd's and Janis's breathing were audible—not Null's. It seemed like he wasn't breathing at all. When he spoke, it sounded dry, hollow.

"Like everything in life, it all comes down to need."

"I don't follow. What is it that you need? It doesn't even play that you want anything. You don't want to get high, don't want sex, don't care what you eat, where you live. You have more money than you can spend, apparently, from your meth operation."

"I put the meth in Methuen."

"I guess you do, and you seem to part with it easily enough, like it makes no difference to you. You had no problem paying me off to help you do whatever the hell it is that you're doing. What's Boyd get out of it? You paying her off too?"

It was as if Boyd were fighting hard to suppress a belch. "Null—Do. Not. Go. *There.*"

"Kay has her own reasons, Janis. She feels it's worth her while."

"Yeah. I do. And that's all anybody needs to know.'

"So, what's this need, Null? What's the point for a strange-o zombie fuck like you?"

"I have no needs, really, but what's necessary for me to stay alive. The trouble with me is that I really have no actual reason to stay alive. No real need for that either. So, I have to think very hard about what would be the substantive need for me to exist, to be alive, to be in the world, functioning in this world. Boyd was good enough to provide me with some of that need. Her need. And then that led to an even bigger need, a very simple, basic need."

"Well, what the hell is it?"

Null spoke softly, but clearly without hesitation. "The children. The soft, small, vulnerable little children, innocent of right and wrong even when they do either, innocent of the foulness and filth of this world even when its driven into their lives like an aggressive cancer. The goodness and decency missing from the world? Well, they have it in spades. They don't know it, but they do. And what do we do with the ones who crush that— debase it, kill it? Listen, they need me, those kids, with a need that's huge and palpable. A desperate need. This need is something I can satisfy with my unique skill set."

"You only do one thing."

"That's right. Just one thing. And when I do it, I can make it stop. Stop the rape, stop the destruction, make the violence go away. Set the children free. Maybe keep a little goodness and decency in the world. I can actually do this, factually and very effectively. The need in Boston and all of New England is great. Vaster than anyone might have known. This is what we're all signed up for, and this is what we're going to do. And now, we have no choice but to do it, otherwise Hebe Group will slaughter all three of us as casually as snuffing out the life of a child."

"Thanks to you, they will."

"Setting them free. Through Ruth Coelacanth, you mean," added Boyd with acid.

"That's right. Ruth. She'll help whether she likes it or not. But I think she likes it."

"I don't get how that satisfies *your* need, Null. Just what's in it for you? There has to be something. You're not a charitable organization."

"The simplest need. The most basic human need of all. So deep and intrinsic I believed I never had it, and since having lost it, the act itself has in some way given it back to me."

"I don't get it."

"You'll get it, Janis," Boyd said without sarcasm.

"To be needed, Janis, is the need. For human beings to need you to be alive for them, to rescue them from something terrible, to be there for them so their lives can be lived out. So that those with no chance can finally have a chance. Otherwise, no one else in this cesspool of a world, this abattoir of relentless filth and cynical violence, needs me at all for anything. I could be swallowed up by some Charybdian pit and it wouldn't matter at all. Or it wouldn't have. Because now it does. It matters that I'm alive, and it matters what I do."

"You kill, therefore you matter."

"Kay, I couldn't have put it any better."

"So, now you're going to be the self-proclaimed savior of children tricked out for kiddie porn, sold burned, and snuffed? Is that it?"

179

"Yeah. That's it. Can either of you think of anyone better suited to give these children what they need?"

"No," said Janis with a lilt in her voice as parked the Altima in the back of Boyd's condo building. "Not if what they need is corpses. When it comes to that, I really believe there's no one better suited than you."

Boyd chuckled quietly, shook her head.

"No Janis, not corpses, but justice. I am here to give the children justice."

"What, by killing their kidnappers, torturers and rapists? By torturing them and killing them like you just did to Phyllis. Is that how?"

Null might have smiled, only he didn't. His voice was like a low hiss.

"Yes, Janis. That's exactly how."

TWENTY-TWO

The Warren Gardens on Walnut Avenue in Roxbury had less to do with gardens and more to do with slums, drug runners, denizens of micro gangs, the elderly, wayward youths struggling not to be beaten up and made gang-bait—almost exclusively black, alienated from anything remotely resembling the American main chance and taking as much diminishing public assistance as was available. This was where Null wanted his meeting, directly in the heart of Gangsta Boyz territory. The carbolic-scrubbed scent mixed with that of urine, marijuana and miscellaneous greasy food might have caused a person unused to Roxbury projects to reflexively gag, making the arduous climb up five flights as the elevator was marked unusable by bright yellow crime scene tape. Null was, as admitted by all, far from normal.

The late Edgar's brother, Dominic, a few inches over six feet, stood watch at the door to Desi's apartment. He stepped forward and put himself in front of Null before he could reach the door, blocking him.

"Do I have to pay a toll?" asked Null ingenuously.

"You in the wrong neighborhood, homes. Get your skinny ass outta here."

"Oh, I can't do that. I called this meeting."

"You—a skinny little white dude, are the motherfucker killed Edgar? You? That's a joke."

"It's not a joke. I don't even think I could joke if I tried, yet I know some things must be still be funny even if I can't laugh."

"Get the fuck outta here."

"I can't. This is my party. I'm the one throwing it. You don't want to deprive the boys of my presence, do you?"

"Who the fuck you callin' boys, motherfucker?"

"Gangsta Boyz. They all should be in there. If anyone's late, there'll be trouble. And I don't want to be late myself."

"What if I just tossed your boney freak ass down those flights of stairs, seven-thirty motherfucker?"

Null pulled the Heckler fast as an impromptu summer breeze.

"Better take your shot while you can."

Dominic moved away from the door, hands up. He had no weapon, just size, which wasn't much against a hastily pulled Heckler and Koch VP9SK nine-millimeter with its OEM suppressor. Null looked to be all business with it and had the business end of the Heckler aimed squarely at Dominic's face.

"Shall we dance?" Null asked, without the faintest hint of irony or sarcasm.

"No, homes. We cool. You can go in."

Null didn't waver with the Heckler.

"Dominic, I regret what happened at the clubhouse."

"Grandma's house? Who the fuck are you?"

Null took a breath, narrowed his eyes.

"You know who I am."

"You that netted-up motherfucker? So what—you gonna smoke my ass or what?"

"No, I'm going to give you some money, Dominic. Condolence money. My fixer, Do-rag, is handling that."

"You think you can run GBs, seven-thirty bitch?"

"I'm running them as it stands. Now step aside and continue doing such a bang-up job as gate security. But don't stray too far. I think I have a job for you."

"It don't involve killin' do it?"

"What do you think?"

"I get to do the motherfucker who did Edgar?"

"A distinct possibility."

"Shit, homes, yeah, I'm in the car, you want me in it."

Null was still holding up the Heckler when he walked through the door which led right into a good-sized living room with clear plastic-covered furniture that was also covered with all manner of Gangsta Boyz, lounging around, goofing on each other, drinking beers from a case of Stella Artois whose remnants were on an otherwise spanking clean olive shag rug. When Null entered with his Heckler drawn, the ones who sat and lounged didn't stand, but they all jerked to attention. Do-rag looked especially nervous.

"So is this grandma's house actually a real grandma's house?" asked Null without irony.

Desi, a weedy, rail thin youth of about nineteen in a white tee shirt and black vest with the requisite baggy prison jeans, stood shakily and approached Null. "This my moms's place," he said. "She gone visitin' somewhere, left me in charge."

"Good, Desi, you be in charge of that then. I'm sure we'll all try not to make a mess."

"Everybody respectful up in this bitch. No cigarette burns, stains on the rug or rings on the end tables. Real talk."

"Excellent."

"Cut this motherfucking shit homes, why you call us all in here for—etiquette lessons?"

"You all know why we're here."

"No shit."

"You do?"

"You don't even know who in your own crew, you chatted-out motherfucker."

"I have a lot on my plate."

"I'm Ronald, and I think your time running GB's be about up."

"I'm holding a gun on you, Ronald, you realize."

"Yeah, so the fuck what? You won't use it in here."

"You're testing me, Ronald. I know who you are—valuable guy, about twenty-seven, no substance abuse problems, juvie record only, doing a good job running the sling up there in Methuen."

"They should call that bitch Meth-town by now."

"You're slinging out all over the Merrimac Valley, staying away from the kiddies. And away from the all-too-white Andover."

"Don't want to stand out too bad."

"And yet. I notice you now."

"Yeah, and what thanks do I get?"

"Money, Ronald. You get money."

"I don't run no skim."

"Why you're still alive."

"It's not fucking enough. We'd make a killing hitting the high schools."

"I said colleges only, Ronald."

"Who cares what you say, motherfucker? Why should a cracker like you run things? You got Edgar and Howard roasted 'n' toasted."

"You're right. I'm responsible. Even though I warned you all to stay away from the club on Tremont, they defied me. Now they're scrap. Do you want to defy me too, Ronald?"

"I ain't got no gat, homes."

In a sudden motion like an owl jumping a rat, Null tossed him the Heckler. Ronald made a smooth catch.

Jo-jo, a slight, pear-shaped bespectacled boy who had driven the stolen bus down to Dapper O'Neil's with the rescued children, stood up, waving his hands. "Don't be stupid. I've seen him before. He settin' you up right to die, J-Cat! He fifty-one-fifty! Fuck!"

"Fuck him," said Ronald, pointing the Heckler at Null like he knew how to use it.

"Don't mess up my moms's carpet wit' blood, yo!" Desi cried.

In an instant, Null shucked off his shabby drab, black coat, pulled up the Bushmaster 90291 and put a line of rounds into the drop ceiling. The loud sound caused Ronald to bring his arms up to protect himself, still managing to hold tightly onto the Heckler. The rest of the Gangsta Boyz refused to move a muscle.

Null was coolly holding the Bushmaster 90291 chest level with Ronald.

"Going to take your shot now, or step down?" He sounded like a voicemail time-date stamp.

Ronald aimed the Heckler back at Null's bony torso, albeit shakily. Unable to stop shaking, he dropped the Heckler to the rug, yanking his hand away as if the steel were red hot against his skin.

"See," said Null flatly. "Now we're all friends again."

"Y-you want a beer, boss?" asked Do-rag. "We got a case of Stella Artois."

"No, thank you," Null said, shouldering the Bushmaster 90291 and picking his coat up from off the rug. Do-rag handed him back the Heckler, which quickly went into the coat pocket.

"You sure you don't want no beer?"

"Yes, but I think I'll do a couple of lines of our Methuen meth right here and now. How are the boys handling manufacture, Ronald?"

"Riley is all over that. He and that Northeastern kid Ricky are cookin' on the line. Hardly stop. Lucky they don't splode for sure."

"That may explain their absence."

"They too busy, man—they playin' on ass. Could be rough."

"But you'll see to that for me, Ronald? Won't you?" Null was wide-eyed and as ingenuous as an empty plate.

"I-I guess I will." Ronald knew Null was giving him his dignity back, and he was quick to take it and let Null be what he obviously was: the shot caller.

Null laid out a pile of greenish white methamphetamine on the glass coffee tabletop, chopped it and lined it up with a credit card from his wallet. He rolled up a dollar bill and snorted the gak quickly and efficiently as everyone in the room watched quietly, not daring to say a word.

"Cops go'n' come!" whined Do-rag.

Null finished his last snort with a long inhalation.

"They won't come. This is Roxbury. You really think anyone'll call the cops? Nobody remembers "Bloody April?" I don't think anybody here is particularly worried about that."

"What 'bout they *do* come?"

"Well, then, we'd better talk business right now."

"That gonna be 'bout Edgar 'n Howard?"

"Yeah," said Null, adjusting the machete on a lanyard and the Bushmaster 90291 beneath his coat and the Heckler in the pocket. "You remember what we did in Allston?"

"Fuck, yeah. I drove the motherfuckin' bus, if y'alls remember," said Jo-jo.

"How could I forget?" Null assented.

"Lotta blood, but a lotta good wallpaper, too," added Jo-jo.

"You could decorate your bedroom."

"Lotta joog, no doubt," said Alec with the shaved head, lounging unmoved all this time on the couch. "No doubt."

"If we think the cops are on the way, we can finish up quick."

"Go dawg," said Alec. The entire room muttered and grunted approval.

"All of you that don't have special tasks to do like Ronald have been very busy slingin' gak pretty good in Merrimack, Lynn, Lowell, greater Boston, avoiding Southie, Allston, getting Roxbury, Dorchester all the way up to Brockton. No busts, no high school trade that I know about, no problems. Why do you think that is? You know why, Ronald?"

"Yeah, I do."

"Why is that, Ronald?" Null was frigid, far to an extreme below cold.

"Nobody wants to fuck with us, I guess. You kill anyone —*every*one."

"That's right. In a heartbeat. In a New York minute. You should know that's how we'll handle Edgar and Howard. But we're not going for an eye-for-an-eye. I don't much care for the Bible. We're going for the same effect we had in Allston. Nothing left standing."

"Not for fuckin' free, homes, that's real talk!" Ronald barked.

"Did you do it for free last time? When you work for me, do you do *any* of it free? Do any of you feel right now you might like to try and negotiate a raise with me?"

Dead silence.

"I thought not. Still, money's coming in pretty flash, all due to you gentlemen. GBs as a business has plentiful cash reserves. I'm going to spend some of them. On you. My question of the moment is this: *are you down for business?"*

Shouts of assent went around the room.

"The business is killing. Literally. You good with that? Because you have to be. You want out now, say so."

"Every man here knows y'all can't avoid dat shit. Real talk, homes," offered Jo-jo. "You want the weed, do dat deed, yeah!"

"Do-rag, bring Dominic in here. He should be standing directly in front of you all. Edgar was his brother."

Do-rag was out the door before Null had finished the sentence. He reentered with Dominic striding in just ahead of him. He towered over Null, though his posture was slumped, head slightly bowed.

"Wassup, cuz?"

"You're not really in the GBs, are you, Dominic?"

"I catch a ride sometimes."

"You want in the car?"

"For what homes?"

"For blood. Do-rag is going to pay your family with cash. A death benefit. Isn't that right?"

"Money come tomorrow, boss. True dat."

"My moms 'n' sisters sure could use it."

"That leaves blood. You want blood, Dominic?"

"I'm a vampire, homes."

"They call me zombie fuck Null out on the street, you know that?"

"I heard that. Wouldn't never tell you that."

"No one would. You know where that leaves us?"

"You tell me, homes."

"Only one way for us, Dominic."

"What way?"

"New hope for the dead."

Then Null was gone from the Warren Gardens apartment like a whisper of confession that came just before the sirens of the Boston Police grew loud enough to swallow up the room.

TWENTY-THREE

The Muddy Charles was a modest former "no tell" motel built in the fifties located on a large traffic island right on Soldier's Field Road between Market Street in Brighton and the Eliot Bridge in Cambridge. The sounds of swishing traffic were nonstop, unabated either by the hour of the day or routine catastrophe in the street. It was a sound indifferent to the human suffering contained within it, and certainly indifferent to the human suffering that took place within the precincts and rooms of the Muddy Charles.

The Muddy Charles used to be a Best Western Hotel, a Comfort and then a Red Roof Inn, but all the franchising failed due to its obnoxious location. And there were only so many daylight assignations to be had. So now, it was the tacky, slightly grimy Muddy Charles. Named with the type of outré irony that had fallen from fashion long ago. It didn't seem that too many people actually stayed there. The parking lot was never full.

But the Muddy Charles nevertheless stayed in business.

And the lot was empty by the time the ancient boat pulled up.

Null was dropped off at the registration entrance by a flat black painted Buick LeSabre. He made it to the front desk, revealing a slight limp to his gait.

A portly, jolly man obviously watching TV in an adjoining room answered Null's single push of the call button on the wall without delay, with twinkling eyes and a broad, white smile. Null spoke first. He put both his hands on the counter and leaned forward to address Null.

Null spoke before he could say anything.

"Show me a room. I'd like to see a room."

"I'm sorry, sir. But we're full up."

"I'm sure you are." Null paused, looking through the clerk as if he weren't there. The clerk frowned. "Show me anyway."

"I'm sorry, sir, but our residents need privacy."

"No, I'm sorry. They won't be needing it anymore. You know who I am, right?"

The white-haired, cherubic man behind the counter frowned and sputtered.

Null interrupted him.

"No need to pretend otherwise. Right now, you're pressing a panic button on your cell phone in your pocket to alert the gunsels upstairs to come down heavy. You don't have to say yes."

The clerk backed away.

"They won't be coming down."

"Fuck you!"

"Don't be afraid. It's too late. Fear won't help you now. Neither will god. No doubt god made his decision about you long ago. If he exists. I'm betting he doesn't. And you are a chip sitting on the red."

The man fumbled for something in his desk.

Null shot him twice center chest with a dismissive shrug. The clerk gagged on the floor. Null cooled him out with a single shot to the neck, then quickly snapped the deathly grimace with his cell phone camera.

The man sputtered and gagged.

Ronald burst in through the door behind him, Smith and Wesson standard thirty-eight drawn. Several of the Gangsta Boyz were filing in behind him. They had to stand and wait in the coffee area where the continental breakfast was to be served daily. That matinal event hadn't happened since the nineties. Null recognized the faces of Ronald, Desi and Jo-jo.

"They comin' down or what?" Ronald asked, as if boasting. "Cocked and locked."

"No, we're going up. Dominic and the others go up to the emergency exits?"

"My green light on the walkies?"

"Don't tell them yet. Not until we've looked in a room or two."

"What if they in the motherfuckin' hall?"

"Jo-jo's going to play canary in the coal mine. You hear him yell and fire shots, you give the signal. Meanwhile, we have three floors to cover."

"Why ain't they comin' down yet? If they know you're here?"

"Because they know I'm here."

Jo-jo nodded and took the elevator up one flight, his Ruger forty-five drawn. Null and the others crept up steps. It was quiet all the way up. Jo-jo met them at the landing. None of them spoke. Jo-jo nodded and led the way. Null followed with the others seeming entirely unconcerned. Everyone else was jumpy but Jo-jo. It seemed he was getting off on the moment. He exchanged looks with Null, nodded at the first door. Null nodded back. Jo-jo kicked it in awkwardly, taking four tries to finally get it.

A shirtless teenaged boy smoking a cigarette stood in the center of the room, looking vaguely surprised, but more resigned than anything else.

"All you had to do was knock," he said quietly.

Ronald was impatient. "Got thirty rooms up in this bitch— we gonna have the bus driver kick 'em all in or what?"

"You have a point. Signal Dominic and whoever else is with him to pile in and start hard on the second level. Kick in all the doors, get ready for a firefight. Greenlight the pervs."

Ronald spoke the order through the phone.

The rest of the Gangsa Boyz each took a door on the first floor and kicked them in, so far with no shots fired and the only sonic responses being wailing and yelling. Null went back downstairs and let himself in behind the counter where the clerk lay dying on the floor. He located the master pass key card on the clerk's desk that was marked as such by the antique computer dominating it and stood over the clerk for a moment as he lay begging for help, uncannily still alive and noisy. Null stared at him for a long minute, then sprayed a line of fire across his body with the Heckler.

"There. That ought to help matters."

He bounded upstairs to join the Gangsta Boyz on level one. The Gangsta Boyz stood back as Null opened all the remaining doors that had stubbornly refused to kick in and joined Dominic and the others, opening the doors for them as well.

Each room had a teenaged boy in it, each one emaciated, some in a state of undress, some dressed in fetish leathers, harnesses and several in kiddie pajamas. They were all submissive and compliant when revealed from behind a kicked-in door, so no further shots were fired by anyone. Dominic looked perplexed at the second level. Null spoke softly, as if pointing out some minor architectural flaw of the building.

"They're all up on the third level. No second guessing. Just go up there and start shooting."

"Where you go'n' be?"

"I'm taking the roof. The gunsels are playing cute up there. I'm going to play cute too—see just how cute I can be."

"Sounds like fun, dawg."

"I'll take your word for it. I wouldn't know."

"You wearin' a vest?"

"Of course. I'm the one who expects to get shot."

"We need 'em too."

"Time was an issue. I'll see about it for the next run. Meanwhile, I believe you have some killing to do."

"Clowns blew up Edgar."

"They did. Make 'em laugh."

"I'm your vampire, homes."

Null gave Dominic the master room key card and backed out a window at the end of the hall that led to the fire escape that led to the roof. He paused while climbing to listen to the gun shots and the attendant shouting and screams. He noted that he'd have to climb back down again and make sure that any surviving gunsels wouldn't stay that way for too long, and he had to snap their pictures with his cell phone and send the images off to Brother Ray to stuff them directly into the faces of the users of the dark web.

Plus the kids.

Always the kids.

What to do with the kids?

He was about to heft himself onto the tar roof of the Muddy Charles, the fingers of his hands holding firmly to the metal ledge, but brash impact and a white-hot flash forced him back down and he all but lost his grip, nearly entering an awkward plummet down to the empty parking lot below.

He had just been pistol-whipped in the face.

"Zombie Fuck Null, die already!"

Four gunsels on the roof, Null guessed, dizziness and shadows obscuring his vision. A booted foot was coming fast at his face. Null pulled a move. With one hand free, he yanked the boot and its owner off the roof, smashing him down to the tarmac. With the other, he came up on the roof in a high vault, rolled low when he hit the tar, shooting until the Heckler was spent.

Two rounds grazed his right side near the broken ribs just skirting the flak jacket, which cut his breathing shallow.

Two of the three gunsels left had sunk down to the tar. The one left standing held an outsized pistol, a Browning Hi Power single-action, semi-automatic nine-millimeter. Null stood, his left leg seeming to buckle, pocketed the empty Heckler and raised up both hands.

"That ho check wasn't no thing to you, was it?"

"All the same to me."

"You're a creepy little fucker, Null."

"No doubt. You going to insult me to death?"

"Real talk, motherfucker. I'm takin' you to see Legere. He go'n' party wit' yo ass."

"He's going to fuck me?"

"He go'n' fuck you up!"

"Doesn't he just want you to kill me? Why the elegant plan? What am I, Batman?"

"You a J-Cat motherfucker. You a lame duck fuck."

"So, mow me the fuck down already." The reports off a few different pistols in the middle distance broke the pause of the stolid silence. "Or do you intend to bore me to death?"

"Da fuck?"

"Hear that? That's the sound of your buddies getting blipped off by my crew. You're molly whopped."

"The GB's *your* motherfuckin' crew? Shit, they a fuckin' laugh! Punk ass d-boys slingin' gak is all."

"Today they're slinging lead."

"Meth king of Boston!" The gunsel laughed. "They say zombie fuck Null's a chatted-out motherfucker. Fifty-one-fifty shit. They got you and that's a fact. Yeah, Legere and everybody pretty much want you chilled off. I get a fat bonus if I make you die. I get a even *fatter* bonus I bring your punk ass down for Legere to party with. And that dude likes to par-*tay.*"

"Good with that gat, are you? A trip-wire trigger finger, the Browning all condition zero and everything? Cocked and locked?"

"You talk way too fuckin' much for a dead motherfucker."

"I hear that a lot."

"I bet you do!"

"Usually I hear it just before death, which comes at you hard like a wrecking ball, knocks you flat on your ass and humiliates you while you pathetically question life, which all the time was the actual answer. But you never got it."

"Tell it to Legere, zombie Null fuck."

"Greed killed you. Ultimately does in the end."

"I'm still alive, chatted-out punk!"

In a seamlessly easy series of quick moves, Null shucked off his coat, brought up the Bushmaster 90291 and made a crater in the gunsel's chest, the force of which caused the Browning to fly off useless to the side and put the gunsel's back up against the brick of some roof utility before he sagged down slowly to the roof tar. His mouth remained open though: a gaping black hole of hopelessness, clearly discernable even against the shadows and darkness of the night.

Null climbed back down the fire escape, hitting the rungs with tentative steps to account for a possible concussion.

He had a harder time maneuvering his body through the open window at the end of the third level hallway and fumbled into Desi, who almost went down as he went in.

"Yo homes, I ain't no diaper sniper."

Null dusted himself off, though there was no dust to be seen. There were gunsels splayed out in the hall, some of them in the half-open rooms. Blood had soaked the gray carpeting in numerous spots. He quickly took each one's picture.

"Anybody we care about dead?"

"No, cuz," volunteered Ronald. "No injuries even. These guys was playin' on ass."

"Where are the kids?"

"They on the second level. Punks every single one."

"Any of them dead?"

"No homes. We alls know 'bout dat. You gots da keys. Nobody here interested in dyin'."

"Not today, anyway. There'll come a time, though I'm sure."

"Wallpaper says no."

"You're an optimist, Ronald. An excellent quality that can get you well and truly killed."

———

"You're not a john, are you?"

"Are you kidding? *I'm* not one of them."

"One of them. You mean like your friends? The ones dead on the floor?"

"Yeah, obviously, I'm not one of them. I look at you and *your* friends and I could say the same about you. You're not one of them."

"Appearances can be deceiving. I assure you, I am exactly one of them. I'm one of them more than I'm one of anything else."

"Who dies next, homes? Which one dese ofay motherfuckers *goes?*" asked Ronald with alacrity.

"Not me. Oh, no. I'm not going anywhere but home. I'm too important. You need me for whatever it is you're doing you ugly fucking piece of shit."

"You were found anally raping a teenaged boy in a hotel room. Who really needs you for anything?"

"I can pay you."

"I don't need your money. What's your name? What is it that you call a mope like this, Ronald?"

"He a diaper sniper."

"Thank you. You know, Ronald, I think you're developing a taste for this. I'm not sure that's a good thing."

"Adapt or die, homes. Adapt or die."

"True enough, Ronald."

Null turned to the man and eyed him hard. He was big, wearing a cable-knit, maroon-colored sweater and khakis, florid faced, gray-haired, blue-eyed and overweight. He looked bored and on the verge of yawning.

"Alright, diaper sniper, what do I call you before you I kill you?"

"You been punched in the face once too often, you know that?"

"Name?"

"Hal. Everyone calls me Hal. I'm popular. Even you're going to like me, because you're going to *need* me. You need me right now, in point of fact. I'm one of the people owns this smorgasbord."

Null scanned the hall. It was a crowded, stifling scene: Bodies of older men mixed in with younger hired gunsels, some from Roxbury, some from Mattapan, maybe one or two from Andover, all unmasked with lolling cartoon faces. Twink boys huddled in every room, afraid of what was in the hall. Gangsta Boyz dominated the dead and soon-to-be dead. The older men were there for a party. Hal and four others still alive were zip-tied on their knees on the bloody gray carpeting while Null, Do-rag, Dominic and Ronald stood over them. The rest of the crew either sat on the steps or loomed, lurking at the far end of the hall. Two sat carefully on sections of unbloodied carpeting.

"This bitch do, Edgar?" Dominic wasn't hiding his anger. He pointed at Hal.

"No, Dominic, I don't think so. Not that he didn't play a part in it."

"I'll blip him off anyway, dawg."

"Not yet. Let's see what Hal has to tell us, or should I say, sell us."

"You da shot caller."

"Try again, Hal. I don't remember seeing your name on the list I got from Finnerty the day I stabbed him in the heart, nor did I get any data from Franking before I blew the back of his head out through his eyes. I also was given the idea Hebe group was run as a business—no allowance for staff or equity partners sampling the goodies."

"Yeah, well, I'm the exception that proves the rule. I *dote* on the goodies."

"I can see that. You have a taste for raping young boys."

"My flaws don't define me. Besides, I pay in just like any john. Although the cameras are all off when I pay for a room. Our dark web end users don't really want the privilege of seeing me *in flagrante delicto* with a boy of my choosing."

"What have you got for me, Hal?"

"I'll serve you Legere on a platter, for one, then I'll tell you about all the other silent equity partners you don't know about, and a guy so high up on the totem pole you can't begin to touch him. But at least you'll know. How does that sit with you, your *sty*-ness?"

"That was funny, Hal, I bet. Any of you think that was funny?"

"Ain't no one laughin', homes."

Hal spat at Null. "Now, untie me, shit-for-brains, and I'll tell you everything you need to know so I can blow this popsicle stand permanently."

"Permanently? You mean, like, you'll be giving up your

equity stake in the Hebe Group partnership also? That kind of permanently?"

"It's not like it was such a great moneymaker after you came along to fuck things up. Took you to mess up a good thing. You know what you are, scumbag? You're a category killer. That's you."

"Not a good use of the term. I don't specialize in the rape of children, teenage boys and girls. No, I do one thing. Just one thing."

"Like I care, fucknuts. Just untie me and let me get my pale white ass on the road."

"I see," Null said, somewhat animated. To look at him, you might have even said he was cheery. Unless you knew him. If you knew him, you wouldn't know what to say. "Cut his zip ties and get him up on his feet, Do-rag, if you will."

Do-rag did so and helped the man up.

"I knew you'd see it my way, fucking punk. Everyone does sooner or later, and you're nothing special. You're actually nothing at all. Just like your name."

"Now, Hal, as far as I'm concerned, your little insults have no effect on me. I don't really mind them at all. They're an interesting show of character. But now you've put me in a kind of a predicament. A dilemma, really. You see, in my line of work, I'm what they call the shot caller of this crew. If I were to just let you go now, my crew might start thinking that I'm getting to be too weak to be the shot caller. I mean, allowing myself to be insulted by such a punk ass monkey mouth piece of shit like you wouldn't be a strong show of leadership, now would it? If I just let that go and let you walk out of here untouched, free as a bird, even if you happen to give me valid, useful information, I'd likely have a fight on my hands anyway or at the very least a chin check. Maybe even a ho check. It could get positively violent. We can't have that, can we?"

"You're telling me that you actually *run* this circus of niggers?"

"Hal, you're not really helping yourself."

"Tough shit if you lose face. That's your problem."

"No, Hal, now it's *your* problem."

Dominic moved his bulk to stand directly in Hal's path. "This bitch don't move till da man wit' da keys say he move." His face smoldered, far darker than the pitch of his skin.

"Hal, you weigh, what, a pot-bellied, somewhat out-of-shape two-sixty-something? Athlete in college?"

"Started cornerback at Colgate."

"See? What did I tell you? Now, take me. I'm, what? A buck-seventy-eight, maybe? Not really what you would call a team sports kind of guy."

"Like I care."

"Goes to your advantage, Hal. You see, you and I are going to settle things, right here, right now and, most importantly, right in front of the Gangsta Boyz on this bloody carpet amid all the corpses."

"Fine, if that's what you want, I'll cream you. I'll kick your fucking ass right into next week."

"That's the spirit, Hal! That's what we all want to hear."

"Tell your goon to back off and we can start pronto."

"Don't you want to hear what's in it for me first?"

"Why would I give a shit about anything you want, you sick, pathetic fuck?"

"Of *course* you wouldn't give a shit. No one in their right mind would expect you to. Perfectly reasonable. But, for the sake of manners, indulge me anyway?"

"Whatever."

Null's tone of voice became so matter-of-fact and soothing as to be almost affable. "Well, just for you, Hal, and the guys behind me, I plan to beat you to death. I'm going to beat you blind, but not deaf nor dumb. Oh, no. I'm going to require that you'll be able to tell me everything I need to know, clearly, concisely, accurately. And believe me, you'll beg me to let you tell me, plead with me to let you tell me. Do you have any idea why you'll be begging and pleading so badly? Any idea at all?"

"You're really out of your fucking mind, you know that?" Hal was sweating, disquieted. He swallowed hard.

"You're quite right about that, Hal. No use arguing the point. Right on the money, to be sure."

Null relieved himself of his coat and all its weaponry, the Browning Hi Power he took off the gunsel on the roof, falling to the rug with a thud, making a couple of Gangsta-Boyz jump back, worried it might go off. He unshouldered the Bushmaster 90291 and removed the machete hanging around his neck from a lanyard, handing them gingerly to a very twitchy Do-rag. He gave his porkpie hat to Ronald, who held it respectfully.

He left the flak jacket on.

"Okay, you got toys. So, what? Big fucking deal. Why would a prick like you think I'd ever beg you for anything anyway?"

"Why? So I can kill you, of course."

Hal made a disgusted face, like a drunk in a bar gulping a watered-down drink of cheap whiskey. He shook his head as if to clear the cobwebs. "I thought we had a deal."

"We did. This is something else. This is heart-check territory."

"I just want to check the fuck out of here."

"Sure. You'll check out. Oh, you're going to want me to kill you, alright. You'll beg for it. And I'll oblige you, but any way you slice it, it's going to seem like forever when I do it."

"You mean like this conversation?"

"No. Like the collective screams of all the young boys you abused and anally raped."

TWENTY-FOUR

The bilious, misbegotten orange sign—the brightest fixture of the entirety of the Muddy Charles Hotel—went dark, possibly forever. Even the "Vacancy" sign below it was turned off, including the "No."

Window-shaded dim and shadowed—lights off in the registration office—the Muddy Charles betrayed no inkling of the flurry of activity occurring within it. The Gangsta Boyz were now transformed into the most expensive cleaning crew in the history of the greater Boston area. Meanwhile, Brother Ray drove in from Methuen, bringing more cleaning supplies, a short store of meth and an enclosed utility trailer hitched up to his Grand Cherokee for the hauling and transport of corpses. The corpses were to be bound for deposit in the quarries around Cape Ann and Gloucester, also Fletcher Quarry in Milford and Merrill Quarry in Westford.

All the decent quarries more conveniently located a stone's throw away in Quincy had since been filled in with 800,000 tons of dirt from the Big Dig in back in 2000, doubtless hiding more of the uncounted human detritus and debris of incarcerated Boston gangster supreme Whitey Bulger.

The Gangsta Boyz were working up a sweat, scrubbing out blood, cleaning up gore and, wherever necessary, ripping up carpet to be incinerated. Policing of the Muddy Charles was going to be an all-night operation.

Null presided over the scene, a grim specter of doubt and assurance, fish-eyed and brooding, silently calculating. No one thought to ask him to pitch in; it never occurred seriously to anyone. He was the shot caller.

He had the keys.

No one had any inkling of disputing this when they saw what he did to what once had been Hal Champerty, kiddie porn equity partner of Hebe Group. Null took him long past any beating into some other plane of extreme torment.

An astonished solemnity had descended upon the scene when Null had not only passed the point of no return, he had already arrived at his planned destination.

His destination was punishment.

The bare-knuckle brawl in the second level started conventionally enough. The bigger, huskier, albeit older, opponent against the much shorter, impossibly scarred bag of bones. It really didn't look like Null had a chance. From a numbers standpoint, no other conclusion could be expected than a catastrophic loss for Null. Ronald had already calculated the numbers and craned his neck forward with eager anticipation to watch the utter deflation of the shot caller. Do-rag shifted nervously from one foot to the other, not knowing whether working for a stone psycho like Ronald would be any better than working for Null.

It was clear Null wasn't going to survive this; that much was made plain after Hal landed a piledriver dead bang to the face that nearly knocked Null off his feet. Null countered with a surprise roundhouse kick to Hal's gut, but that only served to anger him. After that, Hal went to town on him with big fists hammering punishing blows, not letting up until it appeared Null was about to go down.

Only he didn't go down.

He went up.

Somehow, Null effected a weird flip that put him on Hal's back, his arms now wrapped around Hal's bull neck.

Hal was frantic, bouncing off the walls of the corridor, but

Null, in the act all the essence of odd calm, merely squeezed his arms together progressively tighter. This coupled with Hal's frantic motions, starved his brain of oxygen and so down he went.

And when he went down, he never got up again.

Slowly, methodically, with icy purpose, Null beat Hal until he flopped over loose with surrender, his tongue lolling out of his mouth.

You would have thought that would have ended it.

It didn't.

The best way to describe it simply and without dwelling over the searing, naked horror of what the Gangsta Boyz and the twinks were witnessing was this: Null took Hal apart with his bare hands, taking his time, doing it slowly while Hal made noises that were as clearly not human anymore as Hal was not human anymore—piece by piece, bit-by-bit, minute-by-minute until the crackling death rattle emerged from Hal's ravaged throat that at last signaled the dead end.

Hal's dead end.

And all the while, just as Null had predicted, Hal had begged him to let him talk, to stop the anguish so he could tell Null everything he knew. Null encouraged him to talk and proceeded to disassemble him anyway.

It was like watching a preying-mantis demolish a beetle. Fast, subtle—ruthless.

Null listened intently, absorbing every word, yet not missing a beat in the inexorable destruction of Hal Champerty.

No one spoke or hardly moved at all until Null had—as if in attendance at some holy mass, some ancient ritual practice whose effect would be tainted by even the slightest, understandable human reaction to it—finished with Hal. Not even Do-rag turned away and vomited his guts out at what he was seeing. He forced himself to look. Dominic stared hard into it, gulped, and swallowed harder. Ronald had the shakes and stuck his hands in his pockets to hide them.

At the final sigh, Null bounced up from the rug and motioned for Do-rag to help him on with his coat and for

Ronald to remove his hat from his head and place it back on Null's.

"Uneasy lies the head that wears the hat," said Null to absolutely no one laughing at all.

———

The twinks were gathered in the biggest suite at the head of the third level, where some of the worst clean-up had yet to be done. Brother Ray had busily rigged the phone system to an outgoing message of shutdown, took the website offline, set-up auto-pay on all the bills, insurance and the mortgage. He rigged the phones to give an outgoing message stating the Muddy Charles was closed due to extensive renovations. Null had instructed that the Muddy Charles continue to exist, causing no uproar among creditors until he arranged to have it torched, or perhaps something better. All the other Gangsta Boyz cleaned and scrubbed all evidence of death away. And Null had the twinks assembled before him as if a general reviewing his troops.

"Alright boys, as you probably figured out, we're into a brand-new ballgame."

One shirtless twink with long auburn hair and a face full of stubble piped up in a voice that broke, "So what. That means we work you now, right?"

Fourteen other twinks milled and murmured assent.

"No. That game's rained out for keeps. You don't work for anybody anymore, at least not doing what you've been doing."

"You're not a pimp, like Oliver downstairs?"

"You mean the late Oliver. No. I'm nothing like that. I just sell meth. Good, old-fashioned straight up drug dealing."

"Holy fuck! I'd take a bump of some of that shit," the stubbled, shirtless twink commented.

"It's good you said that. Most certainly you'll all get some bumps, if that's what you want, on the house. No charge."

A chubby twink, also be-stubbled, moved up to the front and replied, "Dude, that's sweet. We all like a bump from time-to-time. Usually comes out of our money."

"Not this time, it won't."

"So, what do we have to do for that, kill somebody?"

"As a matter of fact, yes. You do."

———

They were there again in the same conference room at the top of One Beacon. Steve and Martha Privilegiata, looking like they had just stepped out of a J. Crew ad, Beatrice, looking like an apple-sculpture kitchen witch in her oversized hoodie, wizened and feisty Mike, still radiating the jar head, marine feel, his cheeks red with irritation.

Steve broke the silence and the tension. "Where the fuck is Hal?"

"He's never late. I tried him on his cell but nothing," said Hortense at her most mousey, backed with thick glasses, a puffy face and stringy hair. Hard to believe she had over a million salted away in various offshore accounts. She wore fuchsia crocs. The rest of the equity partners of what was left of Hebe Group weren't doing nearly as well.

"This meeting's not a joke—we're not fuckin' around!"

"Did anyone catch the death face page? There's a bunch of new entries." Mike was impatient, his wattles jittering as he spoke.

"We all got the link, saw the faces, counted up the bodies. We all got the message: Null's the new owner of the twink hotel. The Muddy is lost," said Steve.

Martha cleared her throat. "There was a face on the page, or it was supposed to be a face, but wasn't really a face, more like a bloody skull. You don't think—?"

"Hal's not that stupid. He knew better to fuck around at the twink hotel when we're in the midst of a hostile takeover by the meth king of Boston," Steve said rubbing his chin.

"Is that who the little prick thinks he is?"

"No, Mike. It's who the little prick fucking actually is, unfortunately. And he runs the Gangsta Boyz crew in the bargain."

"You know this how?"

"Seems like everybody knows this but Boston PD."

"They're always the last to know."

"If there was money in it, they'd know for sure. But the whisperings in 4chan and 8kun online say Null, who's officially dead, they say, would rather kill a cop than pay one."

"A prudent policy."

Hortense smashed her fist down on the table. "Don't you fucking idiots know we're hemorrhaging cash? Hebe Group is cash negative and so are we."

"Well, we'd all know that if Bernie Franking was alive, we'd be getting weekly statements."

"I make my own statements," snarled Hortense, no longer seeming so mousey, "and they're telling me that we'll be going broke if this takeover doesn't end soon."

"Maybe we should all just call it a day and pull out," Beatrice said, lighting a long thin cigarette, taking a drag, waiting for a complaint about her smoking in a non-smoking area. She exhaled when no one bothered to make it.

"I'm for pulling out," Mike grunted.

"Let's vote on it," Hortense suggested, ratcheting back down to mousey.

"Vote on what? Ending a veritable cash machine?"

Beatrice's voice was husky and troubled. "Ending a deepening loss, Steve. I don't see Hebe coming back from this. And who's running things anyway? This Null fuck seems to have killed off management."

"We're managing it for now, until things get back on track. I'm managing things, maybe, because I don't see anyone else here doing jack shit."

"I think we should take what's left of the principal that we put into this thing and cut our losses. Steve, at this point, I think you're the only one, and maybe your wife I guess, who says we shouldn't. You can't justify our taking any more hits."

"I have a vote too," Martha seethed, "and you're right. I'm with Steve. Before this clusterfuck, we saw astronomical profits, literally *scads* of cash roaring in until this wannabe gangster came along and pissed all over it. Well, there's way too much money in KP for you to pull out now. Kiddie sex trafficking is the great goldmine of the twenty-first century. It's the future! Cast-off neglected, unwanted kids made into little cash machines then sold off at a profit. There's no end to it! There's no end to *them*, especially now that the Republicans are running the show. The whole social safety-net was turned into tax breaks for people like us. Finally, we're their best bet. Their only hope. And they just keep on coming."

Hortense leaned forward, energized, her eyes wide behind coke bottle glasses. "So, Steve and Martha, you're saying you'd like to buy us out?"

"We don't have the liquidity to do that."

"It doesn't matter, it's two against three, so you're out-voted. Sorry, Privilegiatas," Mike offered coolly. "It's done."

"Yeah," Hortense said before yawning, "as of today, Hebe Group is shit-canned."

Then there was a sound, a click that was thunderous in the pause of silence.

The door to the conference room swung open and just at the cusp of where the fluorescent light coming in from the hallway hit the dimly shadowed, unlit conference room, an outsized figure loomed in dark outline. He was both shaded and indistinct. In a low, near choke of a voice he said with a hint of menace:

"Now it's a draw."

———

"The days of rape for money are over. You birds are all free. As of right now."

"Free to do what? Starve and die on the street? Find another pimp? What? You have no clue. Nobody here has a degree—some not even a high school diploma. Killing us won't solve that." The chubby twink, whose physical incarnation seemed to be that of a modern cherub, had a smiling, benign face that belied his complaint. Null didn't have to think about it to answer him precisely when he finished.

"That's all true. In this lousy economy, even the PhD's are

turning to crime and the shady underground world of profiteering. The straight world has nothing to offer you but hypocrisy, indifference, and bureaucratic contradiction. I can't offer you anything better, and I don't see any of you seeking to join The Gangsta Boyz crew."

"Ain't we a little bit too white for that?" the first, shirtless, stubbled twink piped up.

"I'm an equal opportunity employer."

"Can we just go?"

"Certainly, but if you go to the cops, I'll find you and kill you. Believe me, I will. As I've shown you tonight, I'm very, very good at it."

"Nobody here wants nothin' to do with the cops anyway. They'd probably buttfuck us, too."

"You have a brain. Got a name to go with it?"

"Angelo."

"Okay Angelo, and all of you, this is the deal: You can stay here for a couple of months. I've got some of my crew here running the things you can't, seeing to provisions and payments, food and money for you. The rest will all be handled by you, however you want to divide it up. Maid service, laundry, cleaning and whatever else has to be done. Nobody gains admittance to this place but one of my guys and you. Nobody. Rule infractions will be handled only one way. Just one way. And I think you all know what that way is.

There was a low murmur of assent.

"You need anything; money, meth, food, cleaning supplies, anything like that, you can call a number I'm leaving for you at the front desk for Brother Ray. Or you can use Facebook or any other social media, including 4chan and Reddit. Brother Ray is on all of them most of the time under that name."

"Do we really get free meth?"

"Yeah, you do, but you're so skinny and wired I hardly think you need it. What's the name, kid?"

"Norman."

"You'll definitely get your meth. Hopefully, Brother Ray can use some judgment and prevent you from killing yourselves with it. One thing we don't need is a cop car, a fire truck and an ambulance parked outside to save your scrawny ass, calling attention to our little set-up here. Right now, Boston, Cambridge and Brighton PDs are blissfully ignorant. Let's try and keep them happy."

"Where do we go after this?" squeaked Norman.

"Well, after you've completed a little task for me, you can take the money I'll be shelling out to you on a weekly basis that you didn't spend and go anywhere you want. I have a friend who takes care of neglected, abused kids and gets them as much of whatever the social programs that haven't been savaged by the Republicans as are available. I'll set you up with her and she'll find a place for you somewhere doing something, what, I can't say. School might have to be involved."

There were some noises of distaste accompanied by mild laughter that died down fast.

"We ain't kids," spat Angelo.

"Okay, anybody in this room but me over the age of eighteen?"

Silence.

"All you kids are eligible for something, and though my friend Mrs. Coelacanth may seem grouchy and unwilling, she will in fact pull out all the stops for you. If you don't want to go that route, then I suggest when you leave here that you go buy yourself a bus ticket and get the fuck out of town, because Boston's done with you. Probably, by then, I'll be done with you too."

"What does that mean?"

"You know what that means."

"So what? What kind of future do we get? What the fuck happens to us?"

"You get the future you get, make one choice or the other. Make no choice and see what happens. Making no choice is always the worst choice. I'm not Nostradamus."

"We want the gak first," said Angelo firmly. "Then we can negotiate."

If Null were more human, if he had had the slightest sensitivity or basic empathy within him at all, he might have laughed at that. He didn't. Instead, he enunciated his response with the dead tone of a computer text-to-speech program:

"This isn't a negotiation. This is an ultimatum."

"Nobody else is talkin' much, so tell me, what do we gotta do?" asked Norman in a reedy, high voice that had yet to fully change.

"You're going to have to kill somebody for me."

"You're fucking kidding—out of your freaking mind!"

"I'm not kidding, but you're most likely right that I'm out of my mind. Nevertheless, your choices about how to deal with that are limited. So, unless one of you has a gun on you somewhere and is ready to shoot me, I suggest you go along with it."

Norman shuffled his feet and frowned for a moment. "Who do you want me to kill?"

"I don't want you to kill anyone. I want all of you to kill someone—collectively."

"Who is it gets the 187?"

"No one important. One of your old clients."

"That might be okay then if he's one of the sicko's."

"I don't think you'll have a problem with it."

"Who is it then?"

"Just a guy," Null said, apparently distracted; the only response to that being the labored breathing of everybody else in the room. Then he added, "Just a guy who likes to fuck little boys to death."

TWENTY-FIVE

"You're not an equity partner, Legere," said Steve nervously, unconsciously rubbing his smooth, spatulate hands. "You got no say."

"I got a stake in this fucking thing."

"You blew your stake when you failed to make the kill on Null, blew a wad of our drastically diminished cash straight down the toilet."

"Can he actually vote on this?" challenged Hortense. "From Franking's numbers, I don't see he owns jack shit."

"I got papers if ya want 'em, girlie, otherwise, I got no time for your mouth."

"How do we break the tie?" asked Mike, both irritated and bewildered.

"Easy-Peasy," said Legere. "Fuck the tie. We kill him, then we bust up his crew and scatter 'em. That's how." Legere was a rough man with a fat, jowly face, pig-slit eyes, no discernable neck and a bulbous nose long past broken. His cheeks were full of rum-blossoms, but not from alcohol. No, they were there from a lifetime continuum of hardcore violence. When he spoke, it sounded like a foghorn blasting right in your face. He was pushing sixty but looked older. His hair was gray, thin and slicked back. If there was one word to describe him, it would be imposing. He stood a broad, thick six-six.

"Can't we buy him off?"

"That'd be great, Steve," said Beatrice before entering a coughing jag in a gout of her own cigarette smoke. "Hasn't that cocksucker taken enough of our money, costing us money, basically just about wiping us right the fuck out? *Ya think?*"

"You can't buy off a sick fuck like Null, so save your pennies, boys and girls."

"We are saving our pennies, Legere, because we're not paying you a dime anymore."

"That don't matter. I'll do it for my equity stake in the profits once we're back online. You can vote to give me a bonus if you think I deserve one by then."

"Can't we just vote to get rid of this jamoke?" whined Hortense.

"Sure, but you can't do that legally. Not that any of what we're doin' here is legal by any stretch."

"But we have ethics," said Steve absently, distracted by the hunt for a solution. "If Legere has papers showing an equity stake, then he has voting power, and that means we're deadlocked."

"Not necessarily. There's one voice we haven't heard from. He has the largest equity stake remaining. Maybe we should get in touch with him. Ain't he like a Skype call away from any laptop with good WIFI or what?"

"We're *not* doing that."

"Why not? Wouldn't he just *love* to hear from us?"

"You know he wouldn't," Steve said gravely.

"Get to the point. Nobody wants to contact him, nobody wants to disturb him at all. Just what are you trying to get at, Manny?" Mike asked, trying to contain his unrest.

"Simple. We kill the fucking mutt."

"What do you mean we?" Steve sneered.

"I'll do it."

"Like you've had so much luck with that up till now," Beatrice countered.

"I've learned a few things since then," Legere grunted.

"Why should anyone have to kill him?" asked Martha with

seeming innocence, smoothing back strawberry blonde hair. "Isn't there some sort of deal we can make? You said he's the meth king of Boston, right? So he does business. Maybe we need to do business with him."

"He's doing business with us already, in case you didn't already know it—his kind of business."

"What's that supposed to mean?"

"You're inexperienced, Steve. You just don't know, so let me lay it out for you. This guy's a psycho. He's not like a regular human being, more like a machine. A cyborg, a fucking zombie. Boston PD has him listed as officially dead, info I got from a friendly uniform down at One Schroeder. He does what he does because he does it and for no other reason than that. He doesn't care about money, he doesn't mind pain, and he doesn't make deals. He's like an act of god. Maybe he even thinks of himself *as* god."

"He's an agent of chaos, like the Joker in that Batman movie? Doing it just because he can? For its own sake?" Martha asked, actually fascinated.

"That's just a fantasy out of a comic book. This mutt's got a purpose, that much is clear. He's got one fuck of a king-sized vendetta against kiddie porn, against the trafficking we do, and he's not going to stop until Hebe Group goes belly up. Maybe a relative, maybe his own kid, somebody he knew was affected by it. So, he focuses on us."

"Maybe it was a lost love," sighed Hortense.

"That's what you don't get. That's why he's such a problem. He doesn't love, he doesn't hate, he doesn't feel anything. Just like his name. Null. That's what this fucker is—Mr. Nobody. Which doesn't at all stop him from being a man with a plan."

"Yeah. Some plan. Take us down. Well, this is one fuck of a way to go about it!" Steve said, getting up to pace about the conference room and walk off some of his mounting frustration. "Just brilliant!"

"Ain't it though?" Legere asked ruefully. "Lemme give you an education."

"Just dandy," shouted Steve. "Go ahead, professor, educate us."

"Gladly, Steve, gladly," Legere said with a smirk and winked. "We've all seen the streaming video captures from the playhouse in Brookline to the twink hotel on Soldier's Field Road. He's a capable sick fuck, handy with weapons, good in a brawl, and he's got heavy funding from a meth operation we can't touch with a crew of vicious niggers backing his play. He's got one of the not-so-clueless BPD ranking cops to play along with him. So far, he's killed off management and just about every Hebe employee of record, including the comptroller so that our cash transfers and Bitcoin conversions are fucked, just about all the playhouses are down, either whacked out by Null or turning themselves in voluntarily to the cop. I still don't get what their deal is."

"Is that it, Legere—is that what you've come to tell us? As someone once said, it's a null set."

"Funny. You're a freakin' comedian."

"I try."

"No, Steve, there's more." Legere spoke like he was reading items off a to-do list, instead of Null's successful assault against Hebe Group. "Null's burned down most of the dark web servers; the chatrooms are disabled and the most heavily trafficked of our websites is a page showing cell phone cam shots of all the people this fucker whacked out. Worse, he co-opted a hitwoman I hired to ambush him who's now palling around with him and the cop. Meanwhile, your independent hitman's up on the page, my two snipers are down at Mass General and Hebe Group at this very moment is officially cash poor. That do it for ya?"

"Like we didn't know that?" Steve answered.

"Yeah, well, here's an item or two that may have escaped your notice. He's not done yet."

"What do you mean?" Martha asked in a small voice.

"Zombie fuck Null, as they call him on the street, is coming after everyone that's left, and that means all of you and definitely me. He won't stop until we're dead. And if he's the kind of psycho I think he is, he'll go after your children and relatives too. Even your grandparents. He's got time, money, a crew and a psychosis we can't even begin to understand. If we don't stop him, nobody will."

"But doesn't he realize all the good we do for the children and even the teens?" Martha asked with genuine conviction. "Without us, they'd starve and freeze to death out on the street, overdose on drugs and die, or get into foster care and wind up sexually abused. Can't he see that we give them a purpose and hope for the future? Medical care, nice clothes, food, shelter, even toys? He doesn't get what an actual *blessing* we are to them!"

"No, Martha. He don't see it that way. He thinks that if you pimp children out as whores and profit from it, you should die for the privilege. That's the long and the short of it."

"But we're not even involved—we're just equity partners, investors. We don't *do* any of that."

"Problem is, Martha, he thinks that by making money on pedophiles fucking kiddies or getting off watching that on the dark web, you're just as guilty as the ones doing the fucking."

"But we aren't."

"What about Hal?" said Steve. "He was a little more, um, involved, you know?"

"Funny thing," Legere intoned with his foghorn voice. "I don't see Hal here at all. Wasn't he supposed to be in on this meeting?"

"He never showed," Steve said, puzzled.

Martha's eyes went wide, and she spoke in a loud whisper, "Jesus Christ, you don't really think that—?"

"Yeah," Legere interrupted, blowing hard on the foghorn. "I really do."

———

"What the hell happened to you?" asked Janis, expressing seeming motherly concern. "You're sweaty, filthy, and bloody as fuck!"

"It's not my blood," said Null.

"I guessed that."

"Do you think I should shower?"

"Definitely. How many years has it been do you think?"

"I lost count. Better go and do it then."

"Sure. But first, where's Kay?"

"Down at One Schroeder, having her KP investigation taken away from her."

"They got wind of the dark web activities, didn't they?"

"You mean the FBI?"

"Who else?"

"Well, it wouldn't be BPD, and that's for sure. They were all happy making KP OC. But the FBI wants their cut, take over the operation."

"That could cause problems, although nothing too terrible."

"Why do you say that? You do stink, by the way."

"You covered that already. I say that because we're just about done."

"Really, I don't feel like we've done very much of anything."

"Oh but we have. Hebe Group senior management are all dead. Their US server backbone and cloud pretty much shut down, most employees deceased. Their dark web presence has been whittled down to a few small sites and their main site carries the faces of the dead, courtesy of Gangsta Boyz IT whiz Brother Ray."

"Who's he?"

"He works for me. They all work for me."

"They don't give a shit a white guy is the shot caller?"

"They do. But they claim to give more of a shit about the money. I make sure it comes pumping in and I also make sure everyone slinging meth, and even those who don't, get a fair cut. I pay generously. Sure, at least one or two of them want me in the ground – but they don't want to screw up their cashflow. And they also don't want to die in the process. So I'm good. For now."

"Good luck with that. I have no use for a crew—I work alone."

"Maybe in the past, but right now, you're in my crew. I paid you already, didn't I?"

"Yeah, and thanks for that. A little nervous black kid with a red bandana around his head dropped by with a shopping bag full of kale, and not the kind you make soup with."

"That would be Do-rag, a most useful guy. My fixer."

"So, what's on the agenda now, Mr. shot caller?"

"As you so sagely pointed out, a shower for me. Then we have to figure out how Kay is going to deal with the feebs nipping at her heels down at One Schroeder. There are, by my last count, twelve playhouses left. We'll divide them up. I'll take one half, you and Kay take the other."

"What if I want to partner with you instead of Kay?"

"It makes no difference to me. Just as long as you can handle what I'm going to do when I do it."

"What do you mean?"

"Janis. I only do one thing. Just one thing."

"Oh. That. Yeah, I think I can handle it now. Hell, I'll even pitch in."

"You can put the Beretta away, you know, unless you're planning to shoot me."

"I forgot. I've been a bit jumpy, knowing Legere and his little helpers are out to get me."

"You're right. They are. We're down to the wire now. If it wasn't this way before, this is how it is now: It's either us or them. And Legere is going to be particularly aggressive. He won't go after a Boston cop though, not directly, so you're safer here in Kay's place than you'd be anywhere else."

Janis put the lavender Beretta Pico down on the coffee table and gazed at Null, evaluating him. She could only imagine the things he had done during the past two nights, but whatever they were, she was sure they contained all his favorite elements (if Null could be said to have any favorites about anything at all): blood, gore, violence, torture and finally death. She didn't want to think about it, yet it strongly invaded her thoughts, none-theless. She couldn't stop it.

Being close to Null for any length of time inspired in Janis an odd combination of queasiness and attraction. The fact of it made her tremble ever so slightly.

"Maybe he's cooled off. He hasn't tried anything since the snipers, you know."

"No, he's already started, and he's going to figure a way to come at us and come at us heavy."

"You mean he's coming after *you*."

"No, I mean all of us."

"Well, so far there's been nothing."

"I wouldn't say that."

"No, what would you say then?"

"I'd say that Kay's problem down at One Schroeder facing down the feebs is Legere's final opening gambit."

TWENTY-SIX

"Your busts are bogus, Boyd. You know it and I know it," said a sallow-jowled, bleary-eyed, balding man with a mustache that needed a trim badly. His expression and carriage didn't so much radiate authority as the fact that he believed with ferocious intensity that he had authority. And that belief was apparently fragile.

Boyd was going to break it.

"Why do you say that Quark?"

"Special Agent Quark to you Boyd."

"Lieutenant Boyd, to you, dickless."

"You're close to arrest, Boyd, you know that?"

"I know that you don't know dick, dickless. If you did, you'd have a partner with you and some evidence to show me, so I'd flip on whoever you're really after."

"You're in with Hebe Group and goddamn kiddie porn up to your eyeballs, Boyd. You're cleaning house for them with quick and dirty busts of the pervs they want to get rid of. They're going to ground to regroup and you're giving them the cover to do it."

"I thought you had to be smart, have something on the ball to be in with the feebs. But that's not you, Quark. Oh, no. You're just a grade-B dumbshit."

"Sure. Meanwhile, you wonders at the Boston PD are always so smart and on the square. You're not dumb, corrupt, dirty as fuck, committing crimes if not taking down outright

219

scores. Now, is it just my imagination, or didn't the DEA bust about forty of you back about fifteen years ago off *our* surveillance?"

"That's before my time, Quark, and I was never part of any steroid ring, including that one."

"News to me. You look like you've been on the shit for years, and that's a fact."

"Appearances can be deceiving, you know. For instance, when I first laid eyes on you, I thought you were an asshole. Now I know you're just an idiot. You can't even make the *cut* for being an asshole. And by the way, I seem to recall a pretty cozy relationship between the bureau and that mass-murdering fuck Whitey Bulger. Does the name Steve "The Rifleman" Flemmi mean anything to you, dickless?"

Quark gritted his teeth at this and his rheumy eyes blazed.

"How about I just haul you down to the JFK building right now and set you up for arraignment in federal court?"

"How about you get an indictment first?"

"I got a CI says you carry water for Hebe Group."

"And I got one who says Hebe Group is on the ropes and done for."

Quark laughed and rubbed his puffy face. "You mean you have a dead CI—who does what? Sends you messages from the great beyond?"

"No, he tells me how much he likes fucking your mother."

"If you were a man, I'd paste you one."

"Same to you, Quark."

The air in Captain Parseeman's office at One Schroeder was close. The office itself was cramped and dumpy, looking more like an adjunct professor's at Bunker Hill Community College, and a shared office at that. Crammed with books and out of date files going back to the last century held by furniture adorned by a tragedy of walnut wood veneer. Boyd absently cracked a window, which did nothing but break the standoff silence between her and Special Agent Wilmer Quark.

"So, dickless, I guess Special Agents like you happen when we have a corrupt moron in the executive interested in running the FBI hands-on. You add dimension to the term '*Special Agent.*'"

"Fuck all, Boyd. I'll give you special. You're off kiddie porn as of now. You're done. It's officially removed from your OC task force agenda until the bureau clears you, which might well be sometime before you retire, or after you get locked up."

"I haven't heard a word about it. Nada. Zip."

"You will after I talk to your captain. Then, I'm gonna go over each and every one of those bogus KP busts of yours personally until I get probable cause enough to bring you into *my* house. Then, when you're well and truly mine, you and I are going to have a little party. Do a little dance, maybe." Quark had given up trying to emulate mocking superiority and settled for an easy sneering matched only by his frustration. "Yeah, you'll dance alright."

"Listen, Quark, I've known inchworms more threatening than you. Go shoot your pathetic wad. Everybody *knows* what the outcome's gonna be. Your fishing expedition will wind up leaving you on the hook and not me."

"That's rich, coming from you. Your angle's pretty damn obvious. You're taking payments from whoever's running Hebe, keeping them anonymous and looking legal. Clearing away any of their bothersome deadwood. Well, I'm putting an end to that as of right now. We don't have a clue who's running you yet, but we're getting closer. Help us now and you might be able to steer clear of a jail cell, otherwise, you're headed straight for federal gen' pop'." He grunted. "And the girls will *love* you!"

"One problem with that, Quark. There ain't no "we." The bureau's not behind you. They may be looking into this Hebe outfit for kiddie porn—that part's likely true—but this line of inquiry is all your own doing. Not official. Wanna bet if I get a hold of the Special Agent in Charge, he'll be surprised at your doings? Maybe even a little pissed you didn't clear things with him first? I'm pretty sure the bureau's not running this investigation out of the Chelsea office. This is all about your making a pathetic effort at a promotion and transfer. Like this discussion, like your dick, it's gonna fizzle like a wet noodle."

Quark failed at adopting a poker face betrayed by reddening cheeks and ears; flecks of saliva fired out of his mouth when he opened it to speak.

"Maybe not. But okay, I heard you're in pretty thick with Boston's so-called meth king. Some psycho I can't get so much as get an ID on from your local crowd. Every CI's shit scared to say so much as boo. Some wise ass compared him to Dracula. The most I could squeeze out of anybody was the phrase "zombie fuck Null." What's that supposed to mean? He's part of the zombie freakin' apocalypse? Null's actually his name, maybe? I think they take it to mean absolutely nothing, just like I do. A null fucking set."

"You mean like this conversation?"

"They say you got a mouth on you, Boyd. They're not wrong. And my SAC is a woman, by the way. One just as obnoxious as you are."

"Go file a complaint with my captain. Blow your load."

"I was going to do that anyway." Quark wiped spittle from his lips with the sleeve of his ill-fitting, off-the-rack baby-shit brown suit jacket. "You wouldn't have a name on your meth king crony, by any chance, would you? That might help ease your upcoming suffering a bit. Because, whatever you think, any way you slice it, it's in the cards for you, Boyd. Bank on it."

"Like I haven't suffered enough?" asked Boyd, without a hint of irony.

"Yeah, I heard some unsub piece of shit offed your foster kid. Sorry for your loss." He spat this with blatant anger.

"You mean my adopted child."

"Yeah. Terrible shame. You gonna link that shit up with Hebe Group for me? Give me a couple of names or what?"

"Go fuck yourself, Quark, is what."

"You'll be singing a different tune at your arraignment, Boyd. And that's a fact."

Boyd said nothing and just stared at Quark, which said everything.

Quark threw up his hands in a stiff and awkward gesture of resignation, and without any further words, turned on the heels of his ox-blood tasseled loafers and left the room hurriedly with Boyd still standing there as if frozen, quietly wishing him dead.

———

"You think you're gonna be rescued? *No*body's gonna rescue you!" He was a tall man with a pot belly, craggy face and jet-black hair, obviously dyed. He was throwing a small boy around a large bedroom as if he were a rag doll being tossed about by a dog.

"Lemme alone!" the boy cried.

"Son, you're whatever I want you to be! Come back over here!"

"Just get the hell away from me!"

"You plan to kiss me with a mouth like that?"

"No, you stupid faggot!"

"Is that any way to talk to your father? I'm going to have to discipline you."

"Don't touch me."

The bedroom door was locked, but some commotion could be heard from behind it, muffled and indistinct. The man ignored it. He was too busy admiring the boy, who couldn't have been much older than eight, like a gourmand admiring a rare steak. The room was white, the bedspread was white and the man's shirt was white, but whitest of all was the small boy's face.

"I wanna go back to my parents."

"They were your *foster* parents, kid."

"I have a name!"

"You do. Whatever I choose to call you is your name. Maybe I'll call you Alex."

"Robbie! Robbie's my goddamn name."

"You learn that language from your foster parents?"

"You're a gross pervert — get away from me!"

"Don't say such things. You'll like it here. I'm going to show you what love really means!"

"Screw you!"

Robbie had run to the other side of the bed and now that the man was approaching him, he tried to make his way across the king-sized mattress to the door. When he made that move, it was all over. The man grabbed him with ease, held him up, and shook him like a ventriloquist's dummy. The boy screamed so hard and loud it made the man squint. His hair was light brown, and he was freckle-faced with blue eyes. He had a pug nose which made him look somewhat comical, like the plucky sidekick out of an old boys' adventure story. That wasn't the story he was in now.

And what he was in for could only be called an adventure by someone nefarious, someone repugnant, someone obscene like the man with the jet-black hair.

Crying hysterically, screaming the words, "Help me!" over and over again savaging his throat until they became unintelligible, Robbie's face went pomegranate red, and he kicked out at his captor with everything he had. The man laughed, hugging the boy tightly to him, genuinely delighted and amused. He kissed Robbie again and again.

The commotion outside the door became louder and voices could be heard shouting, but the man refused to notice, choosing instead to strip the boy naked and toss him on the bed as if he were a stuffed animal, all the while relishing his useless struggle, like it was all part of the fun.

And, for him, it was.

Then it wasn't.

The door opened with a loud bang, startling both man and boy, causing them to jerk into a freeze.

Janis stood in the doorway pointing her lavender Beretta Pico directly at the man's crotch.

"Somebody in here say something about a rescue?"

———

The first floor of the house was awash in blood, bodies, and commotion. Plush wall-to-wall carpeting was ruined. The room carried the copper stink of blood and the bruised stench of sweat. A bunch of children were huddled in the center of the large open den, bodies of full-grown men lay strewn about and Null hovered over the children, brandishing the Bushmaster 90291, eyes glazed and lips drawn tight in tragicomic style. The man with the jet-black hair plodded down the flight of stairs into the well-lit foyer with heavy footfalls, Janis right behind, her lavender Beretta jabbing him in the ribs intermittently. The children were whimpering, and some were outright crying, none of them over the age of twelve.

"Where's the kid?" Null asked, his voice raspy and dry like the cracking of brittle twigs.

"He's upstairs, dressing. This piece of shit was going to rape him."

"Maybe he should join his friends on the floor."

"Maybe he should."

"I didn't do anything. I love children," said the man. "This is a misunderstanding. What you interrupted was a loving consensual act." He was wringing his hands with sincere, anguished perplexity, or the habit of mimicking that. His face was plaintive, eyes beseeching. "The little ones *love* me."

"Can I shoot him in the face, please?"

"Not yet, Janis. Go back up and collect the kid. We'll use the two station wagons I hot-wired from down the street to take them all to Dapper O' Neill."

"I'd still like to shoot him."

"You can't shoot him," stated a stern, feminine, authoritative voice. It was Boyd. "He's mine." She had come in through the open door, her Sig-Sauer drawn.

"That's true," Null acknowledged as Janis bounded up the stairs to collect the spoils of the tall man with jet black hair. "You definitely have some things to work out with Mr. Goodnature. And so do I."

"I recognize the hair and the body from the video they sent me, after they—" She simply couldn't finish the statement. Her throat locked with a perceptible click. She aimed the Sig at Goodnature's head.

"Is this what you want, Kay? Think hard. You're on camera, you know."

"I'm fucked anyway. They put me on suspension for making too many suspicious busts."

"You mean for showing up the feebs. They tend to resent that."

"I can just plant a quick one in his brain and that'll be that. *Blam*."

"Be my guest."

Boyd squinted hard and pressed the barrel of the Sig up against Goodnature's temple. Her arm trembled not with fear but with rage. Then, instead of firing, her face relaxed, and she turned her head to Null.

"You have a plan, don't you? You have something worse in mind."

"I always do, even when I haven't quite figured that out myself."

Boyd lowered the Sig and let her shoulders slump a little bit.

"You're right. He deserves worse."

Janis came down the stairs carrying the squalling, writhing, struggling Robbie close to her to keep him from slipping away, the keen pitch of his screaming harmonizing with the whimpers of the huddled children in the center of the den. At the bottom of the stairs, Janis clapped a hand hard over his mouth.

"He's a wild one," she said.

"Let him go. If he wants to run around screaming, let him do it. He'll get tired, then we'll put him in the station wagon with the rest and let Mrs. Coelacanth handle him."

Null thought for a moment to ask either Janis or Boyd to hunt up whatever drugs had been keeping the children quiet and subdued up to this point but decided against it. The children had had it rough enough.

"She's gonna be pissed, Mrs. Coelacanth," Janis observed.

"Can you blame her? If I could be pissed, I'd be pissed too."

Janis let Robbie go and he rocketed around the den and foyer, screaming incoherently.

"You're not going to kill me. You're not going to do anything, are you?"

Goodnature smirked, making his craggy face become even craggier, with a set of debauched dimples.

"You're whistling in the dark. That won't make things any brighter for you."

Without so much as taking a breath, Null hit him with an uppercut no one could see coming. Goodnature went back on the heels of his expensive shoes, then fell to the bloodied rug on his ass. When he focused his vision, he found himself looking into the angry face of a very large black man. Dominic was looming over him.

"This the motherfucker, homes?"

"No, this isn't him. Not that he isn't just as bad."

"Why he still alive? You killed everybody else."

"If you'd have gotten here earlier, you could have helped."

"Real talk."

"You'll have your day, Dominic. That's real talk."

"Now you're sayin' somethin'."

"Kay, you and Janis want to herd the kiddies into the station wagons? We don't have too much time before some concerned citizen rouses the Belmont police. We don't really want to have to kill them as well, do we?"

"No, we do not," Boyd said with fierce declaration. She went over to Goodnature, who was still lolling on the floor, and kicked him hard in the ribs a few times. "Nobody's forgotten about you, Gorgeous George."

"So I'm aware," he whined.

Livid, Boyd directed her anger at Null. "How the fuck did you know? How did that happen?"

"I was privy to the life story of Hal Champerty down at the twink hotel. He got very detailed while I was taking him apart. We know quite a few things we didn't know before."

"I must be out of my mind to be here with you tonight. I'm batshit crazy!"

"Usually, that applies to me. Why would anyone think you were crazy?"

"Jesus Christ! I'm on fucking suspension!"

"That'll clear up when Legere runs out of juice. And he's bleeding pretty good as it stands."

Still shouldering the Bushmaster, Null reached into his coat pocket and withdrew his smartphone. He offered it to Dominic, who seemed dumbfounded at the array of corpses on the floor. Janis was busy chasing down Goodnature's screaming would-be victim while Boyd stood glaring at him. He was too fearful to try standing unless cued to do so.

"Dominic, do me a favor and take pictures of each of the faces of the dead men on the rug, then send them on to Brother Ray? You know how to work the thing, don't you?"

Dominic smiled and said affably, "Cuz, you gotta be half-dead not to know that."

Dominic took the phone and obliged him, sweating visibly. He worked carefully and quietly. For a moment, the only persistent sounds were a gaggle of upset children trying to whisper, and failing, and the awful tone of a lone boy screaming.

"You're going to insist I do our deal suspended or not, aren't you?"

"Of course, Kay. No reason not to."

"How does that even work?"

Janis joined the conversation, holding Robbie, her hand now clapped firmly over his mouth. "We'd better get those kids loaded before things start going south."

"We will, Janis," Boyd snapped. "Don't worry. I just need a word with Null."

"The risk of this escapade is hitting critical mass, you realize," Janis warned, still controlling the boy.

"You expect me to go arrange busts when I'm on suspension? Do you *really?*"

"No, Boyd, I don't."

"Then what the fuck am I doing here then?"

"You're going to visit each of your six houses and convince those who run them to give themselves up voluntarily."

"And why would they do that?"

"Janis videoed tonight's proceedings. I'll text you a copy. You can show your roster of participants exactly what'll happen if they don't. You can't be held to account for suggesting they give themselves up. You're not arresting them."

"They'll point a finger right at me, claiming I threatened them."

"With what—a boogie man coming for them at night? A video? You don't think Parseeman will jump for joy when they show up and beg to be arrested? Meanwhile, you, with no gun or badge, used your free time productively, aiding law enforcement in a civil way as you've perfect a right to."

"You really are unbalanced."

"Why litigate trivia now?"

"Too late for that anyway."

"Getting too late for the cops too, if you don't hurry and get those kids into your station wagon. You know how to get to the Dapper O'Neill, right?"

"How could I forget?"

Dominic tapped Null gently on the shoulder from behind, and when he turned his head, offered him the phone back. Null took it, pocketed it. Before he could say anything, Janis let loose of the boy and he started screaming again. Null knelt down to him and said, "Listen, kid. You don't know the situation and it's too complicated to explain to you right now, but if you don't keep quiet and do just what these two ladies tell you to do, I'm going to have to take drastic measures."

"Like what?" Robbie sneered, as if mimicking a gangster.

"Like knocking you the fuck out."

"Oh," the boy said quietly, credulity easing his facial expression down to blank.

Boyd convinced the other children to grab whatever they needed from upstairs and meet her in the foyer. She accompanied them. Robbie stood quietly by Janis, who led him into the foyer. For lack of anything more comforting, he had chosen in the precise moment of crisis and fear to bond with her. She was a woman who hadn't yet tried to hurt him. A good sign. He was docile, and also tired, as they walked together to the point of rendezvous in the foyer by the stairs.

"Dominic, did you secure all the items on the shopping list I gave you like I asked?"

"Done deal, dawg. What y'all want me to do next?"

"When the kids, the women, and I are clear of this house, I want you to finish things up for me."

"What y'all mean?"

"You don't see it?"

"Yeah, homes. I see it."

"Torch the place."

Not much time had passed before two station wagons pulled slowly away from the curb down a quiet, residential street in Belmont, followed by an outsized, twenty-year old gold-flake Lincoln, a beautiful, impressively huge, orange bloom of fire gracing the street with its soft glow barely making the smallest sound.

TWENTY-SEVEN

"Tell me that you did it."

"Let me the fuck go!"

"You're a lucky guy, George as I fully intend to let you go. Usually people in your current situation with me don't get let go. What they do get, you don't need to know about right now."

Goodnature was sitting in an old, half-splintered wooden chair, zip tied securely in place. The room he was in was huge, empty and shadowed by a single dangling lightbulb that swung. It smelled dry and musty. A warehouse of some kind—perhaps an abandoned factory. It was industrial, he figured, and in his mouth was the curdling, desiccating taste of sawdust. His now soiled clothes and his body were both saturated with sweat so that, despite being tied up, he still could slide in his seat somewhat.

"Lucky you," added Null.

"Where am I?"

"You're in Limbo. A place that doesn't exist, according to the Vatican. You're in a unique state of double nowhere, a place of non-existence that itself no longer exists. A perfect place to find yourself no longer existing as well. The end of reality."

"You're not going to kill me."

"You're absolutely right, George. I'm not. I have no intention of killing you."

"That bitch cop wants to kill me."

"That's true. But don't worry, she's not going to kill you either. Kay Boyd has many fine virtues, but cold-blooded murder isn't one of them. She tried it once, I think, but it didn't go so well."

"Chickened out, huh?" asked Goodnature, trying in vain to preserve a brave face.

"Oh, no. She did it alright. Splattered the guy's brains all over the wall behind him. She just feels bad enough about it to lose considerable sleep over it. Maybe try to drink away the nagging memory of it when she shouldn't. Now, take me: I'm not like that at all. I could put two in your heart, two in your head, then go somewhere and have dinner without a second thought. Easy-peasy."

"But you said you're not going to do that."

"And mostly I don't lie. Quite right to call me on that. But as I said, I have no intention of killing you."

"That's good, right?"

"It might seem the right thing to say yes, but it really depends on how you look at it."

"How else can you look at it?"

"Oh, there's more ways than one, but here you are tied up somewhere you don't know after having been drugged with enough Thiopental to knock out a moose, then being hammered on by some unsympathetic goon like me. It's understandable that you can't see it—amazing you can focus on anything at all, really, after I already just slugged you a couple of times so hard you can't even remember."

With that, Goodnature started feeling the pain in his jaw that had been waiting for him to connect with it all along. The reminder from Null made him spit blood angrily at the dusty floor.

"I guess it doesn't really matter how you see it, George, because this really ends for you only one way."

"Yeah, motherfucker? And what way's that?"

"You're going to beg me to kill you, and I won't do it."

Then Null reared back and punched Goodnature straight in the face for good measure.

"Let's get back to basics, here, shall we? Now, tell me that you did it."

Goodnature just sat there, breathing angrily.

Null smacked him again with a jab to the jaw, but this time not too hard. He needed Goodnature conscious and his mouth still capable of speech. Goodnature laughed a laugh that was much closer to a sob. "I don't know what the fuck you're talking about!"

"The Thiopental left you a bit groggy, perhaps desensitized to pain. I'll have to put a little more into it, I think."

"You don't have to do that. I'll tell you anything you want to know. Anything. Ask away."

"Just don't tell me what you think I want to hear. Be honest. Your life doesn't depend on it, true, but your sanity might."

"I need to piss."

"Do it in the chair. I don't mind."

"What if I have to do other things?"

"Do them in your pants."

"You think I fucked a kid—okay, so I did. Big deal. I fucked a lot of kids. Which one do you want me to conjure up for you?"

"You tell me."

Null nonchalantly walloped Goodnature in the midsection, snapping his head forward, causing him to heave and gag both at once, pathetically. Miraculously, he managed not to vomit, but only drooled copiously.

"I think I went a tad too far on that one, George. Oh, well, maybe while you're busy recovering, you can start formulating an answer for me."

Null made a move toward him, which inspired Goodnature to bounce in his seat and force himself to speak in a stertorous, halting way. "Th-the—the! Cop! The cop—the one with that kid. The bitch who was with you when you torched my f-f-fucking house!" Goodnature again spat blood.

Null clapped. "Grade A, George Goodnature, just grade A. Why didn't you say so in the first place?"

"I didn't because I was unconscious and when I woke up you were beating on me, for fuck's sake!"

"That's a very good reason. I can't argue with your logic there. Tell me more. Tell me in detail. Spare nothing. Don't be shy."

"I'm n-n-not f-fucking shy!"

"I didn't think you were. Please continue."

"What more do you need to know?"

"All of it."

"Then what? You kill me?"

"No, George, as I said before, I'm not going to kill you. Even when you beg me to. And I guarantee you that you will. Now, continue, please."

"Sure. Okay. The kid—he was pretty banged up by the time he got to me."

"He had a name."

"Ya. They all have names."

"His was Rudy. Rudy Boyd."

"Rudy, okay, whatever. Anyway, Rudy was all played out when they gave him to me."

"Tell me who they are."

"You know. Everybody knows—Hebe Group. They did it to protect the business."

"The business that ran your cozy little house in Belmont."

"That's right. The business. So, since I'm cooperating, maybe you can see your way to getting me out of these bonds? My hands and feet are losing circulation already."

"That's a shame. We'll see how far that goes. Back to the point. Played out from what, pray tell. By *whom?*"

"You know what they did. They whored him out. They made him a dark web Internet superstar—movies galore. The poor kid was damaged, drained, and out of it by the time he came to me. Docile, beaten."

Null stared and didn't blink. He let the silence fill in the blanks.

"You felt sorry for him, you're saying?" he said softly.

"How could I not? Poor little kid." Goodnature grinned

sheepishly.

"Who gave him to you?"

"You know who."

"Say it."

"Legere. Legere gave me the kid, okay?"

"With instructions. He gave you instructions, didn't he? Tell me what they were."

"You know what they were."

"I think if I went at you just a little bit more, it might defeat the whole purpose of this interview, because you'd probably be incapable of further speech. That wouldn't help either of us. So talk as if your life depended on it, which it doesn't, of course, but certainly your continued health and well-being does. Count on that."

"Fine. So, it has to do with me."

"I know that. Tell me how it has to do with you."

"I'm a little embarrassed."

"There's a time and place for that, and this isn't it. Spill it." The words were impatient, the tone was dull if not suggestive.

"It's like this…" And Goodnature trailed off, chuckling to himself as if at a private joke.

"If I have to start yanking out your teeth, I guarantee you won't be laughing."

"So here's the deal."

"I have patience, but I don't see why I need to waste any of it on you."

"Okay! I like to do it, really. I do. And that's the truth. It's a treat. I don't get much opportunity for it, being what it is. Legere knew all about that, though conniving fuck that he is. He had the four-one-one on me long before we ever met. I was his target as much as you, no matter what you think. Maybe more. It's a sickness, you know. I can't help it. But once you do it, once you know you can't ever really go back, well then, you are there. You can't undo what it does to you. You can't take it back and be the same ever—how it takes you, owns you, shapes you."

"How what takes you? What exactly did you do? Tell me. It's necessary—so that I know. So that we understand each other."

"You don't understand shit."

Null slapped his face to get his attention, leaving a welt, yet not too hard. It worked. George's eyes opened wide at attention, and they burned.

"You need to know. Really? Okay. Well, here it is, fucker. I like to feel them die when I climax. I kill them at my orgasm, break their scrawny little necks with my two hands. Their death is my life. It's fantastic! It's what I crave, so perfect, so rare and decadent. It's the best, like it or not. Legere wanted to end your bitch cop's efforts at busting Hebe Group, as if she really could do that anyway. Put her totally out of commission without killing her. So, he chose the next best thing. How do you go after a mother, right? He gave me her kid as a reward, a present, meant to send her reeling 'round the bend. It worked. She wound up in the spooky house. Probably where she belonged in the first place."

"And you think she was the crazy one."

"Sure! Thinking she could ever stop them. You can't stop human desire. You can't stop need, no matter how sick or wrong stupid morals say that need is. It's undeniable, like god. You're fighting freaking wind and smoke. Punching out at the fucking holy spirit, for Christ's sake! "

They glared at each other for a moment. An odd, tenuous connection.

Then Goodnature smirked and drawled, "Are we good? Are you letting me go, now, or what?"

"Sure. I'll let you go. And I'm also going to hold onto you until you beg me to kill you. We're not there yet, but we're definitely on our way. I have some loose ends to tie up first. Then I'll focus on you."

"Don't do me any favors."

"Don't worry. I won't."

"Loose ends. You're really a stupid fuck. You'll never wipe out kiddie porn, here or anywhere else. It's gonna be around forever, getting bigger all the time. You think poor children will ever cease being a commodity for trade on this earth? You actually believe that? Because that's the way it's been since the first

Cro Magnon man paid for sex with a fish. You admit you're mentally ill, right? Isn't that what they say? Well, that's pretty much a sure sign of it. Legere will finish you off. And if he don't, they've always got the money to find somebody else happy to do the job. Strangle your whacky fucking mouth with your own entrails, you try ending their guaranteed money machine. You got no clue who you're dealing with."

"Maybe, but right now I've got Hebe cash poor and desperate, and the bitch cop you proudly cite is saner than the both of us put together and she's out for blood. Your blood, in fact. And I have to tell you, she's not going to lay a finger on you, but when she sees what's in store for you, believe me, she'll be satisfied. After what you did to Rudy."

"All this drama over one little piece of chicken? Are you fucking *serious?* Jesus!"

"That's right. One life. One little, insignificant life is going to make sure you all die in agony."

"So what I did to the kid you're going to do to all of us?"

"No, not by a longshot. You've all fucked yourselves to death anyway, just like you did to Rudy—the difference is that, for him, that was it. The end. In your case, however, you don't really know that it's the end, and I'm coming to make sure you know it and collect what you owe every single child touched by you in torture and pain."

"Melodramatic, doncha think?"

"Only if you feel it. And you will."

"I suppose nobody's tried buying you off yet, have they?"

"Why would they? What would I need money for?"

"Because that's why anyone does anything, dipshit."

"Well, not me. Haven't you heard?"

"No. I haven't. Heard what?"

"I'm the meth king of Boston."

Null moved suddenly close, and he flinched, cut him loose in a few jagged gestures with a bright orange box cutter and left him sitting there in the splintered wooden chair, uncertain, as he limped out the grated security door like a battered machine into the gray and compromised cold light of day.

TWENTY-EIGHT

"Pretty cute, Legere, I'll give you that."

"Praise from Caesar," Legere said in a guffaw. "You're definitely the cutest of all."

Null stood in front of Legere, his Heckler & Koch aimed at his forehead. Legere was seated in an ancient swivel chair that rolled on casters next to a ruined wreck of a roll-top desk. He wore an overcoat, his gray hair slicked back and his jowly, florid face dimpled with amusement. He had the classic Magnum three-fifty-seven aimed straight at Null's heart. His size thirteen shoes were resting on a milk crate used as a stool, legs crossed at the ankle.

They were on the fifth floor of a dilapidated commercial building on A Street in South Boston. Noises were coming up from the stairwell on the other side of the door but had to be ignored for the moment. The room they occupied was a bombed-out shell hardly resembling an office at all.

"If you could turn my head, Legere, I think it'd pull a three sixty."

"You figure how this plays yet, genius?"

"Mostly, I think. Firstly, though, I think you might want to aim your pistol more toward my head. I'm wearing a flak jacket just as you are. I have a nice clear shot at the frontal lobe of your brain."

"Think you can fire before me? Or do we both pop each other off at the same time? This'd make a nice scene in a movie, don't you think?"

"I'm pretty sure John Woo covered this in a more exaggerated way in one of his movies. This is pretty tame compared with that."

"I'll take your word for it. Although what's added here in the low budget edition is that death is very much in play. Your death, fuckstick."

"Then I have you at a disadvantage, because death is a well-established ally of mine."

"Maybe, or maybe you've just been lucky and right here and now, your luck has run out." Legere chuckled, with an amused facial expression analogous to that of an alligator.

"We all have luck, Legere, you included. It's one of the great features of the seemingly endless chaos we're all subject to."

"Yeah, you're right about that. That's something you and me have in common. We superimpose order on that chaos."

"That's right, Legere, that we do. And the order we impose is death."

"What's the play, Null? It's your call."

"Is it? This little set-up of yours in an abandoned office building was your call, not mine."

"That's right. In the here and now, I'm the shot caller, and you're not."

"I yield to your logic. What's next?"

"Well, we either shoot each other or talk each other to death."

"So far the latter prevails. I think it bothers you much more than me, though."

"Maybe. I have a hunch you're pretty human, though. You're one of those tough guys really ain't more than a little scared bitch projecting a façade. You wanna take your shot now? I'm pretty old, you know. I might miss."

"I bet not. My headshot will come first, but yours won't be too far behind."

"Play this out the old-fashioned way? No guns?"

"What about knives?"

"I don't have any. You?"

"I got a machete."

"Leave it on the desk?"

"Sure. We both strip down to bare chests and pants in front of each other."

"What if I have a small knife in my pants pocket? That'd end it all fast."

"Don't worry, Legere. I can handle it."

"Pony up, Null."

Legere stood, tossed off his coat, removed his shirt, timing it to coincide with Null's shucking off his topcoat. Both removed their coats and shirts, still holding their handguns. Null laid the Bushmaster, the machete, and the Browning on the desk.

"You're a prepared little fucker, ain't you?"

"Yeah. I was a boy scout once."

"Not anymore."

"Put the pistols down on the desk on a three count?"

"Nerves will tell what happens at three."

"I think you want a hands-on experience, Legere, but I'll be just as ready at three as you."

"Do it then."

Both slammed their pistols down on the desk at the same instant with a sharp report, then they threw down on each other in a soundless collision. They suddenly broke apart for a moment, one of them certainly wounded, but it was difficult to see who actually drew first blood.

"This is too easy," said Legere heaving.

"We're both a mess, Legere. Neither one of us should ever be seen in public without a shirt."

"I've got the height advantage. I've got more muscle than you and I outweigh you. After I beat you unconscious, I'm gonna have what's left of Hebe Group use you as a toilet and an ashtray until you fucking die, you obnoxious little twerp!" Sweat dropped from his torso, neck and face like rain.

"I'm still standing."

The big man charged Null, but he bent down and used Legere's own weight as leverage to toss him over his back. Then he kicked Legere sharply in the face to get things going. Legere grabbed his leg and twisted until Null fell. Legere missed kicking him—Null dodged it too fast. Legere was slow and Null was not. Finally, Null decided to hit him head on and take whatever blows were coming. Legere obliged him enough so anyone else would have folded down to the filthy, ruined linoleum floor. But not Null.

When Null hugged him close under the rain of blows, he felt a hard metal shape in Legere's pocket. He took note of this and persisted.

"What are you, a fucking punching bag?"

"Not exactly."

In minutes, Null had Legere bloodied and panting on the floor, barely able to sit up. Null went for the Heckler on the desk. Legere shot him in the right shoulder. Null seemed not to notice as the blood ran down his side. He stood there with a quizzical look on his face, sizing Legere up.

"Jesus fuck, you stupid zombie. Why don't you just die!"

Null stood looking at him, unaffected with the Heckler in his hand, but lowered slowly by his side.

"Derringer twenty-two, isn't it? Must be an antique. Handy little thing, though."

"It does the job. Think you can make the kill shot before I put next round in your brain."

"Shall we dance?"

Legere out of nowhere and apropos of nothing started to laugh uproariously.

"What's so funny?"

"*You* are, dumbshit zombie fuck!"

"Enlighten me."

"Oh, surely. Do you really think I expected you to come here alone?"

"I kinda didn't."

"So what do you think I did, hotshot?"

"Deployed some torpedoes to whack me out."

"Not just some. Pick a high number."

"They can't be very good. I fucked up Hebe's cashflow

nicely. So, you must have bought volume on the cheap. And you wouldn't shell out for it yourself. You're not the generous type."

"Very fucking good. Now, I'll raise you. You got three gunhands with you. One lesbian cop in disgrace, one disposable contract hitter with a sensitive stomach, and one stupid nigger. That right?"

"No, it isn't. She's not a lesbian. Janis is hardly what you'd call disposable and we don't call blacks niggers."

"Well, nice to see you're a politically correct psychopath."

"We each have our virtues."

"Here's your choice: flap your gums here with me or shoot it out with me and hope you get down there in time to keep your pals from getting blipped off. And I got another round here just for you." Legere rubbed his damaged face with his free hand and revealed a sickly, bloodied smile. "Oh, that's right. You like to torture them to death, rather than make the quick hit. But time is ticking, isn't it? Better blow a hole in me now and be done with it, because I'm betting from those faint popping sounds I'm hearing on the opposite side of that door that your friends are in a bit of a mess."

Legere laughed. Feeling emboldened, he tried to raise himself up off the colorless, distressed linoleum, but Null kicked him back down with ruthless precision, cooled him out.

The bullet wound wasn't slowing him up in the least.

Null hung the machete back around his neck, threw on his coat and grabbed the Magnum, the Browning and the Bushmaster, quickly checking that the clip was secure.

"You're right, Legere, you're not gonna die fast. Not at all. You'll see what I have in store for you after I take care of a few things."

"I'll be pissing on your grave first," said Legere, spitting little flecks of blood then descending into a coughing jag.

Null slammed the door behind him, not hearing Legere's final comment.

"They're on every floor, you stupid fuck!"

———

242

And so they were.

Null must have sensed it, even though he didn't hear Legere say it. When he left the office into the broken lobby of the fifth floor by the condemned elevator bank, he went out blasting, firing bursts from the Bushmaster in his descent. The gunsels came hard and heavy, firing semi-automatic rounds. Null took a few in the flak jacket, but with measured progress and even breathing, he began literally killing his way down to the first floor. He shouldn't have made it. The rounds fired were too many, diverse and wild.

It was like a funhouse, minus the fun.

Yet, with the Heckler in one hand and the Bushmaster in the other, he fired semi-automatic bursts all the slow and murderous way down. When the Heckler was spent, he still had the presence of mind to use Legere's Magnum, and when the Bushmaster was done, he managed to shoulder it under his coat and broke out the Browning, taking two more rounds in the flak jacket for his trouble that should have had him collapsing on the steps or at the landing, barely able to breathe.

It didn't.

He wheezed a bit but kept right on going, gunsel bodies falling or retreating in his wake.

Janis stopped him at the second floor, her face full of blood, yet grinning.

"Where's Kay and Dominic?"

"They were behind you, coming down from the roof."

"Really."

"What—you think you could've gotten down here in one piece by yourself? Take all those fuckers out all by your lonesome?"

Null's breathing was shallow, but his voice stayed even.

"No. It's not the movies."

"Jesus Christ, this isn't even cable!"

"Why the bloody face?"

"I think a round may have grazed my scalp. Head wounds bleed like a bitch, you know."

"I've heard that somewhere."

"It's in some handbook somebody wrote."

"I never read it."

"Me neither. Some people are just naturals, I guess."

"We're clear on the first floor?"

"Yeah. Those assholes took no pride in their work at all. They just booked when things got heavy."

"And the ones who didn't?"

"Gonzo. You can have Dominic take their picture with your phone while you're at it."

"He can use his own phone this time."

"I can hear them sort of, up there. I think this little foray might have given me tinnitus."

"You took them out with the Pico?"

"No, I seemed to do okay with one of Kay's rogue police weapons, a Ruger SR9 nine-millimeter. Light and fast, easy on the reload. Who knew she was a gun nut?"

"She digs the nickel-plated Sig-Sauer." Null paused, cocked his head. "Those voices upstairs are them?"

"Who else? Why, did you leave anyone standing?"

"I tried not to."

"I tend to think you managed. How many rounds did you take in that flak jacket? And you took a round in the shoulder, for Christ's sake. Why the hell are *you* still standing?"

"Practice," said Null, turning his back on Janis and making the slow, beleaguered trudge upstairs with thudding footfalls.

"What about Legere?"

"Don't worry, he's not standing. He's got one more slug left in his pocket Derringer, though. Be sure he'll use it."

"Yeah. Even a pea shooter with a twenty-two round in it can still do some damage. I'll watch it."

The door to the office on the fifth-floor landing had to be kicked in. It had locked automatically behind Null when he slammed it shut—Legere's way of making sure there would be no retreat from the surge of hired gunsels ready to take him out all the way down to the bottom.

Dominic kicked the door in after a few loud, abortive tries. It exploded open on the last and Legere fired off his final Derringer round on reflex, figuring to hit the first person in, presumably Null. He missed. Dominic was first in and he was no small target. Everyone had guns up and ready.

No one fired a shot, waiting for Null.

"Why are you still alive?" said Legere, tossing the empty Derringer to the side.

"Waste of a round, Legere, not that it would have helped you," Null stated flatly.

"It would've helped me if it penetrated your fucking brain."

"It would've helped you if you had aimed it better."

"Don't be too hard on him, Null, headshots aren't easy. Takes skill and control to get it right, especially when you're down to your last round."

"Hey, girlie, I'm a dead shot."

"Well, Mack, you're half right," Janis rejoined.

"So kill me already. Get it done and stop flapping your gums."

"I never figured you'd beg for it, Legere."

"Anything to not have to listen to you fucking jabronies yap."

"How does this go down, Null, since you're shot caller? Isn't that what they call you on the street? How much disgusting mayhem do I have to gape at?"

"None, actually. You don't have to stay, Kay. You can go."

"I want to know how this plays out."

"I think you have an idea about that."

"Yeah, I guess I do."

"I could take him out with a twenty-two from the Pico. I won't need a nine mil for this—what did he say? Jabroni."

"What do you think, Dominic?"

"I think y'all fifty-one-fifty. I don't know why I ain't killed yet either."

"You handled the Smith & Wesson just fine," Boyd countered.

"And I'm helpin' fuckin' five-o on top of shit!"

"Not really. I'm on suspension. I'm just another girl."

"I ain't never see no bitch crazy like you, and I seen some

bitches." Dominic was still trying to catch his breath; his clothes were soaked through with sweat and his face was pale. He was struggling to adjust to the perverse scene of the bodies, blood, fear and now a garbage strewn office with a huge old guy lolling on the floor with his shirt off.

"Well, Dominic, here we are at last, your moment has arrived."

"What you mean?"

Legere pushed himself up off the debased linoleum floor, shirtless and trembling slightly.

"You pukes had your day. Now, I'm gonna scram, so get the fuck out of my way."

"I could knock you back down again with a feather," said Null.

"Better be a two-ton feather, pally."

"No, just a young man who has a bone to pick with you."

"Get out of my way."

"Keep still, Legere. You aren't going anywhere."

"This fucker's BB filler!"

"You couldn't be more right, Dominic. You wanted to know who killed Edgar and Howard? Well, there he is. Meet Emmanuel Legere, Hebe Group chief torpedo. He did it."

Calm descended upon Dominic's face. He squared his shoulders and got his breathing under control.

"This punk nigger gonna stop me?"

"I think so, Legere. I won't lay a finger on you and neither will the women. Your fight's with Dominic. Think you can handle it, Dominic?"

"Yeah, dog. I'm your vampire. Here. I don't need no gat for this fool."

Null took the Smith & Wesson forty-five semi-automatic, nodded, and Dominic moved forward.

"No point to this. Null. You win. I'm gone. As of now, I'm history with Hebe Group, and they're pretty much history as it stands, thanks to you. I'm leaving Boston. You won't hear from me again."

"Why didn't you say so earlier? Oh, well, I'm satisfied, thank you very much."

The blood spot at the shoulder of Null's topcoat was increasing in size, though he ignored it. No one else did.

Legere grabbed his shirt off the roll-top desk and put it on, looking sallow, and bedraggled in the inadequate yellow light of the single bulb hanging from the ceiling. All shadows were immense. His face was bloodied and swollen, and his nose was like a bulbous tomato in the center of his face. "Can I take back the Magnum?"

"Sorry, Legere. Spoils of war."

"Get out of my way then."

"I don't think so," Boyd seethed.

"I don't beat on women."

"You won't have to," added Null.

"What the fuck is that supposed to mean?"

"Well, Legere, I have no quarrel with you. You're no child molester, you're just an enabling exploiter."

"Yeah, well, you usually murder those too, otherwise what you've done to Hebe would make no sense."

"That's true. But I have no intention of laying a finger on you."

"Then move aside, zombie fuck!"

"No. I won't. You see, even though I don't have a problem with you, my friend Dominic here does. It seems you murdered his brother when you blew up the Gangsta Boyz clubhouse. Dominic has a bone to pick with you, don't you, Dominic?"

"Real talk, homes!"

Dominic was breathing hard through his nostrils. His blood was up.

"Go through Dominic, if you can, and you're home free."

"Fuck that. This chomo's mine!"

"I don't fuck the kiddies."

"Might as well, cuz I'm gonna fuck you up anyway."

"You women don't have to stay for this, you know. You know where it's going."

"We're getting used to it," Janis sighed.

"I want to see it. You know, I've been feeling better since we started. It's not rational or fair. But I do. I'll watch this play out. Because I need to know they're not getting away with it. I have to see it."

"I promise you that you will, Kay."

She could hardly hear him.

Before Boyd could finish her last sentence, Dominic stepped forward, grabbed Legere into a bear hug and lifted him a foot off the floor, squeezing hard, not seeming to feel any of the punches leveled at his ribs. Legere got a few punches in at Dominic's face and it looked like they rattled him.

But they didn't.

Legere was already wounded from the struggle with Null, so it wasn't long before an unschooled roundhouse right to the chin put Legere down on his knees. That was when Dominic rallied and really started to go to work on Legere. He had seen what Null had done to Hal Champerty and decided to duplicate it on Legere, who by then had lost consciousness, which didn't slow Dominic up one bit.

Before he lost consciousness, Legere managed to gurgle like shouting an epithet through a fountain, "I didn't do it!"

Hammer punching Legere in the face until his voice box could only produce a wet slosh, Dominic answered him, with an inflection more of pity than anger. "I know, dawg. Edgar and Howard didn't do it neither."

TWENTY-NINE

The twelve playhouses remaining went fast, and Mrs. Coelacanth was somewhat less than pleased about it. She had to dicker and dodge, connive and overpromise, delivering care and housing to the flood of squalling, disturbed, damaged and psychically horrified children. Dealing with Department of Youth Services in Concord, New Hampshire for two houses full of underage children was a week of maniacal sweat-work making a triangle of her, DYS and the extremely reluctant Derry police. Often foster care was the best answer, although it was often a bad answer.

The same proved true of Boston.

And each time she had to deal with Null, he reminded her that his cure for reneging on a deal with him was casual homicide, and she had no doubt that he could do it. Or would do it. He was a worry and whenever the anonymous caller ID popped up on her cell phone screen, she would stiffen up with fright and unease.

Her hands trembled, fumbling the phone.

Null and Janis took six of the potentially hardest playhouses to hit and left the softest ones for Boyd, who would kindly convince their staff that it would be better to turn themselves in to Boston PD than face a duo of psychopaths who would without hesitation torture them to death (or in Janis' case, outright slaughter them, something Null grudgingly made peace with). If that failed, then Detective Third Grade Byron Wurdalaka would make the collar. After they saw the cell phone videos of Null deconstructing humans, the same video streaming all over the dark web world of kiddie porn and not just on the servers that Brother Ray enslaved, they were quick to flip.

Knowing that Null would come.

Knowing that Null was inevitable.

Null was becoming an umbral legend of the street—something unseen you never wanted to see. A name you didn't want to hear spoken in connection to anyone you knew, anything you remotely cared about, anything that might come back to you. It was becoming bad luck to even mention the existence of what had once been easy to call "that zombie fuck Null." Whatever humor had been once attached to the name had given way to literal terror. You could talk about the Gangsta Boyz as the reigning meth operators in Boston, make jokes about how they put the meth in Methuen. It was becoming clear, though, that to even refer to the shot caller of that gang might actually wind up getting you tortured and killed without ever knowing why.

He was insane and just did things like that.

The man with the name you don't say.

If videos and posts about something as heinous and evanescent in specific knowledge as the Tall Man, Slenderman or The King in Yellow could go viral, then that's what happened to the grotesque, gore-soaked and vengeful exploits of Joseph Xavier Null.

The day when Mrs. Coelacanth finished with the kids, was the same day she took unscheduled leave and seriously contemplated her retirement.

Any cell phone tone from then on triggered dire palpitations.

Any tone at all.

And Null wasn't done.

No, there was still work to do.

There were going to be runners.

They never had any sense that they would be running straight into Null. A decisive demurral was the best bet. Why would that guy care? They were just equity partners, investors in an operation that had gone from being an outpouring of staggering profits to rudderless dysfunction and then at last to being completely belly up.

A dead loss for everyone.

Thoughts of the children never entered their minds, even once.

To the equity partners, the children were simply the wrecked and damaged inventory of a business that now had no further use for them, unable to monetize even their basic resale value.

The problem simply stated was this: Null actually remembered the children. The late Legere had affirmed that Null was seeking retribution and that he was a stone psychopath. If that were true, then there would be no reasoning with him, no buying him off, no reliance on common sense to give them the protected exemption they were used to.

The remaining equity partners realized, after viewing the gruesomely visceral stream of Hal Champerty's confession, without collusion or even an exchange of emails, social media postings or DMs, that it was time to be anywhere but Boston. Massachusetts. The east coast. America. They were all on Null's list—which was, as the streaming video captures confirmed—one of the worst places to be anywhere on this earth.

However, like most people who are encouraged to evacuate a place by an indisputable set of facts, they procrastinated. They felt somehow that they had a window of time.

They didn't know Null had slammed the window shut.

Beatrice Bronfein was looking to park some of her trust fund assets into an REIT and was being shown a commercial property, a parking garage in Brighton, when for no apparent reason the broker who was enthusiastically trying to sell it to her just ran off. She turned her head to locate him but found Null instead.

"You're smaller than I thought," she said, mustering false bravery.

"The hype makes me look that way. I'm actually of average height."

"How much do I gotta pay you to get rid of you?"

"Oh, I don't want your money."

"Think if I scream loud enough, someone will come?"

"Why not try that? You'll be screaming soon anyway."

"You want me to scream?"

"I do. As much as I want anything."

They stared at each other for a long, silent moment.

In the distance was were the echoes of the cars.

Beatrice—looking like some oddly dowdy, overaged millennial in yoga pants, hoodie and watch cap—dropped her handbag and started screaming. She put everything she had into it, her body quaking with the force of it.

Null made sure she kept screaming until he crushed her voice box at the end.

———

Hortense Gallimaufry had just finished shopping at Whole Foods, hefting two full grocery bags as she waddled out to her Saab in the crowded parking lot.

She felt a gentle tapping on her shoulder from behind and a firm hand grabbing at the handle of one of the paper shopping bags.

"I'll help you with that," said Null.

Hortense recognized him and her heart sank, yet she continued grasping the shopping bag full of groceries. "Thanks. My car is right over there."

"Let's go then."

She opened her hand and let him take the bag.

They walked slowly together to where the Saab was parked, and for all the world, looked like friends, gabbing cheerfully.

The world is seldom the way we see it.

Hortense looked like a distressed elementary school teacher, homely, coke-bottle glasses, beige & olive drab clothing, a cardigan, an ill-fitting blouse and skirt. Her face was puffy yet unlined. Null carried the aspect of a dingy, homeless man.

"Really, you're going to kill me right here, in broad daylight? In a Whole Foods Parking Lot?" She tried her best to seem amused. She wasn't.

"Well, that was the plan," said Null, as he loaded her bag of groceries into the back of the Saab after Hortense opened the hatch.

"You must be crazy. There's too many people around. They'll stop you. Now that I know what you're going to do, when I leave here, I'll disappear before you can try it again." She laughed a strained, nervous laugh. "You didn't really think this through at all, did you?"

"I admit I was a little fuzzy on the details."

"I don't see how you managed to fuck Hebe Group up beyond all repair. Just look at you. You're a joke. But everyone's so shit scared of you they won't even say your name. How does that work?"

"My reputation precedes me."

Null took the other bag from Hortense, which she was gripping so tightly that her fingers were turning red and the knuckles of each finger were white and loaded it in as well. She let go of it easily. Hortense was sweating and her breathing was heavy, labored. The sun beat down on her with unusual heat and when the breeze blew, she felt annoying pinpricks on her skin where her sweat had gathered.

"I'm pretty good with improvisation, though. Would you like to see?"

"No thanks. I need to go anyway."

"Yes, Hortense, quite right. You really do need to go," he said pleasantly.

Null opened the driver's side door for her and as she was climbing in, he pushed her down suddenly in a rapid, cruel movement, pulled an old-fashioned, spring-loaded switchblade from his coat pocket and went to work on her.

Null was right.

No one stopped him.

Her hopeless screaming was simply swallowed up by the casual, bustling activity of the Whole Foods parking lot in the warm afternoon.

———

Mike Withers was just leaving the Downtown CrossFit gym, covered with a light coating of perspiration still dressed in his fatigue sweats and striding with purpose and swagger toward the gym exit. He looked like a hawk, with his close-cropped head craned forward and his aquiline nose pointing the way like an arrow. Null stopped him in his tracks.

"Sorry, man, I'm not carrying any cash on me. Just finished my workout. I'll get you next time, okay, buddy?"

"No need to worry. I don't want any money."

"Get out of my way then."

"No, I don't think so."

"I'll make you, then."

"Do you really want to do this here? In the lobby of your gym? If so, it suits me."

"Dude, you're a little guy. I'll take you apart."

"It might seem that way, but it won't work that way. Maybe you don't recognize me. Take a look and think for a minute."

Mike squinted to cut down on the glare from sunlight streaming in through the picture windows of the lobby of the gym. The guy was a shapeless, overdressed hulk, medium height, scarred face in the shadows of his hat. Then it slowly occurred to him what he was meant to see. The man looked confusingly different in bright daylight—the grime, shabbiness and dark shapelessness of his attire; his middling height; the ridiculous porkpie hat that shadowed a face distorted by scars, recent swellings and contusions. Mike's heart was seized with fear even as he swallowed back on it.

A reflex occurred like a spasm—a small hiccup—causing Mike to take a half-step backward.

He felt a chill consume him.

"Holy shit! You're him!" he shouted, not caring who heard him, and although they did hear him clearly, onlooking passersby simply quickened their pace to get out the door that much sooner. Mike started reaching frantically for something in the gym bag that was slung over his right shoulder.

"By the time you pull it, Mike, I'll have emptied a full clip into you. I already know where my iron is. Don't bother trying to find yours."

Mike let his arms go limp by his sides.

"That's better."

"Yeah, you're armed. I can see that. You're always armed. So the fuck what? You want to go and hold court with me right here and right now?"

"Your choice, Mike. We can either do it here or you and I can go for a ride in that SUV of yours. It's a fancy one, right? What is it?"

"It's a Land Rover."

"A bit too much car for Boston and all its cow paths and rotaries, isn't it?"

"It's handy in the winter."

"Take me for a ride."

"I thought that's what you were doing to me."

"It's all in how you look at it."

"Fine. Follow me."

"Oh, I know where you're parked, Mike. I'll be right alongside of you. And I'll take that bag. You're probably tired after your strenuous workout."

Mike half-shoved the bag at him, hoping it would throw Null off balance and he could make a run for it. It didn't. Null prodded him hard in the side with the barrel of the Browning Hi Power through his coat.

"What is it that you do in this gym again? What kind of workout?"

"Crossfit," mumbled Mike. "You know, like the name of the gym?"

"They say that's rough on the joints."

"At this point, does that even really matter?"

"No, not at all," Null replied, prodding him toward the door.

The cheerful young brunette receptionist in her tight, sparkling white Downtown CrossFit tee shirt at the check-in counter through the window that separated the lobby from the gym spied them both. She waved goodbye to Mike with a great, toothy smile. Null waved back at her, without returning her smile.

"Why are you laughing, Mike?"

"Jesus, don't you have a sense of humor?"

"No, Mike," Null said as they walked together toward the parking lot in the crispness and golden light of the late afternoon. "I don't. But I'm glad you have one."

"Why?"

"So you can fully appreciate the irony of the next few minutes."

THIRTY

"We have time, so don't stress, Marty," said Steve Privilegiata, dragging an American Tourister Bedford suitcase down mauve carpeted steps to the light-filled, airy den of his split-level house in Wollaston. His wife, Martha, was in the upstairs bedroom packing, frantic. Her voice was a keening wail when she responded, stuffing clothes in another American Tourister bag.

"How can you say we have time? Didn't you see the streams? The motherfucking *streams!*"

"He only got Hal. Not the rest of the partners, and you know what he was doing down at the twink hotel. Don't worry. We have plenty of time to bail."

"You're underestimating the guy who destroyed our business, our income, and put us in the hole. He's killed everybody involved—why not us?"

"The other partners aren't showing up on the dead-face page yet or in the streaming emails, you know."

"Legere did! Your fucking so-called "Expert" did! We'd better get the fuck out of here before we do too!"

"I don't think this Null fuck wants us. Did you check with Hortense and Beatrice?"

"I just got voice mail."

"Do you need any help with the other bags?"

"What do you think? Of course I do; get your ass up here!"

"I will. Did you get a hold of Mike?"

"Voicemail there too. He's probably long gone by now. Where we should be!"

"You see? That asshole didn't get any of them."

Steve's chuckling was cut short.

"Oh, but actually I did," Null said calmly, standing in the center of the room, making a long shadow in the sunlight. "My IT guy Brother Ray hasn't had time to update what you call the dead-face page yet. Good name for that, by the way. He's been busy helping me run the twink hotel, helping me get it ready for conversion to new management. As for the videos, there couldn't be any of your friends, or even of Legere. It wasn't expedient at the time to capture their final moments. But even if there were any, you wouldn't be able to view them. No matter."

Panicking, but holding it together weakly, Steve said with quiet rage, "You've got a wounded shoulder, Null. That says I can take you."

Null leveled the Heckler at him, the silencer still attached. "Ten rounds a second says you can't."

"Is that actually even true?"

"Give or take."

"That suppressor will still make a loud noise. What will the neighbors think?" Steve didn't notice it himself, but Null did. He was hyperventilating very quietly.

"It's louder than I would like, that's true, but through these walls it should just sound like a prominent popping. And I won't need too many pops to deal with you. Response time won't be all that fast, regardless."

"Jesus, Steve, are you coming up here to help me or what?!" called Martha from the upstairs bedroom in exasperation.

"Tell her to come down, Steve. Nicely, if you please."

With a hesitant lack of cheer, Steve did exactly that.

Martha didn't come down.

They stood there silently for a minute, the only sound being a slight, wooden creaking.

"Oh, you two are just so sly," said Null in his flat lack of inflection. "Stay there for a moment, won't you?"

"Umm, sure."

"No, I suppose you won't."

Null fired two quick rounds from the Heckler into Steve's midsection, which caused him to topple down immediately to the plush mauve carpeting, groaning and clutching at his abdomen. Blood pumped out in a thick gout from his belly and stained the mauve rug a brighter color red than that of Null's injured right shoulder.

"That'll hold you."

Null walked out the front door where he had first entered and stepped off the flagstone walkway onto the freshly trimmed lawn to survey the perimeter of the house. He found Martha dragging herself forward like an arm baby, one of her legs visibly twisted and swollen. She made grunting sounds, moving herself forward toward the street. Null blocked her progress.

"You won't make it that way, Martha."

"I can try, can't I?" she grunted.

"No, Martha, you can't."

Null knelt down, maneuvered both his arms under her, cradled her, rose up and carried her over the threshold like a bride and deposited her onto the bloodied mauve rug near the wailing, writhing Steve.

"You're a smart one, Martha. You sized up the situation right away and made the best move you could. You had something like a twenty-five percent chance of not injuring one or both of your legs when you hit the ground. A reasonable risk, considering that right now you have a zero percent chance of getting out of this alive."

"Fuck you, sonofabitch!"

"I suppose I'd feel the same if I could feel anything."

"Please, call nine-one-one! Get me to a fucking hospital!"

"No, Steve, that would only happen if you had any expectation of recovery. Let me make it clear—you don't."

"Jesus Christ, help me!"

"No one's coming to help you, Steve. Call to your god all you want. I'm the only answer you'll get."

"You're no fucking answer!"

"Well, I'm certainly not the question. Maybe the question was what you were actually doing to make such easy profit for so long. If not me, then maybe this moment is the answer to that. I don't believe in god, or anything for that matter. But if you want to believe god answers the cries of the wounded, abused and tormented, don't you think he might have heard the cries of the children you whored out to pedophiliac perverts and scum? And if your god doesn't answer your cries for help, don't you think it might just be because he's answering their cries instead? And maybe, just maybe, I'm the actual answer to your cries as well?"

"You're the cause of the problem, you fucking lunatic!"

"No, Steve. I think you caused the problem by selling the rape of children for money six ways to Sunday. If it weren't for that, I'd be no problem at all."

"We'll just pay the fucker!" Martha cried from the rug, moving herself to the nearest chair—a Bentwood rocker—and awkwardly hoisting herself into it, nearly falling off as it tipped abruptly forward. "Steve, give him the accounts, whatever we've got. Pay him off and get rid of him!"

Steve interrupted his loud wailing to say with pinched grunting, "I'm dying!"

"No, Steve," replied Null casually. "You're just in pain—terrific pain, no doubt. But just pain. You have quite a few hours before you actually die, and I intend to make good use of them."

"Hospital! Get me to a hospital, for God's sake!"

"No, it appears God has other plans for you."

"Hey, fuckbag, address your attention over here to me. I'm the coherent one. Steve's out of his mind with pain. He can't help you."

Steve returned to inarticulate wailing and sobbing.

"It's a matter of opinion, but you have a point."

"I'm the lucid one. Poor Steve can't handle it."

"It shouldn't be that bad—he's certainly in shock by now. Endorphins should already have been dulling some of the pain."

"Steve's always been a bit too sensitive for his own good."

"I don't doubt it. But not very sensitive to the needs of children, though, was he? No, he was perfectly callous enough to make bank on kiddie porn, kiddie sex trafficking, white slavery. That was all just a matter of business. Nothing personal."

"It wasn't personal! Not ever! We never touched a single child. Not once!"

"Oh, I haven't forgotten about you, don't' worry."

"I didn't think you did."

"You felt okay about that, then?"

"Why not? Who knows what atrocities a money market fund underwrites these days? For all we know, Fidelity Investments makes recurring gains off Boko Haram and ISIS straight into some wage-slave's 401k."

Steve continued writhing noisily on the ruined carpeting.

"How's the leg?"

"Broken, I think."

"Comminuted fracture, probably, judging from the petechiae on the lower thigh. Should be painful, shock or not."

"So I guess I'm in shock too."

"I guess you are."

"It's not that bad."

"You're tougher than Steve."

"Who isn't?"

"Okay, Martha, tell me how you were all right profiting off kiddie porn, how—"

"Oh fucking save it, Null, will you? Grow up! Do you want to hear my spiel about how we're actually helping the little rug rats? Giving them a better life than they might have had otherwise? How we saved them from terrible abuse in foster care and a living death on the street? You wouldn't buy that, would you?"

"No, probably not."

"Of course not. You've heard it all before, right?"

"Sure. Something about kids as commodities like loaves of bread?"

"Bread? Are you fucking kidding me? They're *livestock*, baby! And you're a pussy if you feel sorry for the pig you eat. You're not a pussy, Null, are you?"

"No, I don't think so."

"Right fucking on! This is capitalism, you fucking cretin!

Capitalism, do you get it? The savvy, the advantaged, the predators, the alphas—*us!* The ones with the real balls! We make fantastic money on the backs of sad human victims. Workers, wage-slaves, laborers, disgusting dregs, human sweatshop livestock suffering all over the world, from here to China! The lowest of the low. It's a *ginormous* pyramid scheme and unwanted, abandoned children are at the very base of it, just like their parents, uncles and aunts. Is it class warfare? Fuck, this is the real new world order. Winners and losers, makers and takers. That's the new world order. That's how it's done. Don't you get it?"

"I get it. You're the actual takers and preschool children violated on the cheap, whored out on the dark web, then sold into slavery in their teens are the actual makers."

"Ya think? That's the big joke, you stupid schmuck. We flipped Marx: we're the takers and we grind the makers into the dust. We even have them believing that they're the parasites! The takers! It's a fucking feeding frenzy, a goddamn party, and you had to come in and piss all over it. You're a fucking menace to society. You're the one who should be bleeding on the rug."

"I admire your honesty."

"I knew you would." Martha smiled at Null flirtatiously, opened liquid green eyes wide. "Now can we talk deal?"

"Sure we can. What do you have in mind?

"What is it you need?"

"I'm a funny kind of guy you can't really understand. I don't need anything you have. I definitely don't need your money. You can keep that."

"Terrific. Okay, then. So, what do you want? Me maybe? I'm pretty great in the hay, you know, fractured leg notwithstanding." She smiled and winked in a strained way.

"You have me there too. I really don't want for anything in that way either, no offense meant."

"None taken."

"We're somewhere near an agreement," Null conceded.

"See? This is progress. The art of the deal. Tell me, what can I interest you in, then?"

"Interest me? Oh, Martha, you're definitely the shrewder one of the two. No doubt."

"So tell me."

"Well, I'm curious about something. How can someone who has all the human feeling in the world, all sorts of empathy, someone who cries at sad movies and adores babies—"

"You know that's true. And Steve and I were getting ready to try to have a baby of our own too, now that you mention it."

"I knew that about you right away, Martha. Indeed. So, please tell me then. People say I'm an unfeeling, sadistic monster, which really can't be true, by the way, since you have to feel something in order to be a sadist. And I don't. Now, how is it that someone like you with all that feeling can be completely indifferent and cold about processing children through a virtual meat grinder for profit. It doesn't affect you at all. And you don't even enjoy it."

"Well, I'm really not all that unfeeling, to be truthful. I actu- ally *do* sort of enjoy our position in the food chain, so to speak."

"That would make me the apex predator in this case, then."

"Exactly."

"An excellent answer! Absolutely wonderful. Well done, Martha."

"Thanks. So, like, is that it?"

"That's it."

"You're right, Null. I really don't understand you."

"I have an annoying habit of being right most of the time."

"You're right again—irony. And that's double fucking annoying in itself."

"I'm tautological."

"So, we're all done now? I can call an ambulance now to get us both to the hospital so Steve doesn't croak on the rug? You'll go?"

Null walked over to the window by the upright piano and gazed out at the afternoon skyline for a moment. It was a pleas- ant, pastoral scene, with a beautiful sunset coming.

"What are you doing?"

"I'm drawing the blinds."

Martha suddenly felt a knot in her stomach. She grabbed hard at the arms of the rocker and her voice went shrill.

"But, but I thought you said we had a deal!"

"No, we never said we had any deal. I said we were close to agreement. And we still are. But you did interest me. Anyway, we don't want the neighbors peeping in."

"What are you going to do?"

"Nothing much. I'm going to give you the same chance you gave to those children."

"But what did we agree to then?"

"That I am the apex predator."

"You can't be serious!"

"The truth is, Martha, I honestly can't be anything but serious. Back to business, though. You obviously like doing business, so, here, let me start you off."

Null drew the Heckler again from the copious pocket of his formless topcoat and matter-of-factly put two nine-millimeter rounds in Martha's stomach. She rolled forward off the Bentwood rocker (that rocked with her) like a comical rag doll. She quickly joined Steve in being well beyond speech, writhing on the rug, blending with him into a dissonant, pinched noise.

Null located the stereo, which had a five CD changer, popped in a disk of Otis Rush's Cobra recordings he spied easily, cranked the volume up high and went back over to Martha and Steve. He removed his coat, folded it neatly and put it on the plush off-white easy chair, rested the Heckler, the Browning and the Bushmaster both on top of it. Then he removed the machete from his neck where it hung from a lanyard, grabbed its handle with the lanyard swinging like a whip, and squatted down on the rug next to the writhing Steve, saying to him gently, though loud enough and close enough to be heard.

"We'll give Martha some time to reflect. Let's start with you."

THIRTY-ONE

"Even if you say you don't want to do it, I know for a fact you *do* want to do it."

"I'm not going to kill the fucker, Null. I told you that."

"Oh? I thought our recent experiences together might have changed your mind."

"You've busted Hebe Group wide open, isn't that enough?"

"I don't know. I can tell, though, that it's definitely not enough for you."

Null lit a cigarette, dragged on it and offered it to Boyd, who accepted. They sat together in the front seat of the half-wrecked Buick under the sole light that shone just above the entrance of the former Muddy Charles. It was anonymous now without any signage at all, except for the black and yellow construction sawhorses that blocked off the entrances to the parking lot and the front office. Null had to get out of the Buick and move one of them aside in order to park under the light. Looking through the glass door and its abutting windows, a chubby black man wearing horn-rimmed glasses could be seen sitting behind the front desk. That was Brother Ray, self-taught hacker of talent like so many of his ilk. Formal education had long ago proven to be a waste of time when compared with the deep delights and emoluments of the machine.

"Nothing will ever be enough," Boyd said in a low, bitter tone. "Nothing."

"We'll put that to the test tonight, don't you think?"

"I don't even know why I'm here."

"No, Kay. You know exactly why you're here."

"I have impulses I should never yield to."

"Take my word for it, sometimes you really should."

"I've reached my limit with your bullshit, Null. I'm telling you now, I'm not going to kill him."

Null blinked, and his face in the shadows presented an imperfect imitation of innocence.

"You won't have to, Kay. You have my word. But I think you'll want to be a witness. It might help with—"

"With *what,* for God's sake? My suspension? My weakness and stupidity? My drinking problem? My vanity in going after those fucks? Betraying Rudy? Just what exactly is this going to help with, Null? You tell me."

Her eyes were glassy, not yet welled with tears.

"All of it," said Null, as he got out of the flat black, broken monstrosity of a car with a loud creak of the driver's side door and Boyd joined him. There was still a chill in the air at night, even though it was spring. Boyd rubbed her hands together to warm them. Null was sweating, possibly due to his untreated shoulder wound from Legere's Derringer. It was likely infected by then.

"He's being pretty quiet, you know. Do you think he survived the trip?"

"Oh, he's alive, Kay. I was extremely gentle with him. He's playing possum, which is the only intelligent thing to do in his position."

"Really? I'd have thought kicking, screaming and making a noisy distraction to call attention to himself would've been his best call."

"True, but that can also get you silenced with a bullet."

"Tough position to be in, no matter how you slice it."

"It's about to get tougher."

"So, get him already."

"As you like. This is all for your benefit, tonight's dithyramb."

"It suits you though, doesn't it, Null?"

"It's a happy confluence of circumstances."

"How you can use the word 'happy' to describe it, I'll never know."

"Poetic license."

"Poetic justice."

"That too."

Boyd flicked her burning cigarette into the mulch of a degraded flower bed by the entrance to the hotel, so it sparked when it landed. Null popped the trunk to silence and nothing stirring. He drew out the Heckler and cocked it.

"Get up, George, or I'll have to drag you out bleeding."

"It's hard to move. I'm stiff from being curled up in a ball trying to fit into that goddamn trunk. And the exhaust fumes were killing me."

"Move along, George. You're not dead yet."

Null yanked the lanky George Goodnature out of the trunk of the Buick causing him to lurch about and stand, wobbling like a faltering, newborn foal in the half-light of the pick-up and drop-off area at the front entrance to the twink hotel. "Shit, man, that really wrecked my knees!"

"Stretch your legs, George. I'll need you to be ambulatory."

"You're not going to kill me?"

"I told you no."

"What if I make a run for it?"

"Then I'll shoot you."

"You could miss."

"Probably not. And I'd hate to have to drag you around with both legs shot out from under you to get things done, but I'll do that if it comes down to it. I'd prefer it didn't, of course."

"Jesus Christ, my hands have no circulation. I can't feel them!" cried George.

Null whipped out the switchblade from his coat pocket and slit the zip ties off his wrists. George immediately rubbed his hands together in brisk overreaction. Boyd emerged from the shadows, smoking another cigarette. Her face seemed uncharac-teristically cruel in the chiaroscuro of the entryway. She glared hard at George, like a patient predator focusing on its prey; an alligator eyeing a mangy dog.

"Do you remember Kay Boyd, George? You met her at your house—you know—before I had it torched. You two have a history, I think."

"Hello, shitstick."

"She's talking to you, George."

"I know, I know!" George made a great show of burying his face in his hands, sniveling wetly and somewhat muffled, "God, the fucking cop! Listen, I'm so sorry – I'm sick. I know. I know I'm a sick fuck! For real. I need help. It's not my fault that I do these things. I'm *compelled* to do them by a force I don't under-stand. I've always been this way. Then Legere—he gave me the kid and paid me to do everything I really, really like, no holds barred! The full boat! I was like a kid in a candy store. I didn't know it was a cop's kid. If I did, I would've—"

"Found some other poor schmuck's child to rape and murder instead?" leveled Boyd.

"How can you make such a beautiful thing sound so ugly?" asked George, as if pleading for his life, because—as he had known in the trunk of the Buick—that that was exactly what he had to do if he was going to survive. Odds of that happening were looking grimmer by the second. His eyes darted about, silently frantic, looking for escape.

"Tell it to the worms," Boyd sneered.

"Aww, you don't have to be like that."

"Yeah. As a matter of fact, I do."

"Let's go inside, shall we?" Null asked. "You both look cold."

Null prodded George into the lobby with the muzzle of the Heckler where the front desk was located just a few feet from the door. The atmosphere gave off an uneven effect—the only way to describe it was immaculately grimy. Its shabbiness was indis-putable, yet it was at the same time immaculately clean. Brother Ray hopped up from his swivel chair at the computer and greeted them all as if he were the manager and, in fact, he was, though hospitality was not his specialty.

"Everything's ready, boss," said Brother Ray cheerfully.

"Good to hear."

"He da guest o' honor standin' next to you 'longside Lieutenant Boyd?"

"Yes, this is—"

"George Goodnature," said George, extending his flat, spatulate, clammy hand across the counter. Brother Ray recoiled from it as if his hand were rotted and foul.

"Hands down, George, if you please. How are we on the final acquisition of the former Muddy Charles, Brother Ray?"

"All the paperwork's done—the LLC filing, the P and S agreement, state forms for settlin' up back taxes, outstandin' fines and utility bills all settled up, property conversion's all set, bribes been paid up to continue the zoning. I signed and notarized everything exackly the way you told me to. A squiggly li'l' thing just like yours. You might gotta put in a appearance at a law office if sumpm come out to doubt. But I don't think that's comin' directly yet."

"I do tend to sign in a squiggly way."

"I do good at that."

"We got an inspection pending."

"Ya. That be scheduled for next month already. Enough time to fix this bitch up."

"You can hire a crew to do that. Or I'll have Do-rag do that. We got someone to cook the books for laundering?"

"We got the same guys as before. They cuttin' you a break on percentage due to volume."

"Good. That's what this place is for. Volume."

"No doubt." Brother Ray seemed relieved for a moment. It didn't last.

"Tell me, Brother Ray, are you able to point and shoot?"

"A camera, boss?" He froze for a moment, vividly remembering the last Gangsta Boyz member who argued with Null. He was reduced to a corpse in seconds without warning. That was decidedly not the way he wanted to go. Brother Ray tried to avoid frowning but failed.

"No. *This.*" And Null pounded down the Browning Hi Power nine-millimeter, onto the counter flat on its side with a harsh bang.

Brother Ray was obviously startled, jittery, did a little backwards hop. No one said anything for a few long seconds. Finally, Brother Ray mustered the nerve to speak.

"I don't do guns, boss."

"You do now," Null answered almost pleasantly. "You can relax about it. I know you're not a street guy, but this'll be easy. A milk run."

"What—what I g-gotta do?"

"The safety's off. Just take the gun, point and shoot. Keep shooting until the magazine is empty. The trigger's a bit hard to pull and has a little bite to it." He held up his free hand; the one with the pinky missing. "It catches the skin right here between your thumb and forefinger in the action. Shouldn't hurt too badly, though it'll probably bleed a little. Just ignore it and keep pulling that trigger until the clip is empty. Dead simple."

"What if I miss?"

"You won't. Even when the gun bucks and your shot grouping is wild, you'll be close enough to get the job done. Hollow point rounds. Messy."

Brother Ray bit his lip and his horn-rimmed glasses slid slightly down the bridge of his nose. "Who—who I gotta shoot?"

"Him." Null indicated George Goodnature with the muzzle of the Heckler. He leaned forward over the counter and spoke crisply and definitively.

"If you see this man trying to leave, I want you to shoot him dead. Aim for the head and then the chest. Thirteen rounds in the clip ought to do the trick. Don't worry about the mess. I'll arrange for the boys upstairs to clean it up later."

Brother Ray licked his lips, looked around for a moment, shook his head, and said, "I don't know about that boss. You ain't seen 'em. They way fucking seven-thirty mothafuckas. J-cats. Real talk: they at a super high-level of crazy—fit for the ding-wing. All tweaked out on gak 'n' shit."

"I know, Brother Ray. Don't worry about it."

"Tell me why I shouldn't?" Less a challenge than a serious question and Null took it as such.

"This too shall pass, the adage goes. And by the time tonight is over, they should be pretty much down to the ground. Tame as exhausted dogs. Nevertheless, just in case things go off the rails, it'll be good you have the Browning. For protection."

"I won't argue 'bout dat. You got a knack for gettin' things right too much of the time."

"I'm glad my little failures go unnoticed."

"If they ain't, I di'n't hear no muthafucka up in this bitch say jack 'bout it."

"Also a hopeful sign."

Null prodded George to go upstairs, a sullen Boyd following just behind. They climbed up to the third level, every floor a grim, spanking, colorless clean, yet also somehow disheveled. Ronald sat on the windowsill at the end of the hallway on the third level that led to a fire escape that could either take you up to the roof or let you down to an abrupt stop twenty feet above the parking lot—a short drop into oblivion. And Ronald had Legere's Magnum three-fifty-seven cradled in his lap as he sat there watching them. He gave Null a crisp nod and Null nodded back.

There were boisterous noises coming from behind the door they stood in front of.

George fidgeted and shifted his weight from one foot to the other.

Null used his key card to unlock the biggest suite in the hotel, and when he did, the noise, the pungent, dank odor of sweat and smoke, hit everyone at once. Boyd coughed and George scrunched up his expression in disgust. Null pushed George hard with both hands into the room, stood right next to him and fired a round from the Heckler into the ceiling, the suppressor noticeably missing from the muzzle of the gun.

"Pipe down boys. Just get up off the rug and get good and quiet for a moment."

The twinks all paid close attention to the gun; the wrestlers grappling on the rug pulled apart and stood up. Then they closed in slowly on the three, tentatively, hesitantly, then suddenly just stopped.

"Never bring a knife to a gunfight, boys. You know what I mean?"

The twinks all assented heartily with scattered laughter.

George looked for an opportunity to make a break for it. His eyes rested on Boyd, whose nickel-plated Sig Sauer was aimed straight at his face.

"You don't get the joke, do you, George?"

"If I laugh, will you let me go?"

"I'm letting you go in a moment, George, so just keep still."

"I have to pee."

"We're not doing that again, are we?"

"What's the point here, Null? Just what are you driving at?" Boyd said restively.

"Denouement is what I'm driving at. Not closure necessarily, nothing complex, just an end to bad events."

"How does that even work?"

"I'll explain the rules. Are you listening to me, George?"

"I hear you just fine, you fucked up sonofabitch. Stupid fucking psycho!"

Null stared at him for a moment of quiet—but for the heaving and whispered milling of the twinks—then picked up where he left off.

"Self-expression must make you feel better about what's happening. I accept that. However, the rules for you, George, are fairly simple. I'm leaving you among these fine young men—all of them former child stars of the rape movies you liked performing in so much—with your face obscured from the camera, of course. Showing that mane of jet-black hair. Most of these stalwarts are boys you paid to abuse. Some of them you did for free—perks from Hebe. You may not remember them, George, but they remember you."

perks from Hebe. You may not remember them, George, but they remember you."

"Listen, boys, you remember our friend George Goodnature here, don't you?"

The group of twinks milled low, angry assent.

"So what?"

"So this: You also frequented the Muddy Charles as a customer, what all your buddies on the dark web delightedly referred to as the twink hotel. You know this place backwards and forwards, no doubt. This might actually help you."

"I think there's been some pitiful renovations done since last I was here," George said with amplified snideness.

"Admittedly, this place is a work in progress. I haven't taken ownership quite yet."

"Are we done? Can I go?"

"Of course. Just a few words before you do. All these boys you raped and abused, made them imitate their own deaths to satisfy you—they're all tweaked out on enough meth to make a donkey win the Preakness. And I gave them all a present. Each one carries a brand new blade. A shiny new knife. Do you ever watch late night TV, George?

"Sometimes. Who the fuck cares?"

"I do. Let me tell you, at about four in the morning, they have this long infomercial called "Cutlery Corner," where they sell big package deals of all kinds of knives. Not just kitchen knives, no, but utility knives. Sport knives. Kitanas, buck knives, tacticals, folders, fixed blades and hunters—the whole schmeer. They want you to make a sleepy decision about getting into the knife business—buy 'em cheap, sell 'em high. Unfortunately, even at their price point, it's not really very realistic. Regardless, I made a small investment, and not for resale."

"Will you get to the fucking point already?'

"It's sort of obvious, George."

"What is?" George was sweating, breathing hard, understanding his situation and hoping to talk his way out of it.

"This," said Null, and pushed George right into the center of the impatiently waiting boys. George tried to go for Boyd at the door, but four of the skinny young twinks took him down to the bare wood floor. It was scuffed and damaged from years of neglect, now coated with blood as the boys stabbed playfully at George, holding off on killing him. They whooped and hollered like make-believe savage natives in an old Hollywood movie.

Dancing adolescent Maxes from "Where the Wild Things Are." No wolf suits needed.

"You're crazy!" George screamed at the top of his lungs. *"Crazy!"*

"I never said I wasn't. Now George, I know it's difficult but try to concentrate. If you can somehow get out of this room and get past me, Ronald in the hallway and Brother Ray at the front desk, you'll be free and clear. No one will even try and stop you. You'll be home free."

The stabbing of the shirtless boys became more severe, deeper, wilder.

"I can't die this way! I can't!" he squealed. "Help me! Please!"

"What would you like me to do, George, put you out of your misery with a quick bullet to the brain?" Null had the Heckler out and aimed and Boyd's Sig Sauer was also still drawn. "Is that what you're asking for?"

"My god, too much *pain!* Pain! Help – *me!"*

"So you're begging for it?"

"Yes!"

If they were children, you might have called it a pig pile as the rest of the boys with various knives drawn joined the others holding George down and stabbing at him with angry, frenzied gestures, laughter; growling and grunting could be heard in an amalgam of fury.

It was an angrier version of "Lord of the Flies."

"I said that you would, George. Just remember that if you can. And proving that my word is still good, I have to remind you, I'm not the one who's killing you. Your former victims are."

George couldn't even emit a wet sigh by then. The only sounds were the boys, earning their reward, seeking their vengeance, letting the methamphetamine carry them into an unleashed frenzy of rage none of them had ever experienced, with the possible exception of the first time they were anally raped.

"You don't have to watch this, Kay. You can take the Buick. I'll get a ride from Ronald to take me where I need to go."

Boyd cleared her throat, still aiming the Sig Sauer where George had stood until the savage twinks took him down. "No. I wanna stay. I *need* to see this."

"You're not upset, disgusted?"

"I don't know what I am anymore, but I do know this. I finally understand how you feel about these things. How you can watch this brutality and find some peace in it."

"Is that how you feel watching these children tear this man to bloody shreds in front of your eyes? You feel peaceful?"

"I think that's maybe true. I'm not as disturbed as I should be, that's for sure."

"You realize that he's already pretty much dead by now and that we're witnessing the postmortem. Not exactly Actaeon torn apart by his own hounds, but not too far off. Maybe you've seen enough?"

"Oh no," Boyd said through half-gritted teeth. "I want to see it all. I *need* to see it all."

"We'll just stand right here then – let the boys work off all that meth."

"That's fine. He's not going anywhere anymore."

"So, you're saying you're feeling better?"

A slight smile played across Boyd's lips, innocent of makeup.

"You know something?"

"What?"

"I actually do."

EPILOGUE

It was the kind of New England night when the darkness itself seems even more black than its definition by scattershot lighting: A pool of gathered blackness whose depth seemed also a heavy weight. The little cracker box house at forty Spiers Road was in the part of Newton that just abutted West Roxbury in a housing development of hills and cul-de-sacs called Oak Hill Park. The house was vaguely shown in shadows from a streetlight high above it like a tiny nova. Null had parked the Buick on nearby Saw Mill Brook Parkway. He walked the quiet road, wary of police cars, but none drove by, not even a single, errant, late night car for that matter.

When Null reached the house, he circled it, peering through windows, gaps in shutters and shades, wary of motion detectors and of low lights indicating silent alarms. There were two cars in the driveway where before there had been none. Two adult shapes were huddled under the covers in the first bedroom, visible through the larger of two shade gaps. It was a possibility that Mr. Quinlan had moved back home once he knew of his daughter's safe return. Or it might have been just a boyfriend. That last thought was dicey and doubtless had to be confirmed.

That would take a daytime visit.

Null moved furtively, gingerly, to where he presumed

Shirley's bedroom might be. He found the blind was entirely open and the streetlight that streaked in partially lit her head on the pillow showing half her face and that of some stuffed animal next to her that might have been either a dog or a moose.

He lingered much longer than he should have, watching Shirley sleeping contentedly through the open blind, unconsciously synchronizing his breathing with hers.

Diastole and systole, like the sea.

After a time Null left in the shadows, walking back to the Buick.

One car passed slowly by him.

It did not stop.

———

Null deplaned at Dubai International Airport just in time for the late afternoon call to prayer. The Airport interior was overly bright and postmodern with commercial middle eastern Sanskrit flourishes—brilliant, metallic and cavernously huge. It was busy with ornate installations as well as harried travelers, and its echoes were thunderous. Null traveled light as usual, but customs didn't bother to so much as touch his carry-on bag. He was waved through deferentially, as if by magic.

A short, slim bearded man wearing Ray Ban sunglasses and a black Armani suit with a deep purple tie met him as he emerged from customs. He had a blinding, affable smile and flashed it at Null. He wasn't carrying a sign, but he knew Null right away.

Null was dressed in a white linen Zegna suit and Panama hat.

His wounds and scars remained prominent.

"You are John Hunter, yes? Nice to see you, Mr. John. Was your journey at all comfortable?"

"It was fine. *Assalamu alaikum.*"

The man smiled at that and extended his hand. Null took his hand and shook it.

"*Wa alaikum assalam*, Mr. John. I am Mansour and I will be your driver for today. May I take your bag?"

"No, Mansour. It's light."

"Very good, Mr. John. Come with me to the VIP area where the limousine will be waiting."

"Okay."

"Not many Americans think to dress for the climate, Mr. John. Very savvy of you." This statement contained a hint of sarcasm that Null missed entirely. Dark clothing commanded respect in the United Arab Emirates.

"Thanks."

They walked for what seemed a long distance in silence, engulfed by the echoes and the cavernous busyness of the airport until they walked out into the implacable glare and arid emptiness of Dubai itself. The limousine was parked in an isolated area by itself, the engine running. It was black with tinted windows, a small flag flying the colors of the United Arab Emirates—red, black, green and white bars arranged like a test pattern. Mansour opened the door for Null and he was immediately hit by the air conditioned cool. Before he could react, they were underway.

The thoroughfare was empty and altogether void of life.

"Just because you know how to dress, Mr. John, does not mean it cannot be made cool for you American business types."

"I see that. Are we headed for the palace, then?"

"Well, his Excellency doesn't receive business visitors at the palace, unfortunately. You are right, though. His residence is at the Za'abeel Palace—very grand. Splendid. Perhaps he will give you a tour while you're here, *n'shallah*."

"Security must be tight."

"Oh yes, very. Did you know that that is where his Highness, the Crown Prince of Dubai Sheikh Hamdan bin Mohammed bin Rashid Al Maktoum resides? Security is very heavy and very tight there. No worries about that, Mr. John."

"Is he popular with the people?"

"Very much loved. They know him affectionately as Fazza. He is a very romantic poet and sportsman and can be followed quite easily on Instagram."

"So where are we meeting his Excellency then?"

"In the tallest building in Dubai—an architectural marvel. We'll be there in a few minutes. You know, Mr. John, that it's actually the tallest building in the world."

"Yes. The Burj Khalifa. I've heard of it."

"You know, they're building one to even exceed that, Mr. John. The Dubai Creek Tower, so stay tuned for that. You know, his Excellency is very eager to meet with you after what that terrible man called Null did to his beautiful business in Boston."

"Yes, as you know, I'm here to fix that."

"Which is all to the good, Mr. John. His Excellency is a man of very peculiar tastes and he does this business out of love, not just for the money, you understand."

"Oh, completely. Security must be tight at the Burj as well."

"Most definitely. Why should you worry? You will be protected for certain. And, of course, you couldn't possibly have any weapons on you, of course." And Mansour laughed at the thought of this little businessman wielding a gun.

"Tell me, Mansour, does Sheikh Hilal bin Rashid bin Mohammed Al Maktoum use a pencil to take notes during his meetings by any chance?"

Mansour laughed again at the absurdity of the question. "Now, why would he do something like that when he has computers and secretaries, Mr. John? Very amusing."

"But we'll be meeting alone."

"About a matter as sensitive as this, yes, definitely, I would assume so." He paused for a moment then added cheerily, "You know, just as a point of interest, Mr. John, his Excellency does keep a *very* nice collection of the famous Mont Blanc fountain pens in his private office, if that might interest you at all."

Null sat silently for a few minutes, lulled by the even hum of the limousine cruising along the freakishly smooth and perfect pavement of the road. It was like riding a long, calming mantra. He leaned back into the soft cushion of the seat and replied almost absent-mindedly:

"That'll do."

———

Don't miss out on your next favorite book!
Join the Melange Books mailing list at
www.melange-books.com/mail.html

ACKNOWLEDGMENTS

The author hereby wishes to acknowledge his small band of supporters:

Nancy Pepin, née Durocher, who's with me in all things and in everything that matters.

Scott Oddo, for his friendship and keen intellect.

Marc Songini, for his wit and his literary japing; Huntley Dent, for all his support moral and otherwise; Matt Bon for his startling artistry; Steve Dooner, for his astonishing breadth of cultural literacy, abstruse and not; Kate Nicholas, for her sharp wit, bordering on slight insanity; Susan Gambrell Reinhardt, whose sweetly acid commentary is always inspiring; Glen Dansker for being a mensch; Brett Hicks for his promotional savvy and Joe Schatzle for always knowing how to crack me up.

This parvum opus is for you all.

THANK YOU FOR READING

Did you enjoy this book?

We invite you to leave a review at the website of your choice, such as Goodreads, Amazon, Barnes & Noble, etc.

DID YOU KNOW THAT LEAVING A REVIEW...

- Helps other readers find books they may enjoy.
- Gives you a chance to let your voice be heard.
- Gives authors recognition for their hard work.
- Doesn't have to be long. A sentence or two about why you liked the book will do.

ABOUT THE AUTHOR

Gary S. Kadet has been a journalist, covering various beats for the Boston Herald, Globe and even Playboy Magazine, which also published his fiction. He was a contributing editor for the nationally-read Boston Book Review where he covered crime fiction in his "Trouble is Their Business" column. In the 90s, he was a trailblazer on the Internet, running the 10th largest adult website in the world, appearing on MSNBC commenting on the future of adult material on the web. His novel "D/s - an Anti-Love Story" was the first novel to portray the real-world BDSM scene without prurience or sentimentality and was a Book Of The Month Club main selection.

GarySKadet@protonmail.com

facebook.com/CleverNovels
twitter.com/GaryScottKadet